COMPOST MORTEM

LOUISE GAZZOLI

outskirts
press

To my husband

1. OBITUARIES FOR EUNICE

It was hard to write an obituary for someone you had once loved and now were suspected of murdering. Cuppy was trying to compose himself while composing a summary of his late wife Eunice's life. Making frequent reference to a bottle of brandy, he wrote the following:

KINGBLADE – Eunice Lucretia née Naboth of Deer Creek

She did not die peacefully at home surrounded by her loved ones. What loved ones? She died brutally at the Deer Creek Mulch Site, an inconveniently damp location, surrounded by leaves. Dedicated enemy of many, she was in death as she was in life: unpleasant and combative. She rained on more parades than a monsoon in Bangladesh. She was so negative she could repel magnets at fifty paces.

It was indeed fitting that Eunice died at the Deer Creek Mulch Site. As President of the Deer Creek Garden Club, Eunice was a crusading zealot for the production of mulch, the sale of defective kink free hoses, and the promotion of violence against invasive species of flora, fauna, family, friends (what friends?) and real estate developers.

Eunice was also a founding member of the Pollyanna Parrot Cage, an organization apparently devoted to teaching annoying vocabulary to parrots. She excelled at training her avian students in snide remarks and insults. Her cynically gabby parrot Lulu survives her (but not for long).

Her nonartistic talent found an outlet in photography. A local gallery is refusing to host an exhibition of her work: Offensive Fences in Deer Creek or How to Report Your Neighbor to the Authorities.

A member of the Red Cross Thousand Gallon Club, Eunice was a top motivator in getting others to donate blood, usually at emotional gunpoint. She proudly called herself "a bloody nuisance." You should hear what her victims called her.

Married for 29 (once endless) years to the long-suffering V. Pimms "Cuppy" Kingblade. On tyrant wings she sped her children to the far corners of the earth: Sophie of Tendon, Alaska; Kevin of Hong Kong; and Lynn of Cape Town, S.A. She would never want her age (53) revealed.

Eunice was founder and CEO of the Amateur Herbal Tea Brewers Association (AHTBA) and its Executive Vice President in charge of world domination. In lieu of artificial flowers, uncharitable contributions may be made to AHTBA. (Note: Contributions to AHTBA are not tax deductible.)

Feeling purged by writing that summary and mellowed by brandy, Cuppy set about devising another version of Eunice's life. He was quite proud of the final result and it was certainly no more euphemistically laden than many other such eulogies.

KINGBLADE – Eunice Lucretia née Naboth of Deer Creek

Beloved wife of V. Pimms (Cuppy) Kingblade, devoted mother of Lynn, Kevin and Sophie, she dedicated her life to the care of her family, friends and community.

As President of the Deer Creek Garden Club she led the crusade for the preservation of the mulch site and the distribution of irrigation systems. She also worked tirelessly for the Red Cross and the tropical bird rehabilitation center at the Zoo. Her lovingly lyrical parrot Lulu survives her.

Eunice's hobbies included landscape photography and homemade blends of tea. Many recall the delightful tea bags she made with herbs and flowers that she grew herself.

Memorial contributions may be made
to the tribute fund of the Deer Creek
Garden Club.

2. THE DEER CREEK GARDEN CLUB

"Gently chaotic with civilized overtones," said Ivy with satisfaction as she surveyed the scene.

Grace's voice came up beside her, "Sounds like a wine."

Ivy gave a shout of appreciation, "Ha, yes, but what else could we say about it?" Grace considered this question as their fellow Deer Creek Garden Club members bustled around the almost empty mulch site. The indisputably pleasant women were laboring under enormous old percolators, trying to figure out where to find an electrical outlet. After a great deal of polite confusion, they discovered the outside socket on the side of the office trailer and muscled the card tables into place. A collective sigh of great relief greeted the starting up and reassuring glub-glub noises (not unlike English plumbing) of the coffee pots.

"Oh, I'd say well intentioned but containing quirky notes that hint at something darker, perhaps?"

Ivy Wilcoxen tilted her head in acknowledgement and smiled at Grace Mere. The two were longtime acquaintances and colleagues in gardening matters. As members of the Deer Creek Garden Club, they had worked on many village beautification projects together. Not much could be done to beautify a mulch site, however, so Ivy was in a reminiscing sort of mood.

"Remember when we planted the grammar school herb garden and then the next year they dug it up for a parking lot? Oooh, I could have killed someone! And then there was that flap about the inflatable snake and the empty wine bottles." Ivy continued with the memories of past glories and present indignities involving turnips, artificial flowers, drainage, kink free hoses and mulch.

Grace was happy to stroll along beside her, listening and glancing at her every now and then. What on earth was she wearing? Ivy usually appeared in such non-descript old clothes that you could never remember them and sometimes not even identify them as recognizable garments. This morning, however, an effort had been made. Grace analyzed the look as vaguely Bavarian Art Deco with a dash of samba thrown in.

Grace had dressed carefully for the occasion (because she always did everything carefully) in a tailored shirtwaist dress in a discrete pattern and light but somber tones. A cashmere cardigan that matched one of the dress's colors was over her shoulders. English brogues, in a pale tan called "King Alfred's Oak," kept her feet dry and well balanced. She had drawn the line at pearls however.

Ivy picked up the main thread again. "The Deer Creek Garden Club: something darker? Do you really think so? Well, with Eunice Kingblade as President, maybe so. It certainly can be overly complicated at times. Why on earth we couldn't have the business meeting and coffee at the village hall first, as usual, then come here is beyond me."

"Well, Eunice does tend to make things as difficult as possible," said Grace.

"Yes – and as mean as possible too. But the worst part is that she seems to do it on purpose. How can she not know that she is being so unpleasant?" The puzzled and irritated Ivy was kicking away at a big clump of mulch. "It's for your own good!" she trilled in perfect mimicry of Eunice. "I'm always right," she trumpeted as she kicked another big blob of mulch.

"Where is she anyway? She's the one who organized this field trip to learn all about mulch. You know, Grace, she sounds like an evil Julia Child."

Grace laughed and moved out of the way of Ivy's mulch kicking. "I'm sure she'll be here soon. Eunice always shows up."

"Unfortunately, that is true. Well, onward into the fray! Coffee in the mulch site: how – umm – fundamental. Let's go get some. At least it isn't one of those awful herbal teas that Eunice concocts. Talk about poison."

Ivy led the way to the crowd of ladies twittering around the tables set with white linens, flower arrangements, coffee urns, teapots, assorted muffins and cakes; oh, and the mandatory fresh fruit that was rarely even touched. Grace carefully tucked an errant bloom back into one of the bouquets.

"Considering the location, the Hospitality Committee has done a lovely job of setting this all up."

"Oh, I guess so." Ivy sounded vague because she was looking around impatiently.

By then, the social half hour of the Deer Creek Garden Club had come and gone with no sign of Eunice. After waiting five more minutes, Ivy had had enough.

"This is ridiculous. Let's get this show on the road."

Clapping her hands, Ivy called, "Ladies, ladies, attention please." Eunice usually ruptured people's eardrums with her ferocious whistle – one of those fingers-in-the-mouth kinds – to start the meetings. Privately, Ivy would have admitted to envying the technique.

"In the interests of time, I think that we should start the meeting without Eunice."

There were a number of muttered and un-muttered "Goods."

"You probably all know Mungo Gummers. He has worked for the village of Deer Creek for the last – umm – how long is it Mungo?"

"Fifteen years."

There were appreciative murmurs.

"And you are in charge of the whole mulch operation, as well as the pots – the wonderful village flowerpots…"

There was a smattering of applause.

"…the park and just generally keeping Deer Creek going. Mungo, it's all yours."

Enthusiastic clapping ensued as Ivy gestured graciously to the shell-shocked Mungo. He hadn't expected an introduction or having to say anything at all. Mrs. Kingblade had told him to keep quiet and follow her directions. But he stepped up gamely in front of the riveted garden club ladies.

"Yes, well, umm," he started agonizingly.

Grace called out, "How many leaves do you collect Mungo and how do you turn them into mulch?"

The simple question started him off and, once going,

he delivered a clear explanation of the mulching process.

"Residents can come get the mulch themselves or I can deliver it to your house. It's real popular and we run out fast. Some folks get mad if they don't get any mulch. In fact last year Miz Kingblade…." Mungo pulled himself up in time. Mrs. Kingblade had berated him last year for not saving her some – huh – as if he ever would.

"So by this time of year, most of the mulch is gone. We keep this one pile here for the village – for the beds at the village hall and the Police Department and the fire station." By now Mungo had relaxed and was almost having fun.

"Now I'll just fire up the front loader and show you how I scoop up the mulch."

The big yellow machine coughed and jerked into life. Mungo trundled the beast forward then carefully lowered the huge bucket into the mulch. As he started to lift a heap of the processed leaves, something fell out onto the ground.

Dirty with mulch, the head bashed in, clotted blood and leaf mold partially obscured the body but not the fact that it was Eunice Kingblade. She had been there all along and now even in death was causing distress and consternation, not to mention sickening horror. The village of Deer Creek was constitutionally incapable of hosting a murder. How could something like this happen?

❦

3. THE VILLAGE OF DEER CREEK

Nothing ever happened in Deer Creek. People often described it as a great place to live but they wouldn't want to visit there. It was the kind of town where the inhabitants went on tours of the mulch site. Well, garden club members went on said tours, as well as some formerly skeptical county officials. The local success of the mulch site and the acclaim that it had garnered from national environmental groups had given a resounding comeuppance to the shortsighted critics.

A few months ago, a national study had declared Deer Creek the third most boring village in America. There had been a letter to the editor in the Deer Creek Crier, denouncing the slight.

To the Editor:

It has come to my attention that a national study recently snubbed Deer Creek. This disparaging article requires a response. I am outraged and incensed that Deer Creek is considered the third most boring village in the U.S. It deserves to be recognized as Number One. Clearly the investigative team missed or did not understand the significance of the following criteria.

Deer Creek has three needlepoint shops. It has two Garden Clubs. There is one tearoom. It has its very own mulch pile (the village, not the tearoom). The Deer Creek Garden Club plans to tour the mulch pile. If that isn't the epitome of boring, I don't know what is. The Garden Club of St. James is having tea in the tearoom. Ditto.

Extrapolation of boringly accurate statistics obtained from a traditionally dull private club shows that the per capita consumption of alcohol in Deer Creek per annum is well over the national average. Please note use of the Latin phrases "per capita" and "per annum." Many people in Deer Creek have studied Latin, which, as you may know, is a Dead Language.

Do you know how many stop signs there are in Deer Creek? I didn't think so. Even though there isn't enough traffic to cause a jam, it's stop-and-go anyway. Deer Creek has a full-time employee who is in charge of putting up more stop signs. We do not have signs that say "Welcome to Deer Creek." Heaven forefend. We have signs that say "Now Leaving Populated Area."

I wonder if these so-called experts even came here. If they had, I could not have shown them the sights because there are no sights (see enclosed photo). We don't want sights; they might attract visitors. I think that I speak for most citizens of Deer Creek when I say that we value our boringness. We, however, call it tranquility.

Sincerely yours,
Emeritus D. Wilcoxen, Ph.D.

Most of the readers of the Deer Creek Crier agreed heartily with Emeritus D. Wilcoxen, Ph.D. The village of Deer Creek provided comfortable, easy, everyday life with anything one needed or wanted within a fifteen to twenty minute driving radius. The inhabitants were friendly and helpful but not too much so. They were (in general) very polite, but slow to accept newcomers (who could be someone who had moved there twenty years ago). The most highly valued attributes of Deer Creek were peace, quiet and privacy.

There were lots of nice neighborhoods with big old dignified houses set in well-kept lawns and gardens. Fences had been put up in recent years but more often sowed discord rather than prevented it. Plus then that nasty concept of maintenance reared its ugly head. Another ugly head reared was that of Eunice Kingblade who would go around photographing fences that she deemed unfit to stand in Deer Creek. So most folks left the hedges wide, the shrubs thick and the trees tall to mark their boundaries and protect their sovereignty.

Deer Creek took pride in its good schools with sunny classrooms. The roads showed genteel decay, just enough to project a rural image of a simpler time and to provide evidence of lack of vanity. Indeed, the only strife that occasionally rippled to the surface of civility was precipitated by the chronic internecine warfare between the two garden clubs.

❦

4. IVY

"Ha! That is a myth, instigated and perpetuated by Eunice Kingblade," explained Ivy Wilcoxen as she stirred her coffee. Her husband Emeritus D. Wilcoxen, Ph.D. was reading the morning paper to see if they had printed his latest letter, the one about drainage.

"What's a myth?"

"That we don't get along with the 'Other' garden club."

"Then why do you refer to it so pointedly as the 'Other' garden club?"

"That's what they call us."

"Well, there you are then."

"Oh Merit, it's become so ridiculous. Eunice constantly getting in digs about Gardenia – you know, she's the President of the Garden Club of St. James." Ivy carefully did not refer to it as the "Other" garden club and continued.

"Accusing her of stealing things from the Deer Creek Garden Club's closet at the village hall. As if Gardenia would want any of our junk."

"Then why don't you take over as President? A palace coup or something; a closet coup I guess would be more appropriate. But would you be going in or coming out? Hmmm…"

Appalled, Ivy said, "What? Me? President of the Deer Creek Garden Club? Good heavens, no!"

"Why not?"

"First of all, Eunice will never give up the Presidency before her term expires or she does. But unless someone kills her, there's not much chance of that. Why she's trying to change the bylaws to extend her time in office. Plus, I'd have to buy a Christmas sweater!"

Merit blinked carefully, assuming a façade of profound deliberation, at which he excelled. What a subject: garden clubs that required Christmas sweaters and had members feuding over closets. Deer Creek wasn't boring. It was an anthropological gold mine of investigative potential. This warranted further contemplation and might even provide the basis for a letter to the editor.

"Well, what about this then: you could join the other garden club too and be an ambassador, bringing the two clubs together – doing joint good deeds or something."

Ivy shook her head with sad impatience at her husband's lack of understanding. "Only a glutton for punishment would be a member of both garden clubs."

Breakfast ended quietly and pensively, sending Merit off to his study and Ivy out to pursue her many charitable and gardening activities.

Ivy had inherited a lot of money but didn't seem to realize it. The Episcopal Church thrift shop politely accepted her donations, then took them up the street to the Presbyterian thrift shop. Goodness knows what they did with them.

Her well-mileaged car was a moveable potting shed, filled with shovels, trowels, pruners, sacks of topsoil, bare root trees in tipping over containers and freshly dug up plants wrapped in soggy newspaper. Her Newfoundlands, Lingo and Wooly, slobbered up the windows and down the sides of Ivy's car and left a furry coating all over the seats and plants. Meals On Wheels received the same unhygienic but friendly treatment. Her generous nature caused her to go about dispensing her largesse of plants upon unsuspecting recipients who were sometimes grateful but often overwhelmed.

Ivy loved to tend her own gardens, which had been designed many years ago for her parents. Many of the old flowers and shrubs were long gone, but the classic English country garden pattern provided the bones on which Ivy planted with absent-minded originality. The thick boxwood, bluestone paths and brick walls quietly supported her haphazard but innately brilliant placement of riotous botanical mixtures. The resulting swirly splash of colors, textures, shapes and sizes produced an impressionist's dream.

That interpretation never would have occurred to Ivy and indeed did not even manifest itself until she invited the Deer Creek Garden Club members over for a trough workshop. Always sensing vulnerability, Eunice Kingblade had attacked right when Ivy was in the midst of peat moss, Portland cement and perlite.

"You know Ivy, I guess you try but your garden is really a mess and it is a mistaken notion that the colors of flowers cannot clash. Now I can stay for a while after the workshop to advise you about..." Grace was never one to interrupt others but in this case she cut Eunice off.

"Why Ivy! Monet would have loved this! It's like a vibrant Giverny. How did you go about planning it all?"

"That is what I was trying to say, Grace, before you interrupted – clearly there is no planning." Eunice stretched her narrow lips into a false smile that then flatlined in the direction of Ivy. "Did you ever consider using a professional landscape architect?"

"I like to do things myself, Eunice, in my way, because it is my garden." Ivy concentrated on stirring the sloppy mixture instead of flinging it at Eunice.

"Oh, well, professionals are expensive of course and these old houses are always falling apart so you must have a constant money drain. Or I guess you don't bother to fix things do you?" Eunice sniffed emphatically. "That mixture is too thick. Are you sure you're using the right ingredients?"

THWOCK! Ivy slapped a sloppy splodge of trough batter back into the wheelbarrow and thrust the hoe at Eunice, saying, "There ya go, Eunice. You seem to know everything. Show us how it's done."

"Oh!" Eunice started in coy surprise, "I was just making conversation."

Grace started walking briskly away as she enthused to Ivy about the many unique features of the garden and the glorious herbaceous borders. Many of the garden club members followed them, while others veered off in several different directions – all of them away from Eunice. Left alone, she turned to the task of cement mixing with a sense of sour satisfaction at having had her say.

5. GRACE

Grace Mere really is too nice, smiled Ivy to herself. Quiet and reserved, so old fashionedly polite, always immaculately and appropriately attired and rarely so purposefully chatty as she was being right now, while rescuing Ivy from Eunice. Grace owned Deer Creek Yarns, a small, charming shop that carried yarns and accessories for needlepoint, embroidery, cross-stitch, crewelwork and knitting. The shop building was also her house. It had a welcoming front porch with two beautifully finished oak Adirondack chairs.

The first time that Ivy had gone into Deer Creek Yarns, a bell over the door had jingled musically to summon Grace who had greeted her with polite surprise because Ivy had never been in the shop before. Ivy glanced around with smiling interest at the brilliant colors of yarns in the glass-fronted bookcases.

"What a lovely old house – Arts and Crafts is it?"

"Yes – shall I show you around? I'd loved this place for years and it turned out that Olivier had too. It was going to be torn down. Can you imagine?"

"I'm afraid that I certainly can. People are always tearing down beautiful old houses."

As they wandered around, Grace pointed out some of the exquisite workmanship. The old kerosene (now electrified) copper lamps with mica shades that cast a golden glow on the built-in cabinetry; the stained glass windows; the hammered copper hinges and handles; the tiles around the inglenook fireplace with the hand wrought fire irons.

Grace had embroidered the curtains with Art Nouveau designs. She had needlepointed the William Morris pillows that emphasized the unobtrusive quality of the Arts and Crafts furniture. Lightly scenting the rooms, deceptively simple bouquets of roses, artfully swooping with the air of swallows, filled Weller and Rookwood pottery vases.

Ivy figured that a lot of this stuff probably belonged in a museum, but Grace had captured the domestic patina of time rather than institutional display. "Grace, this place suits you. It absolutely suits you and you suit it. Well, to get down to business. I want to knit a sweater for Merit but I'll need a lot of instruction."

"Well, I'd be delighted to help you." Grace had some private reservations about Merit Wilcoxen deserving (meriting?) a hand-knit sweater, but recommended a heavy wool yarn that resembled porridge with raisins in it. Undoubtedly, he could wear the elbows out of it just by thinking, or by writing letters to the editor.

Ivy was right about not being a natural needlewoman and had gone in for remedial assistance on a number of occasions. She was persistent and enthusiastic, however, and a sweater-like garment did seem to be emerging from the rumpled heap of wool that was now messier than when it had been on the sheep. Ivy did not aspire to produce Irish Fisherman patterns or cables. Sleeves the same length might be nice, and a large enough head-hole. Merit had a rather large head.

Besides, it was just so pleasant being in Deer Creek Yarns. Despite being so tidy, it was very comfortable and restful; restored the soul somehow. People dropped in to knit, needlepoint or embroider or just to gossip over the cookies that Grace baked. It didn't need a sign, although Grace could have embroidered one in flowing Art Nouveau cursive.

Deer Creek Yarns was one of the few houses left in the blocks that constituted the main street of Deer Creek. The others had been razed during the '60s mostly, to put in a row of little shops and small businesses of vaguely bank-like and Williamsburg appearance. They were tasteful, if unimaginative, but certainly clean and well maintained. Victorian wrought iron railings that had been rescued from a dilapidated downtown park separated the parking area from the shop fronts. The fence's original purpose had been to keep cows out of the park. Now it beckoned shoppers with the implied elegance of history.

The shop was a hobby rather than a necessity for Grace and scarcely made even the tiniest profit. Grace had started it after her husband Olivier had died, or disappeared, or something mysterious. He was certainly no longer around. Ivy was a bit sketchy on what had happened to him but she didn't want to ask Grace, who was such a private person. He had been a travel writer, quite a good one actually with articles published in the New Yorker, but he had never returned from a trip to some remote dangerous region: the mountains of Afghanistan or Bhutan or somewhere like that. At the time, Merit had said, "How Nepaling. He was probably up to something. How much do you want Tibet?" Merit could be surprisingly tiresome at times.

Museums and auction houses consulted Grace on the restoration of antique tapestries and all types of needlework. She had even given an expert opinion at a trial as to the authenticity and value of a stolen 16th century altar cloth.

Grace was gently amused that she had become known, not for her historic expertise, but for the Fair Isle sweaters that she knitted for dogs 25 lbs and under. They had become absurdly popular and she could not keep up with demand even though she could knit and read at the same time. Her well-behaved Norfolk Terrier Parsley was the long-suffering model for the sweaters.

6. PARSLEY

"Phlet, phlet. Dlugh. Cghuh cghuh."

"Um, Grace, there's a strange noise coming from under that chair." Ivy had been tangled up in the early stages of the sweater.

"Oh that's Parsley. Come out you little rascal." Then a sterner, "Parsley! Come here right now."

Two little paws emerged from under the skirt of the pale yellow boudoir chair, which was the only anomaly in the Arts and Crafts furnishings. Then a small black nose followed by a mouth with red yarn hanging out of it appeared.

"Now where did you get that? Give. I hope you didn't eat any." Grace pulled the yarn out of his teeth and picked the little dog up. "Well, at least you got a good flossing."

Oh no! She has that "sweater look" in her eyes. Parsley wriggled and struggled against her. Those Feh Rile sweaters that she made him wear. They were too hot. He changed tactics and drooled a bit, nestling against her pitifully.

Oh no! He has that "throw-up-yarn look" in his eyes. Grace ran for the door, holding Parsley out in front of her and dumped him on the back porch. He leapt into the yard, miraculously cured and free and raced toward Digging Corner.

Digging Corner had been Olivier's idea. "Terriers are natural diggers so it would be cruel not to let him dig. All we have to do is set up a certain 'digging allowed' area." So the back right corner of their backyard, just beyond the potting shed, had become Digging Corner.

Olivier had marked the borders with cobblestones then filled the space with sand. Soon sand was infiltrating every room in the house. Sand had not been a good idea. So they'd had Mungo come with his truck to dig up and take away the sand. Then he replaced it with a mixture of topsoil and mulch, which somehow did not track in as easily as sand. Parsley loved Digging Corner and happily submitted to having his paws toweled off before he came back inside. Towels were nothing compared to that awful Doggy Bath. That stuff was terrible, absolutely ruined your sense of smell.

As Parsley zoomed toward Digging Corner, experience slowed him down and he held up at the corner of the potting shed. Just beyond it his Enemy lurked, tightly coiled in its nest, the ridged body poised to spring and golden head ready to strike the unsuspecting as well as the all-too-suspecting; and Parsley was suspecting. He advanced cautiously and peered around the corner of the shed. There it was! "Urr..." Parsely hit the turf with fur up. Wump he went down flat on his stomach, legs out in front. Then up: "Rah Rah!" Darting, charging, feinting left and right, retreating, throwing himself flat on the ground.

"Roo Roo Roo Roo Roo!" The Evil Enemy was biding its time. Parsley struck! He grabbed the kink free hose and shook it like a terrier shakes a rat. He was proud of his terrier heritage and lived up to it with all his might. He dragged the roiling length of subdued but still combative kink free hose out into the middle of the yard, then dropped it like a hot doggy biscuit. Parsley circled it, thunderously proclaiming victory. "Rah Arooo! Rah Arooo!" Parsley had heard of the Jaws of Defeat and he knew that his jaws could defeat anything. "Rah Rah Rah Rah Rah!" He trotted triumphantly to Digging Corner to celebrate, joyously flinging dirt with his furious little front paws.

Grace and Ivy had enjoyed watching the entire battle. "I always think how brave he is to set out every day, sometimes several times a day, to confront this chronic foe."

"Yes, quite an inspiration," said Ivy as Grace opened the door to welcome the grubby little hero. "If those darn kink free hoses didn't leak already, they certainly would after Parsley showed them who's boss. Yours must be soaker hoses by now."

Grace laughed. "My mother suggested that Parsley was the cause of the leaks, not faulty manufacture. He usually doesn't attack things like that but the hose struck the first blow so it is forever his sworn enemy. When I used it for the first time, it started leaking so I turned off the water and was trying to roll it back up, which proved to be almost impossible. It kept bucking and twisting and whacking me in the shins. So then Parsley trotted up to see what was going on and it smacked him on the nose, which he took as a declaration of war and I must say I don't blame him."

"The same thing happened to Merit!" said Ivy. "I mean it didn't hit him in the nose, but it did twist around his ankle and trip him." Grace tried to picture Merit Wilcoxen running through the grass biting a hose. Instead, he had written a letter to the editor.

To the Editor:

It has come to my attention that the truth about kink free hoses will set you free: free from garden irritation if not irrigation. Too much irrigation really because they leak and that is not the least of their offenses. In this matter, I must take Svensen's Hardware Store to task. The product in question is Bluff-Guard's Perfecto Garden Hose: Super Duper Flexible, Ultra Lightweight and KINK FREE! Yes, I fell for those promises: 250 feet of them to be exact.

I happily threw out my old, heavy, dark green murderous hoses that used to lurk behind the shrubs hoping to trip you with their tangled bulk, the kinks hissing at you in derision as they stemmed the flow of water. I was going to enjoy watering with my new, light, carefree hoses. I purchased the beige, which is really more of a Deer Creek Khaki sort of color.

Reality hit hard and fast. The hoses may not kink, and that I must admit is true, but they retain the coil of a rattlesnake. When trying to pull them out at full length or return them to a neat pile, they stealthily slam you in the ankle with the brass nozzle. They leak at the couplings and in random spots. The ridges rip up and retain grass, dirt, moss and mulch so the hoses are always dirty. Then you get your clothes and hands filthy whilst tussling with them.

I think that I speak for the citizens of Deer Creek in denouncing these hoses and calling upon the hardware store AND ANYONE ELSE WHO SOLD THEM to refund purchase money in full.

Sincerely yours,
Emeritus D. Wilcoxen, Ph.D.

Grace did not bring up anything about the garden clubs' unwitting role in selling the kink free hoses. Ivy did not bring up the fact that Merit had appropriated her experience for his own dramatic epistolary purposes. She sighed and said, "Eunice is more to blame than Svensen's. They stopped selling them as soon as we asked them to, but Eunice..." another sigh, "Ol' Eunice: a purveyor of defective kink free hoses. Justifiable homicide in this community."

7. A DRIVE-THROUGH WINDOW

Gardenia St. Cyr, President of the Garden Club of St. James, fluttered nervously into the Badger Tearoom. Maybe this hadn't been such a good idea after all. Eunice Kingblade had invited her. No, invited wasn't quite the right word. Requested? No, that wasn't it either. Summoned was a bit harsh; well maybe not. Gardenia sighed and told herself to think about all the lovely tea cakes that the Badger offered. The heady aromas of toasted almond and pecan, chocolate ganache, creamy caramel, apricot and raspberry jams welcomed and comforted her. They helped prepare her for the confrontation with Eunice: confrontation being the only known form of interaction with Eunice.

Gardenia was a lady in the old fashioned sense of the word and just wanted everyone to garden nicely. Her legendary flower arrangements of exponentially blooming diameter graced the tops of suitably ruinous looking classical columns that lined her spacious front hall and dining room. At a long ago luncheon that Gardenia had hosted, Eunice had snorted at these beautifully artistic bouquets and called them pretentious.

Today Gardenia was dressed in pale blue to complement her eyes and her very prematurely white hair that was still thick and wavy. She gathered herself to endure the inevitable attack and smiled weakly at her nemesis. Someone should put an "Approach With Caution" sign on Eunice, like the one on the Siberian Bears' cage at the zoo. She started to say good morning, but Eunice cut her off with, "Sit down sit down." Gardenia settled in resignedly to listen to Eunice.

A couple of months ago, in a gracious spirit of harmony, Gardenia had proposed to Eunice that the two garden clubs should work together on the upkeep of the village park. The creek handily divided the park in half, so for years the two clubs had each claimed a side and maintained them separately. The Garden Club of St. James's side was a relatively level and open piece of ground with a nice lawn and tasteful shrubs. Memorial trees perforated the perimeter. The Deer Creek Garden Club's side of the park was a steep hill with rocky outcroppings, next to a heavily wooded slope.

Somewhat surprisingly, Eunice had agreed to the collaboration and they set up a joint bank account. This meeting was to determine how to proceed with said account. Gardenia was going to propose that they use the money for a lovely Chinese Chippendale bridge over the creek. It would be useful physically and symbolize the working together spirit of the two garden clubs. More than anything, Gardenia hoped that this whole project would bring to an end the troubling goings-on in the garden clubs' closets at the village hall. Gardenia also wanted to name the park in memory of her mother who had purchased the land and given it to Deer Creek, thus saving the location from becoming the site of a gas station.

Eunice punished the paper in front of her with a stainless steel mechanical pencil.

"Now Gardenia, here is what you are going to agree to. We are going to call the park The Common and use the clubs' joint fund to buy a sign and kink free hoses. We will use some of the hoses in The Common and sell the rest to raise money for its continued upkeep."

Eunice gestured impatiently at a young waitress in a daffodil yellow frock edged with white lace. "Bring me a cup of hot water. I have my own tea bags."

She started to wave the girl away imperiously but Gardenia managed to gasp out, "Oh, may I have a cup of tea please and a slice of your lovely Hollander. It is so delicious. Thank you very much." The moist almond cake with a layer of apricot jam baked inside a butter cookie shell would revive her spirits and bolster her strength. It was medicinal really.

Eunice rummaged through her capacious pocketbook, which almost qualified as luggage, and extracted a plastic storage tub filled with bags of the herbal teas that she concocted. The waitress scurried away but glanced back furiously. That woman was an old tea bag herself.

"Let's see: Mossy Morning, that's good for flatulence."

"Well, really!" Furtively, Gardenia swung her eyes around the tearoom. Eunice had such a loud voice.

"Fungus Future, that has antifungal effects obviously. Yak Butter Substitute, no. Oh here, try this." Eunice flung a disturbingly large and ominous looking tea bag onto the table in front of Gardenia. "Bring her hot water too," she called after the waitress. "That's Kudzu Skullcap tea. It'll make you more alert."

"I am quite alert enough, thank you very much." Really, this was so embarrassing. The smell of the tea bag was nauseating and the scent only intensified as it steeped in her cup. Eunice started rifling through papers and dropping paper clips and searching for pens, muttering away, "I know it's in here somewhere. I've drawn up a plan for

The Common, showing what we are going to plant and where the benches will go – all the particulars of flowers and trees – that kind of stuff. I'm very good at landscape design."

Eunice shoved her drawing in front of Gardenia, although leaving it upside down from Gardenia's viewpoint, elaborating on her ingenious placement of white swamp oaks and bald cypresses, persimmons and paw paws; with inscribed stone steps winding through woodland paths and glades. As Eunice droned on, Gardenia steeled herself to take a sip of the herbal tea. She closed her eyes and took a gulp. The hot and fiercely seasoned potion frothed into her mouth, making her gasp and inhale some, probably causing fatal lung damage.

"But, but Eunice," she sputtered, coughing miserably into a real linen napkin. Thank goodness, the Badger does not use paper napkins; if one has to choke, linen is so much better.

"Now, it is all taken care of. No need for you to do anything except help sell the hoses." In a rare display of altruism and just shy of blunt force trauma, Eunice got up to pound Gardenia on the back. "Drink some water." Not that she offered to get her any. Gardenia was nearly in tears. And the kink free hoses! Merit Wilcoxen's letter to the editor had exposed the truth about them to everyone.

"But Eunice: you know that our garden club asked the hardware store to stop selling those kink free hoses because they are so terrible. And I thought that we were going to put together some ideas and present them to the memberships so they could vote on what to call the park and what to do in it. Perhaps a nice Chinese Chippendale bridge over the creek."

"Oh, that would take too much time and nobody wants Chinese Chippendale these days. I know what's best so I went ahead and ordered the sign for The Common and bought the kink free hoses. Don't be so negative. They're absolutely fine. Some are at my house and the rest are at the village hall. Now, speaking of the village hall, we need to discuss the closets."

Since time immemorial in Deer Creek years, or at least since the village hall had been built, each garden club had maintained a closet there in which to store its paraphernalia: vases, flowerpots, garden tour signs, plastic milk crates full of empty wine bottles and the like. (The empty wine bottles did not necessarily indicate excessive drinking. Not that that was unheard of, but in this case the wine bottles were needed for flower shows. All horticultural entries must be displayed in similar and unobtrusive receptacles.) To the non-garden club member, these items would appear identical or interchangeable and certainly not worth squabbling over. To the botanical cognoscenti, however, they were inviolate possessions of priceless territorial significance.

Then a few years ago, with a fatal blow of eminent domain, the garden clubs had wrested two rooms from the unsuspecting firemen, who knew when they were beaten. For reasons of tradition, the rooms were still called the closets except by Eunice who had recently planted a plaque on the Deer Creek Garden Club's closet door, proclaiming it to be the Deer Creek Garden Club's Head Quarters Office.

"NOW, I am willing to be magnanimous about this,"

said Eunice.

Imposscerous: Gardenia beheld the visage of the Wicked Witch of the West. If only a house would fall on Eunice, or even a Chinese Chippendale bridge.

"First thing this morning, I went over to the village hall to put the kink free hoses into the HQO." Here, Eunice paused ominously. "Some of our vases are missing." After another significant pause, which elicited no admission of guilt from Gardenia, Eunice continued, "So I just happened to peek into the Garden Club of St. James's closet and there they were." Eunice bared evil looking dental work. "How did THAT happen?"

This was just too much for Gardenia. It reconfirmed that Eunice Kingblade meant conflict, unpleasantness and the brutal sabotage of any enjoyment that gardening provided. Now she was accusing her of stealing their tacky vases from the HQO.

"HQO! HQO! Now who's pretentious?"

Gardenia got up so abruptly that she knocked her chair over.

"Eunice, you are, you are... oh, just, just the Limit! And my mother loved Chinese Chippendale!"

Gardenia stumbled out of the tearoom and into her car. She had parked in the best spot: right by the front window, facing in. She stomped on the gas to get away but unfortunately she had forgotten to shift into reverse. Her Oldsmobile crashed through the window. Shattering glass exploded over the hood and the front tables, missing Eunice by inches. It was quite a cause célèbre, people joking that Gardenia had tried to kill Eunice and, although the attempt had unfortunately failed, a drive-through window at the Badger would be so handy.

In discussing the incident that night with her husband, Gardenia mused aloud, "Oh Herbert, do you think that I might have some subconscious desire to kill Eunice?"

"Probably that and a non-subconscious one too. Everybody does. Ghastly woman. How about a drink?"

That wild surmise surprised her with its violence. Killing not drinking. Although why should it? Most people reacted violently to Eunice's browbeating and lethal parting shots, in temptation if not in deed. "Why should I be immune?" Gardenia asked the air.

"Immune to drinking? Sounds fatal. I'll make yours a double. You'll forget all about Eunice. How about a game of Monopoly?"

8. CUPPY, EUNICE AND LULU AT HOME

Eunice came home from the tearoom fuming. She checked her clothes carefully for glass fragments while calling Cuppy at the office. But, of course, he was in a meeting and could not be disturbed unless it was a true emergency. Well, if this wasn't a true emergency, she didn't know what was; but that idiot secretary still wouldn't put her through. That idiot secretary was chronically enraged by Eunice's insulting high-handedness and would not have put her through even in the event of World War III. Besides, she was just following Mr. Kingblade's orders.

"HAVVACUPPATEAHAVVACUPPATEA!" advised Lulu as she shuffled back and forth on her perch.

Eunice turned the burner on and erupted around the Industrial Strength beige kitchen, sending out more steam than the kettle when it finally let out its boiling shriek. She was shrieking herself, telling Lulu all about that idiot Gardenia St. Cyr. Lulu was a receptive, not to mention a captive, audience.

"THATIDIOTTHATIDIOTTHATIDIOT," agreed Lulu, indignantly flinging some seeds against the Band-Aid colored wall.

Eunice dunked two large tea bags of her own brew, Brim Reaper, into the Brown Betty teapot, waiting, just waiting, for Cuppy to come home. She even called the Deer Creek Police Department to press charges against Gardenia but she got that idiot Olney Cowperne on the line. Olney put the phone down and loudly shuffled papers, scrabbled through the pencil drawer and thumped the desk for a while.

"Well, Mrs. Kingblade, I've got the Accident Report right here and it says that it was an accident. If it wasn't an accident, there wouldn't be an Accident Report."

Eunice slammed the phone down. That idiot. She'd call the insurance people, that's what she'd do. They were always looking for ways not to pay claims.

"She tried to kill me! Cuppy, I tell you she tried to kill me!" Eunice stamped around the kitchen snorting and breathing out exclamation points, as Cuppy dragged in late that afternoon.

"What? Who?" (Put her on the Christmas card list!)

"Didn't that idiot secretary tell you? Gardenia St. Cyr

that's who. She drove through the window of the Badger. Right where I was sitting!"

First sensible thing that woman has done in years, thought Cuppy as he tried to make his way to the bar.

Eunice jumped in front of him. "It was murder all right. I could see it in her eyes: they were shut tight and she was grimacing."

Cuppy did not want to risk more invective by pointing out that if Gardenia's eyes had been shut tight, Eunice could scarcely have seen any signs of malicious intent or homicidal mania. He doubted it was either one. Gardenia was a pretty woman with a bit of heft to her: something you could get a hold of. Could be awfully silly at times, but she was all right really. "Oh you know how confused she gets. I'm sure it was just an accident." He leaned resignedly against the dim wall and closed his own eyes.

Eunice was stirring the martinis by now, viciously clinking and clanking the stainless steel wand against the sides of the baja brown earthenware pitcher that they had brought back from Mexico. Cuppy cracked open his lids anxiously, hoping that the pitcher would not break before he could grab a drink. Eunice calmed down enough to pour herself a hefty martini, and then actually poured one for Cuppy, remembering to put in a twist of lemon. Most unusual of her to think of others. Think of them in a nice way that is, Cuppy worried to himself.

All through dinner, Eunice trumpeted on, listing people and their absurd grievances against her. God, what had he ever seen in Eunice? What had once been confidence and command had curdled into bullying and fault finding. Criticism was her only known form of communication.

Years ago, Eunice used to wear pretty dresses, soft, with flowers and fairly easy to undo. Now she was buttoned up and epauletted in khaki like a general at the last stand in some outpost of the Empire. He used to admire her clear, objective appraisal of situations, until he realized that it was not clarity but negativity and always had been. It wasn't that she had high standards, she just disparaged the efforts of anyone else. Instead of making the best of things, she made the worst of things. She also made the worst casseroles, using Campbell's soup. How can you screw up Campbell's soup?

Although the casseroles weren't as bad as her nauseating herbal teas. That time he'd come home mid-morning and found Eunice presiding over a coven of garden club women – some herbal tea workshop apparently. Pots of evil smelling potions bubbled away madly on all four burners. Several of the gals went home in severe gastric distress. Noxious fumes and miasmas from the swamp, partly masked by stinging disinfectants, chronically occupied the kitchen. How much longer could he stand living here? Cuppy had to put her out of his misery.

Eunice strode into the living room, which was two shades darker than the kitchen. "I'm beginning to think that people don't like me," she said, clutching the brandy bottle and glasses that she had snatched from the bar on her way. Cuppy tiredly followed her, thinking now there's a news flash. If she only imagined how much I hate her. Not that he wanted her to know that. He might hate her but he didn't want to hurt her feelings. Her likely reaction of devastated heartbreak would be just too much for him to cope with. Better to keep matters on the uneasy truce level.

Cuppy plopped down into a chair that was even more uncomfortable than a rugged outcropping in the Andes. That is why he hardly ever sat in here. After pouring them both liberal brandies, Eunice continued to march around the room straightening things that did not need to be straightened and fiddling with the ominous venetian blinds that were stained a sort of mulch color.

"Gardenia has taken this ridiculous position over the kink free hoses."

Cuppy pictured a scantily clad Gardenia bending over a stack of kink free hoses.

"And Dash Lethaby hates me for opposing his stupid development of the mulch site. He and I used to get along pretty well I thought back in the old days. He used to listen to reason. Then he married that ballet dancer and he's gone downhill ever since; and he was in a valley to begin with."

Cuppy perked up. "Oh, I remember her all right! Madeleine or something; French too. Wonder what she's up to now that they've separated?" Eunice glared him back into silence. Too bad. He'd ask Dash next chance he got but he'd try to keep a clamp on his mouth for the rest of this endless evening.

Cuppy debated getting up for more brandy but Eunice beat him to it, waving the bottle, which was looking perilously low. This must have really gotten to her. Usually Eunice did not drink much. Maybe he should encourage her to drink more as she was now exhibiting a rosy glow instead of her usual sickly pallor.

"Oh, and back to Dash. There are a lot more lawsuits against him than anyone realizes. There's no way anyone will want any part of that project once I drop this bombshell."

Cuppy could feel hot alarm spreading from his forehead to his armpits and back again, which was kind of disgusting. "What bombshell?"

"I've been talking to an environmental lawyer. He says I could justify filing a lawsuit against Dash to stop the development." Eunice gulped down the rest of the brandy and finally relaxed, contemplating the joy of vindictive legal action. With a satisfied sigh, she settled easily onto the rigid sofa and fell asleep.

So Cuppy went to bed, frustrated in more ways than one, while thinking of his own bombshells: he had invested heavily in the development of the mulch site and had spent a big chunk more on Kimberley in Personnel. Maybe he should give Dash a head's up on Eunice's proposed legal action. "It never ends," Cuppy told the ceiling. Yeah, that's what he'd do. Call Dash first thing in the morning. He could ask about Madeleine too. Cuppy calmed himself down by thinking about coiling some kink free hose around Eunice's neck. Then he pounded his pillow into shape for good measure.

9. EUNICE AND GARDENING

As President of the Deer Creek Garden Club, Eunice Kingblade ruled with a firm hand on the shovel so to speak and liked to make sure that things were done her way; and if they weren't, to harangue the guilty unfortunates who had committed the atrocity. At least you could hear her coming, a penetrating voice that could wake the dead. She would probably tell them that they had died the wrong way. Her stentorian alarm, however, did give one a chance to gird one's loins, hide or run away. Fortunately, Eunice's lack of a sense of humor meant that her laugh rarely erupted. Some had described it as sounding like machine gun fire raking a chalkboard, and had gone so far as to suggest that it be surgically removed.

For Eunice, gardening in general and the garden club in particular were not loves or hobbies; they were missions, crusades, structures on which to hang people, events and ideas. They constituted her major form of social engagement and provided numerous opportunities to tell people what to do. Although for all her touting of gardens and gardening, Eunice's own garden displayed bland, minimal plantings that had been installed (one could not even say planted) by the developer. The shrubs and trees represented a narrow range of medium greens, medium heights and medium widths. The only color appeared in early spring in the form of determined if lonely daffodils.

Her kitchen décor brought beige to a whole new level: coma-inducing beige. She wore beige to the point where maybe she did not exist at all, not even in her own imagination, which was infertile to say the least. She was literal and humorless. Maybe that was why she was so mean: she just could not imagine others' reactions to her blistering comments. After all, she was just trying to help them.

Eunice had her rules on HOW TO DO THINGS RIGHT. She shoved people around like furniture. She had always relished rearranging furniture, or more accurately, telling others to shift the bookcase over here, switch the sofa with the two wing chairs. Reverse the standing lamps. Open the venetian blinds, close the venetian blinds, take them down, put them back up. Take the rug out of the study and put it in the hall. Nothing was ever right, so back it went to the original unsatisfactory location.

Eunice had all ten fingers and ten toes in everyone else's pies: flower shows, kink free hoses, the mulch site and the closets at the village hall. She had to find out who was switching things in the closets. It had to be that devious Gardenia St. Cyr. On a number of occasions now she had seen Gardenia flitting surreptitiously around the village hall, hovering near the garden clubs' closets. She had to be the guilty party. Ever since the tearoom incident, which was possibly a murder attempt, Eunice's antagonism toward that flibbertigibbet had grown. It was her duty to set Gardenia straight. "It is for your own good... I feel it is my duty... I am always right... I told you so..." were the Eunice mantras, intoned in a cold voice, rigidly devoid of caring or concern, not a note, not an echo.

Never had she run into such opposition, however, as in the matter of the mulch pile. Mulch site really – the whole 14.4 acres of it. Hidden by thickly wooded borders and the overgrown banks of Deer Creek, it was a model of the mulching process. A late and lamented benefactress had given it to the village and Eunice considered it the jewel in the crown of Deer Creek. It was also very valuable property that could be developed into a lucrative enclave of luxury dwellings. Now here was a cause worthy of her. This would be her greatest triumph: fending off and defeating the ploys of that idiot playboy builder, Dash Lethaby.

10. A DISTURBING DEVELOPMENT

Dashiell Hammett Lethaby was a man born to wear needlepoint belts, polo shirts and safari boots. Trousers usually sighted at the America's Cup races complemented his physique. He was a non-writing Hemingway, slung about with rifles, flasks and women. Aviator sunglasses caressed his bronzed brow. A watch with five time zones and an altimeter encircled his wrist with platinum and rose gold. Dash could improve the scenery in any Ralph Lauren landscape.

But right now he and his black Labrador Retriever Cole were surveying the local landscape: the Deer Creek Mulch Site to be exact.

"Waddya think, Cole? Look at all this. Almost fifteen acres of pure development gold and they use it to process leaves. The mind boggles." They jumped out of the Jeep Wagoneer with Marine Teak Wood Grain Siding.

Boggles, that'd be a good name for a dog. Boggles, here Boggles! Dash scuffed along while Cole set out to explore. What passel of fatuous idiots had dreamed up the mulch site? And now Eunice Kingblade with her crackpot environmentalism was fighting to keep it that way. At the Zoning and Planning (ZAP) Committee meetings, she kept bringing up all that stupid stuff about water runoff and wildlife habitat and wetland corridors. Parties were his wildlife habitat and Dash liked corridors of oak or tile.

Then she had started dredging up some of Lethaby & Knapps Construction Co.'s professional mishaps. Clasping a bulging accordion file of documents that leaked all over the table and floor, she thumped the evidence down with the weight of justice, detailing case after case of unfinished jobs, faulty drainage systems, flouted codes and tawdry decoration.

"Tawdry decoration? What? You made that up. No one ever accused me of tawdry decoration! And all those lawsuits were settled out of court." She had labeled him an enemy of the environment. "Oh, Eunice, just because I have a better idea for the mulch site does not mean I am anti-environment. I'm environmental!" he had responded indignantly. "I recycle."

"Yes, ladies and gentlemen, I am sure that Mr. Lethaby recycles more beer cans than anyone else in town." A general chuckle broke out, in part due to witnessing the unusual event of Eunice making a joke.

"Ha ha, very funny. Listen, people in Deer Creek want tastefully luxurious places to live and I am going to build them. The location is ideal. Lots of folks are downsizing now, this would be a real boon to them. They could stay in town, near the grandkids, in well built, attractive, turn-key townhouses. Plus it would increase the tax base. The mulch site operation just costs the village money. It doesn't bring anything in except too many leaves. Plus it stinks! A lot of people have complained about the smell. It is time to turn over a new leaf."

That produced some loyal laughs. "So there, I can

make a joke too!" Dash had reached oratorical mode. "The financial climate and market share potential are perfect right now for the village to approve these plans and to invest in the future of Deer Creek. The residential development of the mulch site is for the good of the community."

"Residential development? I call it a disturbing development. Good of the community my foot. This is all about you. You need this project to make a personal killing because you're broke and you've ruined your own family company, you feckless idiot."

The chairman pounded the gavel quite dramatically, in an effort to put a regrettable end to the entertaining squabble. "Mrs. Kingblade, would you be willing to leave your file with the committee so we can study your findings?" Eunice did not trust them; they might conveniently lose the file. So she grudgingly agreed to make copies for them, thereby shelving the matter for another month.

Dash shouted an oath (non-religious and not legally binding) and shoved past the table, knocking Eunice's file to the floor and kicking a chair over on his way out of the meeting. He desperately wanted to save the construction company that his grandfather had founded.

Dash had spent the last decade or so letting his partner run it expertly into the ground. He hadn't had time to oversee it properly what with the summer house and boat in Northeast Harbor and his car habit and his car wrecking habit and some other habits that he saw no point in bringing up. Plus he'd trusted the guy.

Then Madeleine Montluçon had danced into his life. Under duress from his sister Christie (christened Agatha Christie; their mother had been an avid fan of detective novels and murder mysteries), Dash had been at some gala or other to benefit children or a disease or children with a disease. The evening's festivities included a performance by the National Ballet of Canada followed by a five course inedible dinner. Fortunately there was plenty to drink and he was introduced to the most beautiful girl he had ever seen much less met.

Madeleine was the principal ballerina on tour with the company: gorgeous, a bit shy, and (until then) seriously dedicated to the hard work that a career in ballet demanded. Dash was handsome, outgoing and had never been serious about anything in his life until he met her. Their relationship proved that spontaneous combustion does occur. Three months later, after she had danced out her ballet contract, they eloped, spent a month in France and then returned to Deer Creek.

Madeleine loved the basic design and architecture of the house that Dash's grandparents had built and where his parents had lived and he had grown up, but in her eyes it was currently a dump. Plain but dignified, the Lethaby family home was shabby, cluttered with beat-up antique furniture, faded and tattered upholstery and curtains, worn and scarred wide-planked wooden floors, stained wallpaper and an ancient kitchen of interest only to domestic archeologists. Dash admitted that the dear old place needed some sprucing up and feeling happily indulgent he gave Madeleine free rein.

As with his company, Dash just hadn't been paying attention. When they got back from their honeymoon in France, they moved into the Vandenbosch's carriage house while the work was being done. Madeleine was in charge of everything and told him that she wanted it to be a surprise. The word surprise should have tipped him off. Madeleine planned an elegant soiree housewarming party and right before the guests were to arrive she brought him over and teasingly blindfolded him before leading him into the front hall.

The sight of yards of florid furbelows and opulent flounces festooning every inch of the dear old place had knocked him breathless. His sickened stomach contracted into a gallstone as Madeleine toured him around the once gracious and comforting old house. It hit him then that it was a stage set: a theatrical production. He would be living in Sleeping Beauty's Nightmare. The master bedroom and bathroom were Nutcracker Ensuite. Instead of dying, Romeo and Juliet go to Hollywood. This was his childhood home's Swan Song Lake. Those were the few ballets that he could bring to his numbed brain. Worse, everyone at the housewarming party got to see this embarrassment. He had woken up at three in the morning, naked and on the floor of the new swell shower having no memory of getting there.

Truly devastated, Dash hated the travesty that his childhood home had become and planned to tear some of the worst of it out. Madeleine's lack of discernment, or critical judgment or appreciation of what aesthetic qualities he valued, appalled and hurt him. He questioned his own reading of her. Was she not that rarest of birds? A non-decorating, non-real estate selling, non-garden clubbing, non-needlepointing woman? She had lived at school or on the road most of her life. There had been no time for activities other than ballet. Now, it was like she was playing house or worse, was on a glorious holiday: the heady acquisition of unfamiliar vices.

The bills stunned him into looking more thoroughly at the company's finances and business practices. Lethaby & Knapps was in critical condition. He hired different accountants whose research brought to light his partner's wrongdoing. He had taken company pension funds, invested them in high-risk ventures and predictably lost not just his shirt but the whole wardrobe.

Although technically not legally liable, Dash considered himself morally liable, certainly responsible, so for once was working flat out to fix things. When was he going to start thinking, really thinking, about things deeply? Was he terminally shallow? Or only deeply shallow? How much self analysis could he take? The Headmaster back at boarding school had frequently asked him, "Deep in thought Lethaby, or merely becalmed in the shallows?"

"Low tide, Sir. Low tide." Low Tide Lethaby, that's me all right.

Dash had to have this mulch site deal go through. To hell with Eunice. Tawdry decoration – that really rankled – as did her beer can jab. Her sniping remarks had taken this beyond business. Now it was personal. Calling him feckless. He could be full of feck if need be. He'd figure out some way to shut that old bat up or get rid of her. There had to be something he could do.

Cole trotted over to him smelling all mulchy. At least Eunice did not know about the meeting at the mulch site. He was going to put on a presentation that would knock their socks off. Ol' Eunice would be left in the dust, or mulch rather. He patted his best friend on the head. "Right Coley Woley?"

11.   OFFICE PLANTS

Eunice carefully carried the bromeliad (Bromelia voraciana) down the long hall of Tirano BioEngineering toward Cuppy's corner office. She liked to make these forays, these scouting expeditions to see what was going on. All under the guise, of course, of providing Cuppy's office with fresh flowers and plants. It was a point of honor and duty to carry out this service for her husband and the company. Sometimes Eunice was able to see through herself however. She went there to keep an eye on Cuppy. No telling what he might get up to. He was at a dangerous age and she even more so.

Viscount (his real first name – goodness knows what his mother was thinking) Pimms "Cuppy" Kingblade had become more dangerous than Eunice could have imagined. Her relentless negativity and criticism over the years had created his own version of fear and loathing. Sometimes he just wanted to end it all; for her that is. He wanted to start it all for himself. And START it all he had – just as soon as Kimberley had floozed into his life. Her looks had triggered a vague memory of someone, but he couldn't figure out who, just couldn't quite put his finger on it. Now that he had put a lot more than his finger on her, he no longer perceived any possible resemblance. Her innocent cheapness had allured him and she had been grateful for the job. That weekend in the hotel's Clint Eastwood Suite had been great.

As Eunice approached his office, the door opened and laughter and a blond rippled out. Just as she had suspected! Eunice advanced on the target, apparently a sixteen year old girl from Ipanema. The girl smiled blindly in her direction, clearly not taking in Eunice, who as a middle-aged woman, was invisible to Kimberley.

Cuppy followed her into the corridor and turned toward Eunice. The grin exploded off his face and he said loudly, "That will be all. Thanks for all your hard work."

"Whaa?" Kimberley twirled around almost into his face. "Are you all right? You look like you saw –"

"My wife," Cuppy cut her off. "Ah, Eunice. Hi. This is Kimberley from Personnel."

"I'm sure she is very personal." Had she met her before? There was something familiar about the girl. Eunice flowed past, ignoring Kimberley who made a face over her shoulder at Cuppy then stilettoed away.

Cuppy left the door open as a hint to a brief stay and appraised the green spikey thing that Eunice was holding.

"Nice plant. Looks poisonous."

"Kimberley?"

"She does sensitivity training."

"I bet she does." Eunice found a place for the bromeliad and started fiddling with some of the orchids. She whipped a misting bottle out of her bag and haphazardly spritzed a bunch of plants with fertilizer water. The right plants gave such a sophisticated air of gravitas to a business office.

She had offered to install like arrangements in the other offices but only one person had accepted – that rather dim bulb from Research and Development. That jerk was worse than an idiot. He was a moron. That time he had called Cuppy early in the morning at home and she'd answered the phone. Eunice could just see that clown sitting on the bed in his underwear while talking to HER! How dare he! When she asked him, he even admitted it! So she certainly wasn't about to arrange plants for him.

Cuppy had long ago given up trying to persuade her that he did not want plants in his office. She only used them as an excuse to check up on him, always catching him off guard. At first he had tried killing the stupid plants, hoping to discourage her. But the opposite had happened and she had redoubled her efforts to create a jungle in there. There must be some early warning system that Security could install.

Eunice rotated to face him and hit him full on with a blast of Miracle Gro.

"Agh... what the... Eunice!" Cuppy swatted at his tie and jacket. "Jesus Christ. What was that for?"

"Miss Sensitivity."

"Then why didn't you spray her?" Cuppy had grabbed some tissues from his desk drawer and was blotting himself. Christ, he hoped that blue stuff wouldn't stain.

"She must be good at her job because you were sure looking happy."

"Well, you know what, I was! She's a nice girl and upbeat and enthusiastic. It's what this company needs." He continued to fuss with his tie and shirt, then cautiously dared to glance toward Eunice. She was oddly and alarmingly quiet.

Registering cold and tiredness, Eunice's bones were telling her that she was just plain old worn out. As soon as she got home she would have a nice cup of her homemade herbal tea and maybe start that new Stalin biography.

"Are you having an affair with her?" she asked as she continued to molest the leaves.

"What? No! Are you crazy? Jesus Christ Eunice. No!" Cuppy ran his hand down his face to smooth it out and started sending her mental Death Rays. "Listen, McKnight called me, asked a favor. Would I get this girl a job but keep it quiet? No explanation. So fine, I did. I helped a friend. Is that so terrible?"

Eunice was flabbergasted. "McKnight Freemantle! You're kidding me! That pompous, spineless, gussied up excuse for a mayor."

"Aw, c'mon. You always think the worst of everyone. McKnight's a good guy."

"Good guy? Getting involved with a girl young enough to be his daughter?"

"Oh for God's sake Eunice. He said he hadn't even met her. He was doing the favor for somebody else."

"Yeah, right. Of course he would say that."

Cuppy clenched his teeth and stared out the window at the native species meadow of the company campus. He was going to talk to Security as soon as she left.

"Whoo hoo!" It was a cackle of twisted triumph. Cuppy turned around apprehensively. That noise usually heralded the opportunity for Eunice to rub a pillar of salt into her victim's wound.

"Just wait till I have a word with McKnight about this.

He'll change his tune about the mulch site. I'm going over to the village hall right now." The herbal tea would have to wait. Even the Stalin book would have to wait. Besides, that was beach reading anyway. Eunice left, spitting out the worst word she could think of, "Men."

Cuppy grabbed his phone to warn McKnight that Eunice was on the way and on the warpath. That would give him enough time to bug out of the village hall and head for home or an undisclosed location. Cuppy's own office security would have to wait.

As soon as McKnight answered the phone, Cuppy spat out the worst word he could think of, "Eunice!" After McKnight's stunned silence he added, "She's on her way over to your office now. Mulch madness! Time to am-scray." That was all. No point in upsetting McKnight even more. Besides, with Eunice thinking that McKnight was involved with Kimberley, it provided great cover for his own affair with the girl. No, he wouldn't say anything more to McKnight. When it came to women, it was every man for himself.

12.   MCKNIGHT AT THE OFFICE

McKnight K. Freemantle III smoothed his Hermès tie and arched and twisted his neck to make the tie with its subtle design of crossed skis and crutches comfortable and properly placed. As the Mayor of Deer Creek he had to be immaculately attired at all times. But then McKnight had always dressed well. He genuinely enjoyed it. He loved good clothes: their feel, their richness, their caché, that je sais quoi exactement. Although he was starting to achieve a bit of embonpoint, the beautifully tailored suits minimized this middle-aged accessory. With his enviable height and aristocratic bearing he could pull it off. It was the clothes themselves that were increasingly hard to pull off. Not to mention pull on.

To be on the safe side though, McKnight was practicing holding in his stomach. Suck in. Hooold it. One. Two. Three. He counted all the way up to four then slooowly exhaled and the ol' tummy slouched back out over his Russian reindeer leather belt. Try it again.... At home, he did this surreptitiously, not wanting his wife Pinckney to catch him because Our Lady of the Concave Stomach would undoubtedly smirk.

In addition to his stomach exercises, McKnight also hid his writing from Pinckney. He was currently working on a detective novel and was very proud of his clever title *Bet Noir – A Casino Mystery*. He was having trouble with the plot and the characters and the setting, but other than that it was coming along well. Fortunately his assistant, the efficient and self-effacing Miss Sigismonday R. Vellacotton, took care of all the day-to-day stuff, leaving him free to attend to official mayoral functions, do exercises and work on his book. When he'd told Pinckney the name of his new assistant she had snorted, "What kind of a name is that?"

Sigismonday, known to everyone else as Siggy, had been dubbed "Monday" by McKnight. "There's my gal Monday through Friday," he had quipped upon inheriting her from the previous mayor. Singing "Monday, Monday, so good to me," McKnight had charmed her and won her devoted loyalty. He didn't mind Monday knowing about his novel or holding in his stomach, or even knowing about Kimberley.

Monday was so accepting, so low maintenance, with such an inexpensive face. He didn't have to think around her. She was there to think for him and know what to do. The only thing he didn't like about her, kind of gave him the creeps as a matter of fact, was the way she could sneak up on people.

Siggy loved her new name and having only McKnight and no one else call her "Monday" made it even more special. She was Monday for him alone. Alone – she would like to get him alone, for herself; but she did in a way, at the office. She was too objective to harbor that idea for life outside the office. Her power to dream was extremely strong and she imagined all sorts of occasions in which she could save his life or at least his career.

Monday was going to do something extraordinary for him, something so colossal that it would achieve all the political ambitions that she and Pinckney had for him. Her brilliant tactics, cleverly portrayed as McKnight's own ideas, would not only ensure his devotion to her but would keep that silly little Pinckney in the background. She would just have to wait for the right opportunity, but Monday was good at waiting. Then McKnight would see how superficial, not to mention superfluous, Pinckney was. Pinckney, she had snorted to herself upon meeting the mayor's wife, what kind of a name is that?

Monday paused at the partly open office door and

waited, watching him hold in his stomach. As soon as he started looking around impatiently, she silently manifested herself, startling McKnight who suddenly needed extra oxygen as he exhaled sharply and deflated into his swivel chair with the good lumbar support.

"Oh there you are." Christ, why did she have to just materialize like that?

"Listen, I want you to hold all my calls." The telephone had been noticeably silent that morning.

"I need to concentrate on my book. Would you bring me some more legal pads please, then close the door? Thanks, Monds – you're the best."

Ahh, alone at last! McKnight stared imaginatively at the pristine legal pad that pleaded for his immortal words. He could see them now as they would be faithfully typed by Monday.

> "The dame had a décolletage
> that would give a mountain climber
> vertigo. I suddenly needed extra
> oxygen myself as I exhaled sharply
> and deflated into my swivel chair
> with the good lumbar support."

13. MAYORAL SUPPORT

Now that was something that Monday had insisted upon: the proper chair. Pinckney didn't care about his comfort or health, but his dedicated assistant had researched the best chair and ordered it herself. The Revolver, Gold Series II swiveled like the well-oiled machine it was, plus it offered superb lumbar support. It even had an automatic warmer for cold winter mornings at the village hall, which was drafty, poorly heated and didn't have enough closets. There were a lot of problems at what McKnight referred to as "City Hall."

He had recently attended a mayoral conference that had been ostensibly for the purpose of discussing problems common to small cities. McKnight took on the topic of "City Hall Architecture and Design," a subject that had been largely and quite unaccountably ignored. His remarks included the distressing facts that his City Hall did not have enough closets and the few that they did have were quite small.

Encouraged by the surprised looks of the audience, McKnight had explained about the two rival garden clubs fighting over closet space for their vases, flowerpots, Christmas decorations and all those empty wine bottles. Now he may have waxed a bit lyrical, embroidering a few anecdotes, but only as one with a novelist's eye would be expected to do. McKnight had never actually seen garden club members hurl vases at each other but he wouldn't put it past them. The drive-by turnip throwing, however, had been documented by the undeniable evidence of turnips and a broken window in the Building Department. The Deer Creek police had compiled a Weapons Report on the turnips, but the perpetrators were never identified.

An unfeeling and thoroughly urban mayor had responded disparagingly on such terrible problems. All he had were potholes and crime. McKnight had retorted that

Deer Creek was capable of crime. Getting hit by a turnip was no joke. And only thirty-two years ago there was a murder at a private party when somebody (a nonresident) stabbed the victim (another nonresident) in the gazebo. Getting stabbed in the gazebo is usually fatal as was the case in this unfortunate but discretely handled incident.

It was just due to the excellent police force of a chief and four patrolmen that there was so little crime. Plus they had potholes, tastefully small potholes perhaps, but potholes nonetheless. There might be crime. It could happen: high-class crime though. Not to mention high-class litter: none of those cheap beer cans. Deer Creek had premium long necked beer bottles with the occasional Moet bottle thrown in (or out as the case may be).

14.   NO ROOM FOR HOSES

Eunice drove over to the village hall at a reckless 30 mph, hitting only two potholes. She had him now – that idiot McKnight Freemantle. What a nincompoop! Of course he was having an affair with that bimbo. His shirt was so stuffed it was a wonder it didn't explode. It's not really blackmail, not black blackmail, just off-black or gray mail. She wasn't going to threaten to kill him or beat him up (although that was tempting) or even demand money. She just wanted to help him see the light; to raise his consciousness about the true issues involved (like his reputation and political future); to get the idiot to change his position on the mulch site development or she'd tell Pinckney about Kimberley. There, that was straightforward enough so even that lamebrain McKnight would get it.

Her renewed enthusiasm for battle forced back the wave of Damoclesian tiredness and she revved the station wagon and the little red arrow up to 35. She wished that the cops would just try to pull her over.

Eunice putted into the village hall parking lot, slightly disappointed at having failed to achieve a police escort. Several stacks of kink free hoses blocked the front walk. Eunice caught sight of that redneck dolt Mungo Gummers disappearing around the corner of the building, heading for the false security of the Department of Public Works office.

"Hey – Mungo: what are these hoses doing out here? Some are supposed to be in the Garden Club of St. James's closet and the rest in the Deer Creek Garden Club's Head Quarters Office, the HQO."

"Humpty Dumpty!" he said quietly. That woman was poison. He had tried to explain Eunice Kingblade to his wife, Rita.

"She's mean just for the sake of being mean and she criticizes everything I do: the village flowerpots have the wrong color flowers in them, there isn't enough mulch, I don't clear away the brush fast enough."

Mungo sighed. She was impossible to deal with. Nothing worked. His first idea was to be mean back, but he just couldn't do it. He had tried to be mean to someone once, a long time ago, but it hadn't worked and it had bugged him ever since. No one could ignore or avoid Mrs.

Kingblade because she just attacked out of the blue.

Now Mungo wasn't the sharpest knife in the drawer or the brightest bulb in the chandelier or any of those little sayings that pretended to be gentle; but he was a good, kind man. Good, kind men had been nonexistent where Rita had grown up. He worked hard and was a wonderful father to their two little girls Penny and Beth. Mayor Freemantle called the girls the Ladybugs and Mungo loved that cute name. Rita suspected he called them that because he couldn't remember their names. Mungo idolized the mayor, however, so she kept her opinion to herself.

The only other thing that she disagreed with Mungo on was his pet ferrets. She really did not like having them in the house. He had rather sadly carted them away to the Department of Public Works building but then Eunice had discovered them and threatened to call Animal Control. Who threatens ferrets? Rita may not want them in her house but they were innocent little animals. Well, not all that innocent. They had eaten some pillows.

So she hated Eunice Kingblade for Mungo's sake and hers as well as the ferrets'. She had had a few nasty encounters with Eunice at Shady Grove, where Rita waited tables. Unfair complaints about food and service; bringing her own disgusting tea bags; tips so small they were more insulting than nothing at all. That time she had purposely let one of the screen doors hit a bus boy, who was struggling under a full tray of dirty dishes.

Mungo continued, "Then I heard her tell the mayor that I was a redneck dolt. So I figure fine, if that's what she thinks I am, that's what she's going to get."

"Well,   Miz   Kingblade,"   Mungo   slouched

downtroddenly toward her, playing the feebleminded hick to the hilt, "Miz Siggy said there wasn't no room left in the garden clubs' closets. So she tol' me to take 'em to the mulch site and store 'em there. That ain't right?" Mungo scratched vigorously and spat on the pavement.

"No. You take them back inside. I'll deal with her. And stop muttering. Can barely understand you as it is. And stop that disgusting scratching."

"Yes, ma'am, Miz Kingblade," giving his stomach an extra hard raking.

"Hm!" Eunice glared him a slight nod of dismissal.

As soon as she had skirted the piles of hoses and wrenched open the village hall front door, Mungo, suddenly fleet of foot, fled to his nearby pickup truck and backed it up next to the sidewalk. He started flinging hoses into the back, hoping to make his getaway before Eunice came out again.

The village hall's heavy wooden front door was hard to open and then you could not aggrievedly slam it. So Eunice stomped as loudly as she could on the marble floor of the lobby.

"Where's Siggy?" she demanded of the receptionist, Eloise Lutjens who sat frozen in place, terrified of Mrs. Kingblade. Fortunately she did not have to respond because Siggy silently approached, coming up behind Eunice. Siggy mentally mantraed to herself: say nothing, show nothing, say nothing, show nothing.

That age-old warning instinct pricked the hair on the back of Eunice's neck and she jumped a bit, turning around. "Oh, there you are! I want those hoses put back in the Garden Club of St. James's closet and our HQO.

Mungo said you told him to take them to the mulch site."

Through the window behind Eunice, Siggy could just catch sight of Mungo working faster than she had ever seen him before, hurling the hoses into the back of his truck. Siggy had made it clear that he would be rewarded for his help. Cash trumped fear, even fear of Eunice Kingblade. She just had to keep Eunice occupied long enough for Mungo to load up all the hoses.

"Where's the mayor?" Eunice swerved past Siggy toward McKnight's office.

Siggy followed her into the mayor's office, which was dark and clearly devoid of mayor, who had fled immediately after taking Cuppy's warning telephone call.

"Left for the day I take it." Eunice swiveled like a revolving door toward Siggy. "Well, you listen to me missy. You tell the mayor that I want to talk to him about the mulch site and how he may consider changing his tune on the subject. Because," Eunice paused and surveyed the empty room, "I know something that he wouldn't want his wife and all his high and mighty friends to hear about." Her voice dropped to a vicious whisper, "You say just one word to him: Kimberley."

Siggy could see her mother – the purple venom drooling from the witch's lips. The air around her head roiled with orange snakes that whipped the atmosphere into darkness. Say nothing, show nothing, feel nothing, say nothing, show nothing feel nothing say nothingshow nothingfeelnothingnothingnothing.

Siggy and Eunice stared at each other, the latter finally wrenching her glare from the silent flunky and toward the door. Thinking gosh that woman is creepy, Eunice left hurriedly, suddenly cold and tired again. What was the matter with her these days?

Eunice breathed the fresh outside air, turned toward her car, then stopped abruptly. Piles of kink free hoses shook and tilted in the bed of Mungo's truck as it screeched and reeled out of the parking lot. That lout! Eunice ran for her car to take up pursuit.

Siggy kept an eye on Eunice until she drove away. Gosh, that woman is creepy. The frame around her license plate said, "Happiness Is Biting My Parrot Back." That sentiment in itself was weird enough but how on earth had Kingblade found out about Kimberley? The woman should work for the CIA. If she could uncover a carefully kept secret like that, she might have found out about the meeting tonight at the mulch site. Although Siggy had not been planning to attend because it was really more social than business, McKnight might need protection. She better go.

She still had a bit of time on her hands before the meeting started. Time enough for more creative reorganization in the garden clubs' closets. McKnight wanted those old bats out of the village hall and had given Siggy carte blanche to do so. Siggy had hit upon the simple but perfect catalyst for accusations and violence: rearranging the possessions, redistributing tools, causing minor shortages of empty wine bottles; things would go missing then return. The mounting controversies boded well for the departure of one or both clubs.

At this point, perhaps some breakage was warranted to speed up the process. That silly Gardenia St. Cyr had been there earlier that day, hunting almost furtively for something. So yes, this would be a good time to stir up further acrimony.

First though, she would call McKnight to let him know that Eunice had found out about Kimberley. No wait. That would be a mistake. It would put McKnight into a panic. That would require major hand holding on her part. Unfortunately not real, physical hand holding but emotional hand holding which would be nice. First, Siggy would have to figure out how to deal with Eunice, how to keep her quiet about Kimberley. Then present the fait accompli to McKnight. He liked fait accomplis as well as flinging French phrases around. Siggy would think of something. Maybe not French, but something. She always did.

15.   A HAPPY MAN

Like an Olympic discus thrower, Mungo had hurled the last coil of kink free hose into his pickup truck, thrown himself into the driver's seat and gunned it out of there. Even though he went up the hill and round the bend (Mrs. Kingblade was the one round the bend) and was safely out of sight of the village hall, he did not slow down to his usual aggravating crawl.

Now Mungo Gummers did not drive slowly in order to aggravate on purpose. When he wanted to aggravate, he was quite innovative and successful in that regard. But while driving through Deer Creek, he usually liked to enjoy the scenery. He had planted and nurtured a lot of that scenery. Right now, however, he wanted to gain the

sanctuary of the mulch site to counteract the upsetting
confrontation with Mrs. Kingblade. Any contact with her
was enough to unnerve a whole testament of Bible thumping Evangelists. She had probably driven droves of them
into the Jehovah's Witness Protection Program.

After what happened last week, Mungo feared that he
might have to put his ferrets into some kind of animal
witness protection. Since his wife had banished the ferrets from their house because they had chewed up some
pillows, Mungo had been keeping them in a hutch at the
village hall right behind the Department of Public Works
building. Then, that old trout Mrs. Kingblade came
snooping around and happened upon them. Told him he
couldn't keep rats on village property – she'd called them
rats! Mungo was outraged! They were a Special Breed of
Racing Ferret. Her loud mean voice had scared Superman
and Lightning so they raced under their straw to hide and
wouldn't come out until long after she'd left. She said he
had to get rid of them or she would. She'd report him to
the mayor or call Animal Control.

Mungo could count on the mayor to support him –
for the ferret vote – ha-ha. Mungo liked political humor.
The mayor did too and he was a good guy, always said hi
and asked Mungo about Penny and Beth. He called them
the Ladybugs. Mrs. Mayor was sure stuck up. She hardly
ever came over to the village hall, but recently he had seen
her there a number of times with Mrs. St. Cyr. Must be
garden club business. But she'd never go to the mulch site.
Mungo would bet anything on that. But if Mrs. K called
Animal Control, all bets were off.

So he moved the ferrets and their hutch over to the

mulch site where his cousin Reavis could keep an eye on
them and take care of the crop at the same time. Superman
and Lightning should be safe there from Mrs. Nosy Parker.
As would the little patch of tilled earth with its young
plants, hidden at the end of an overgrown path on the
far side of the mulch site. With items that he had rescued from the creek: rebar, fencing, tarps and lawn chairs,
Reavis had built a small campsite there and called it the
Compound. He fixed up a striped canvas awning over the
hutch and fenced in a little exercise yard for the ferrets to
practice in for the races coming up.

Reavis Huckstep was a happy man. He sat down in
the spring sunshine to guard the ferrets and the crop while
eating his apple and reading his book. It was his favorite
book in the whole wide world, the only book he had ever
read. He could recite it by heart, always talking out loud
and looking at every word when he said it.

The Happy Man and His Dump Truck. Oh he just loved
this book. A kind lady had read it to him over and over
again in the hospital when he was there after his father
threw him against the wall of the trailer a few times. They
told him when he got older that he had suffered brain
damage, but his brain worked fine for him and he could
read just fine too – as long as it was *The Happy Man and
His Dump Truck*, which they had let him take home from
the hospital. That had been almost fifteen years ago. The
book was missing both covers and tattered with affection
so he could roll it up and put it in his jacket pocket. He
held it lovingly and continued to read contentedly next to
the sleeping ferrets and the garden.

Reavis and Mungo had started growing the plants back

in February indoors in the Department of Public Works shed behind the village hall. Two days ago they had moved them to the mulch site garden even though it was kind of early in the planting season. They had to get them out of there before someone like that busybody Miz U-No-Hoo found them. Mungo said they should be outside anyway because you need a lot of sunshine to grow marijuana.

Mungo slammed with angry vigor into the pothole opposite the hardware store then tore up to the mulch site entrance and fumbled with the clicker to open the gate. He forgot to close it as he zoomed to the far side of the empty lot, honking SOS on the horn to alert Reavis, who loved codes and passwords. The fact that the only code he recognized was SOS, however, limited this method of communication. Fortunately, it was appropriate for this occasion. Reavis's passwords alternated between Velveeta and Ripple, which were the names of his pet black rat snakes.

Mungo ejected from his pickup truck, shouting "Velveeta, Velveeta," hoping that was the right password for today. To be on the safe side, he added, "Ripple, Ripple." A happy man ran out to greet him.

16.   AN UNHAPPY WOMAN

Eunice drove over to the mulch site at an enraging (if you were behind her) or prudent (if you were her) 20 mph, easily avoiding that pothole in front of the bank and stopping with profound delicacy at every stop sign. She wanted to think about this one. Did it really matter if Mungo had taken the kink free hoses to the mulch site? There wasn't much room in the closets at the village hall to begin with and the hoses were such a disappointment that maybe it would be better after all to have them out of sight. The furor would die down and be forgotten and if anyone brought it up Eunice would gently and sorrowfully imply that it was all Gardenia's fault and deny any knowledge or responsibility.

Eunice preferred to be honest just because it was so much easier. But there were times when one got a little muddled and a hasty, ill-considered lie popped out and then there was no going back. Then sometimes that lie needed subsequent ever larger ones. It did bother her, not her conscience, but the worry of being found out. She ran through permutation after permutation, possibility after possibility of how to kill the problem quickly and neatly. There could be no doubts.

In the case of the kink free hoses, she had known very well before she bought them with the garden clubs' joint fund that they were defective and could not be returned. They couldn't be THAT bad. But they WERE that bad and outraged purchasers wanted refunds.

Eunice did not want them to find out from the outlet guy that he had told her of their poor quality, which is why he gave her such a break on the price. The fact that Eunice had then charged people an inflated price made it even worse. But before thinking about it, she had adamantly denied knowing about the true condition of the hoses; and now she was stuck with that story. As long as the outlet guy was not contacted, she'd be all right. She didn't think she'd told anyone where she'd got them and she couldn't imagine anyone actually investigating. What if somebody went to the police? Not that those idiots would ever prove anything. Nonetheless, maybe Mungo had actually done her a favor.

With a weight of the world on her shoulders sigh, Eunice approached the mulch site. She may as well verify the situation. The gate was open and when she pulled in she could see Mungo's truck on the far side of the large space, almost empty now of the fragrant piles of good leaf mold. Eunice drove across the huge area carefully, hoping to catch that gap-toothed yokel unaware. She parked behind a row of evergreens that separated the mulch site's open space from the heavily wooded area beyond. The enveloping trees sheltered the path that wandered through thick undergrowth in the general direction of the creek.

That blasted bush honeysuckle had already leafed out! Too bad agent orange had been banned. It was just so labor intensive to get rid of the invasive malignant growth plant by plant. Not that she minded. Hacking it down and poisoning the stump suited her just fine, but she couldn't do it alone. Once she got this mulch site brouhaha taken care of, she could resume her anti-bush honeysuckle campaign.

Beyond the bush honeysuckle some other plants had leafed out. They were planted in neat rows, some of the young stalks staked with rusty rebar. Eunice crept closer for a better look and rubbed a leaf between her thumb and first two fingers. Her Master Gardener training and the memory of that college "botany experiment," led her to the immediate identification of Cannabis sativa. That was how she had met Cuppy: he had also been involved in the "botany experiment." What had he said? Something like "Holy Jimpson Weed, Batman, that's marijihoona!" He'd been so funny back then. What had happened to him that had squelched his sense of humor?

Employment at Tirano BioEngineering – that's what had happened. Corporate demands sucked the life out of you. Now he devised ways to test genetically altered plants in third or fourth world countries. Maybe even fifth world countries. Those third worlders were getting too savvy. All those poor starving disease-ridden natives would probably be a lot happier with plain old marijuana anyway, rather than some weird corn or beans or something.

Eunice stalked her prey. Now she could see them: Mungo and his brain wave deficient cousin Reavis Huckstep stacking the kink free hoses into a colorfully patterned wall. Pink, green, blue, beige, red. Row after row in that order. These guys were even more mental than she'd realized. Growing marijuana on village property was just too good to be true. She could have them all arrested: Mungo, Reavis and maybe even McKnight. As mayor, he had to have some culpability.

Eunice leapt into the clearing with a vindictive "Gotcha!"

Mungo, Reavis, Lightning and Superman all screamed. Mungo threw himself in front of the hutch ready to defend the ferrets at all costs, while they cowered under their straw. Reavis ran around in circles yelping and swiveling his ball cap maniacally.

The bizarre scene caused Eunice to pause briefly but then she shouted, "Shut up, shut up you idiots!"

Reavis stopped hollering and ran off into the underbrush toward the creek.

Mungo stood his ground in front of the hutch and dropped the bumbling hillbilly role. "Get out of here you mean old witch. Scaring my cousin like that. Humpty Dumpty! You know he's not right in the head. You are the meanest person I've ever met. Everybody in town hates you. Now maybe you've got personal problems that make you like that. I don't know and I don't care. But I do care about my cousin. Don't you ever come near him again."

Mungo's voice had become progressively slower and clearer and deadlier.

"You leave right now Mrs. Kingblade. Or you'll be sorry."

His serious intent, underlined by the sudden clarity of his speech, hit Eunice forcibly. She squinted at him with suspicious surprise, her eyes going all small and hard.

"I will certainly leave right now. But you're the one who will be sorry. I'm going straight to the police. They'll be very interested in the plants you're growing on village property; and those rats too."

Mungo concentrated on breathing evenly as she slowly moved away. Eunice was keeping her eye on him too but finally turned toward the path; at least where the path had been. After stumbling around somewhat confusedly, she finally found the faint trail leading back to the main part of the mulch site.

Mungo waited until he could no longer hear her rustling through the underbrush, then went after Reavis. He found him huddled on the bank of the creek, slowly rocking but no longer swiveling his cap.

"Hey, buddy," Mungo said gently. "Listen, I'm going to take Superman and Lightning over to the jail where they'll be safe. Heck'll let me keep them there at least for a day or two. Then I'll go home. Do you want to come with me or stay here?"

"Stay here." Reavis frequently camped out overnight at the Compound so this was fine with Mungo.

"Okay, but stay in the Compound. Don't go out into the big area. There's going to be a meeting there with lots of people."

Lots of people made Reavis uneasy, so he would stay put. "I'll be back in the morning as usual. We've got that tour with the garden club ladies tomorrow and they always have lots of cakes at their meetings." Reavis brightened at the mention of cakes and happily returned to the Compound to continue building the kink free hose wall.

17.   MCKNIGHT AT HOME

Well into his third term as mayor, McKnight had started carefully sounding out some folks in the know about higher political office. Congressman Freemantle, Senator Freemantle: they both had a nice ring. Governor? Positive feedback from various movers and shakers had encouraged McKnight to bring it up to Pinckney who had been thrilled at the prospect. Her mother had been one of the Pinckneys of Mobile and her father, Bonn Hagensieker, was a staggeringly rich self-made man who had invented some miraculous bonding substance for dentures.

"Hey Pinks, are you going to the mulch site with me?" he asked as she gyrated in front of the mirrored wall of the dressing room.

"Really McKnight, is that a serious question?" She continued rotating and peering at her reflection to see if her new silk pants fit snugly enough.

"I wouldn't be caught dead in a mulch pile. Think what it would do to my shoes."

"Mulch site, not pile. We're not going to be jumping around in a bunch of leaves."

"Well I should hope not." Pinckney sighed and drooped long-sufferingly, shaking her head and looking skyward. "Didn't you say that Dash is having everyone for drinks at Shady Grove afterwards? I'll just meet you there around six or something. Good, these pants look great. Would you bring me a glass of champagne please before you leave?" Her hands smoothed down her sleek silk flanks.

It had been a while since McKnight had run his hands down those selfsame flanks. These days she was either freezing or boiling; too tired or too busy; had just had hair/nails/teeth done. Teeth done? What did that mean? Her feet/back/head hurt. Stomach kind of queasy, maybe she'd had just a teentsy weentsy bit too much champagne last night. She made him feel like a whole symphony of unwanted overtures these days.

McKnight went downstairs to get himself a fortifying scotch before taking the champagne up to Gyroscope Woman and heading over to the mulch site. Stupid place to have the presentation, but Dash had insisted that it would be vital to show the difference that the residential development would make – the before and after, the now and then, the up close and personal or whatever.

"Ford, Field, here boys."

What kind of scotch does one drink before going to a mulch site? McKnight pondered then consulted his eager-to-help yellow labs, Stafford and Sheffield.

"Whaddya think guys: Old Mulch Pile?" Two tails thumped approval.

"Hmp. That actually sounds like the name of a real scotch. But should it be perchance something more every-day, possibly more befitting a leaf processing operation?" McKnight queried as he clanked some bottles around on the bar.

"How about the Ardbeg Corryvreckan?"

Ford and Field puzzled over this one. Was he talking about a new kind of biscuit?

"Or do I need-slash-deserve something on a higher plane to counteract the lowly location?" McKnight eloquently addressed his furry audience.

Ford trotted over to the door while Field started scratching his ear and then munching sharply at his flank.

"Right you are! The Hankey Bannister 25 it is. Good boys!"

McKnight poured a hefty slug of the scotch into one of the gold rimmed glasses with an old fashioned golfer on it, then shrugged out onto the porch. Ford and Field followed and snorted hopefully as they and McKnight stared at the dead plants in the seashell-encrusted trough, the result of some garden club workshop. He couldn't imagine why Pinckney had gone to it. Her idea of gardening was to call the florist.

McKnight reflected philosophically that he was re-lieved that Pinckney was not coming with him to the mulch site. She would have been aggravated if he had not asked her, but was scornful when he did. Being married to Pinckney had taught him a lot of political realities. He recognized her potential to be dynamite, or even a nuclear missile on the campaign trail. At least he wasn't married to Eunice. Thank God, Cuppy had warned him that she was on the warpath to his office.

"Really McKnight, where's my champagne?"

McKnight gave the dogs some treats and himself some ice before bringing the glass of champagne up to Her Majesty.

18. *PINKS DRINKS*

Pinckney didn't know how it had happened. The drinking had just sort of crept up on her unaware then leapt out of its hiding place. Like that morning when she woke up middle-aged.

Years ago she mostly drank iced tea (unsweetened), certainly at lunch and at dinner during the week. As they went out to more and more parties she started having a drink upstairs while she got ready, then downstairs before they left. A nightcap was always in order when they got home. Lunches were more numerous and longer so she would have a glass or two of wine. Why not? She no longer had carpool and ten million kid activities.

Cooking was boring and she had no one to talk to so she drank while she got dinner ready. She did pride herself on always producing a proper dinner on good china, with flowers and candles on the table and appropriate music playing in the background. That took a lot of work to get together almost every night so it gave her a lot of drinking time. Her drinking just gradually increased over the years like mileage.

McKnight didn't seem to notice that she more than matched him drink for drink. Although admittedly, it was scotch vs. champagne. That had to make a difference, Pinckney consoled herself. Nonetheless, she probably had a liver the size of Connecticut. And now it had come to this: champagne alone in the evening and a Metamucil mimosa in the morning. Maybe she should go over to the mulch site after all. No, too much of a comedown. She still had some standards. Pinckney's reflection in the mirror started to cry.

19.   DASH LETHABY PRESENTS

DASH LETHABY PRESENTS
DEER CREEK MEADOWS
AN EXCLUSIVE RESIDENTIAL ENCLAVE
PLEASE JOIN ME AT THE MULCH SITE TO SEE THE
FUTURE!
TUESDAY, MARCH 25
5:30 PM PRESENTATION
COCKTAILS TO FOLLOW AT SHADY GROVE
RSVP: LETHABY & KNAPPS CONSTRUCTION

Dash and Cole arrived at the mulch site a little after five. Dash got out of the Jeep Wagoneer and Cole bounded after him and started snorting around in the mulch. Oh goody, this place again! This was scent heaven to a dog. The architects were already there assembling the fabulous looking Deer Creek Meadows exhibits. They better be fabulous for what they cost. Large easels held the clear, colorful views and elevations of the tastefully elegant dwellings that would replace the steaming mounds of decaying leaves. For Dash, it was important to hold the meeting there in order to make the biggest impact; to really demonstrate the difference that his project would produce; how much better the mulch site would look and smell. These dignified townhouses would be worthy of Deer Creek, not an embarrassment like the messy heaps of moldy mulch.

Gaily waving a shovel, Gardenia walked toward him. "Dash dear."

"Hey Gardy – you're a doll – thanks for coming." He kissed his dear loyal cousin and gestured toward her. "What's that?"

"It's the Garden Club of St. James's ceremonial shovel. I brought it as a symbol of breaking ground for your project and I polished it all up with Murphy's Oil soap you know they make those wipes now that are so handy and I used up the whole package." Gardenia proudly handed him the gleaming shovel with its shiny ash wood handle.

"Well, cool. Thanks, this'll be great." He held the shovel aloft and waved it around. "Really super, Gardy. What a great prop. This will show everyone that this development project is going to go through. Go look at the displays. I have to welcome people."

Others were starting to arrive so he went to greet them,

shovel in hand. He had invited every heavy hitter he could think of, called in every favor, gone out on every limb to find investors. Cole helped by weaving in and out of the crowd, beating people's legs with his delighted tail.

"Hey, how are you, Bonn? Ho, ho, ho, the Cupster, where's your lovely better half? (Oh God, had he really said that to Cuppy? Eunice wouldn't be the better half of Attila the Hun.) "There's Hizzonor," clasping the mayor's hand as McKnight thumped him on the back. "Hope you brought Pinks!" Lots of folks were showing up, more than he had expected.

Looking surprised and somewhat alarmed at the sight of the shovel, Cuppy asked anxiously, "Whoa! Are we breaking ground?" If Eunice found out that he was involved, there would be so much hell to pay, Dante's Inferno would be just a security deposit.

"No, just something Gardenia brought."

Dash continued glad-handing, chortling and enthusiastically greeting the well-heeled friends and prospects. After a while he banged the shovel against the shed to get everyone's attention. Cole started some hysterically happy excavation: smells great, more digging!

"Welcome everybody." Dash was brilliant at the slick presentation, crediting the architectural firm, briefly highlighting the main points of artistic and commercial value to Deer Creek, commending the investors for their civic commitment and shrewd business investment foresight. He could talk and look the impressive game better than anyone. It was follow-through he always had trouble with, but no one was thinking about that now. Dash could see the approving nods. He would close the deal tonight at

Shady Grove after some liquid persuasion. Oh, the money was almost in the bank.

He ended his talk by thanking Cole for breaking ground. Everyone chuckled and the group fell into relaxed chatting while Cole expanded his area of exploration. His nose led him toward the far side of the mulch site, nearer the creek.

Cole gave a sudden sharp warning bark when he spied an approaching menace.

"What's going on here?" Dash froze. "How DARE you hold this meeting behind my back? Dash Lethaby, you are a coward!" After getting lost in the undergrowth, Eunice had emerged from the other side of the mulch site and gotten closer and closer in disbelief and rage. She jerked people aside to get to the front of the startled-into-silence crowd.

Siggy grabbed the mayor and bundled him into his car. He was the first one out the gate. Nobody wanted to get involved with Eunice but some sure wanted to see the action. Others started to drift toward their cars, heads down, making a strategic retreat to Shady Grove to start building up Dash's tab. Some opted for home, worried that Eunice would follow them to Shady Grove and ruin cocktail time. It was not worth putting up with Eunice for a couple of free drinks.

"What are YOU doing here?" She had seen Cuppy and her voice changed from strident and enraged to stunned and aggrieved. She stared at him while behind her Dash made whacking motions with the shovel, as if hitting her on the head.

"I grack I...." Cuppy couldn't think what to say. The

waving shovel was hypnotizing him. Cole was barking and racing around in a frenzy! Stinky mulch and humans shouting: what a great game!

Eunice recovered enough to berate Cuppy as the remaining and now embarrassed spectators started edging away, then making a downright sprint for it. She turned back to Dash who leaned the shovel against the shed and crossed his arms. Stabbing her finger toward Cuppy, she hissed at Dash, "I blame you for tricking him into this scheme. You are totally unscrupulous! These idiots will find that out," flailing her arm at the departing stragglers.

Gardenia fluttered up, "Eunice calm down. Everything will be just fine."

Cuppy moaned. What a sweet fool Gardenia was. Eunice yelled at her.

"You are a traitor Gardenia! As a garden club member how could you support this?" Gardenia turned away and ran tearfully to her car.

"Eunice for once just shut up." She couldn't believe that Cuppy had said that to her. "Just shut up and go home, right now." He said it through clenched teeth, but it was loud and clear. He stomped rapidly to his truck, the one he took to his hunting lodge and where he was going now. He jumped in and shot out of the mulch site onto the access road toward the highway and freedom. He had had it; just had it. His heart was pounding and his stomach contracting. Over and over, Cuppy ran the sight through his mind of Dash waving the shovel threateningly at Eunice's head. Wham, wham, wham. Ohhh, this was tempting. He could always turn around and go back.

Cuppy's brand new pickup truck of the weekend farmer

hurtled along the highway, the tires hitting a rhythm to fit "Iwishshewasdead Iwishshewasdead Iwishshewasdead, then deaddeaddeaddeaddead when they bubbled over the rumble strips at the exit.

Dash and Cole headed for the safety of the Jeep Wagoneer. The architects were grabbing the presentation panels and the easels and hurriedly stuffing them into their cars. Eunice caught up with Dash and grabbed his arm.

"I haven't finished with you."

He flung her off and ground out with cold spite, "Well, I've finished with you. Get out of my way now and out of the way of this project."

Dash and Cole jumped into the Jeep Wagoneer. Dash backed out fast and rammed it into drive. Eunice was blocking the way. He tried to zoom around her but she jumped toward his car, which swerved away but still hit her. Dash slammed on the gas and reeled out of there. In his rear view mirror he could see her on the ground.

He'd hit her. He'd hit her and he didn't care. He grabbed the flask that he kept in the car for emergency purposes, which were coming up more and more frequently these days, and slurped a mouthful down. He drove around, getting more drunk, talking to Cole, his bestest friend in the whole wide world. They passed the hardware store. He had hit her but not very hard. Went through stop sign. Passed the bank, hitting the pothole. She was probably fine. Passed St. Melchior's. Went through stop sign. It was her fault. Passed the road to the country club. New pothole. Maybe she was dead. Went through stop sign. He had left the scene of an accident.

Dash made a screeching 180 and drove back to the

mulch site and through the open gate. He slowly wheeled around in the dark but didn't see anybody. Certainly no Eunice. Dash sort of fell out of the Jeep Wagoneer to look around and stumbled over the shovel that Gardenia had brought. He picked it up and heaved it into the back seat of the Jeep Wagoneer then headed for the haven of Shady Grove.

20.   LAST RESOLUTIONS

Spurred on by utter disbelief, Eunice got up carefully. Dash had tried to run over her, or at least hit her. Maybe he had meant to kill her. Like that time when Gardenia had driven through the window at the Badger, although Eunice had never really believed that Gardenia had tried to kill her. She was far too silly. But maybe? Maybe it had contained some real intent, conscious or un. And just now Cuppy had yelled at her.

A forlorn and heavy sadness enveloped her, causing her to falter and sway. Mungo's words came back: that everyone hated her. Could that be why her own beloved children lived so far away? Genuine despair poured over her.

Eunice had never experienced such sad exhaustion. Maybe she needed some kind of medicine. There was one they'd been talking about on TV. The word sounded like profiterole, although that couldn't possibly be it. Some may see profiteroles as medicinal however, well maybe fatsoes. Eunice was proud of her trim, muscular, sinewy figure.

Did everyone in town hate her? But she did so much for the community. She never did anything for herself. Who else would take the trouble to come out here and track down drug dealers?

"Gardenia didn't really intend to kill me, did she?" Eunice asked herself aloud. "And all I do for the garden club, arranging field trips like the one tomorrow to tour this mulch site, which wouldn't be here much longer if it weren't for my heroic stand." She was a realist, a pragmatist and stupid people did not appreciate being told the truth.

Eunice stumbled toward her car, which was way at the back of the huge mulch site. Did all these stupid things really matter that much: the mulch site, the park, that ridiculous Gardenia St. Cyr, the empty wine bottles in the garden clubs' closets? Maybe she shouldn't hold others to her own high standards. Maybe she could try to be a bit more forgiving. She envisioned a new role: Eunice as gracious and sympathetic to these other poor souls. Yes, as a tactic it would certainly surprise her enemies – wait, no no. Do not think of them as enemies. They were the misunderstood, the downtrodden and she had to take responsibility for doing a lot of the treading down.

A new beginning opened before her. She'd start with her own dear Cuppy. Yes, perhaps she owed him an apology and a casserole and, as a great sacrifice, a needlepoint belt. And Gardenia too. They could reconsider the Chinese Chippendale bridge together. Eunice could remake herself into the beloved village leader instead of the feared village leader. Was that a car that had just pulled in? Eunice turned with a smile. Oh there was so much to look forward to.

21.   *DASH AT SHADY GROVE*

Dash swerved into the Shady Grove parking lot without hitting Lenny, the valet parker, who was adept at dodging drunks. He ran up to open the passenger door for Cole who jumped out wagging his tail and barking ecstatically. Dash rolled erratically out of the Jeep Wagoneer, clinging momentarily to the doorframe. Somehow the ground fell away to a lower level than it used to be. Cole leaped back into the car and Lenny parked it nearby, although not in the privileged spot right next to the side door. Bonn Hagensieker's Rolls owned that particular space.

If the damn step hadn't moved, Dash wouldn't have fallen in the door that way. It was a good thing he kept that flask and the bottle (flask didn't hold enough) in the car to have while he drove around trying to calm down, think, breathe, drink. Well he didn't have to concentrate to do the last. That was more automatic than walking, which at the moment, was proving difficult. No trouble swallowing though.

Dash went in through the kitchen, the regulars' entrance. The uninitiated or unknowing would never venture into that heated swirling roar of airborne grease, reused cooking oil, shouting, rushing waiters and cooks and looks. The Looks, or the fatal snubs if you were not one of the Accepted. After plunging in, however, he caught himself and followed the polo player into the Men's Bar. As usual, ol' man Hagensieker was draped over one end of the bar, sucking on martinis and his false teeth. Dash kicked one of the beat-up spittoons then waved at Shannon, which meant several of my usuals right away.

Dash's gaze bleared around the room. It was the same old skunk house everyone goes into somewhere. So dark your eyes had to adjust, even at night. Smoked wood, liquor, sweat and dirty hair. Miasmas of youth and funk of old age, bloated dreams, shriveled life. And all anyone wanted was a drink; and someone familiar, even if you didn't like them.

"About time you got here. We had to start without you." Bonn had un-draped himself enough to call out to Dash who flung his arm up in acknowledgement.

"Drinks on me, erry buddy." He waved at the cluster of people who had been at the mulch site and several who had not; or at least he didn't think so; wasn't sure really. Timeworn wooden chairs tilted askew around the battered old tables, repositories of untold meals probably better left uneaten. Candle wax – were there candles? Adding to the smog, always a chance of burning the old place down. That magnificent old dark wood bar with the huge mirror that ran its length – reflecting the glass-fronted liquor cases on the opposite wall. The mirror was like the patrons, once so dignified but now tired and red-eyed, always looking for someone.

People came over and he was shaking hands but couldn't really make out what they were saying. Why was everybody mumbling? Their faces loomed into his, looking like reflections in the back of a spoon. Shapes and silhouettes spun in the spotted mirror. Maybe those were reflections that were trapped in there forever. Your young self was looking out at your old self – what you had become – and it was so horrible you could no longer see and the horror stopped you from remembering. You never wanted to leave the mirror, you could never leave – youth seeing your fate – that was what happened and it could never un-happen and never end, not even when you died. You would always be in that mirror.

Mirrors had scared him when he was little. At night your face became a monster and if you let the mirror reflect that sight, you would look like that forever. Madeleine loved mirrors. She put them up all over the house and he broke them one by one after she left. Seventy years of bad luck. And he'd swept them up and put a pile in a box and sent them to her. A big box of broken mirrors. He hoped she was trapped in there and could never get out and she had only her broken face in jagged bits of light, cracked, not matching up, all wrongly put together – a Picasso you couldn't sell. Time's painting of drunken oblivion. He peeled his eyes from the mirror and took two of the drinks he had left. He moved himself through the crowd like a bumper car with no sparks. He collided with a chair and nearly folded into it but hit the side and it fell over toward the big old print of Custer's Last Fight on the end wall. He jolted into the hall. He could go straight and pass the ladies room. Someone was coming out.

"Oooh, Dashers! How are you?" He kissed somebody who was wafting delicious zephyrs of scent and breathing daiquiri on him, "Love the plans!" She kept on walking and he tried to remember her name. What plans? Had they made plans? He squinted out the back door toward the screened summer huts. Although furnished with metal folding chairs and unsteady tables, they were the most sought after place to eat in town. They weren't open yet, it was late March. But he could tell that they were getting them ready. So where could he go?

He could turn left into the lounge with the print of Union Station and the bird's-eye view of the World's Fair and the small bar, and more smoke and dinner. Past that was the main dining room with the stuffed birds in bubble glass, the area for older folks and families. Prime rib and fried chicken and iceberg lettuce slathered in French Blue Cheese Dressing and rye bread with smetana and bacon and eggs and hamburgers served on Wonder Bread. Dash had grown up on that food, but now the memory and the smell made him feel sick.

He eased himself into the lounge and hugged the bar stool with his legs. His place, his place, yes this was his place and his drink and his next drink and another drink and everything was fine. She was not dead – he had not killed her. He had not run over her he had maybe only slightly gently carefully possibly bumped her with the bumper. "That's what they're for, right? Right? Am I right? Bumpers – they bump and it's all right!"

Dash bumped his drink, sloshing it on the bar and his sleeve. He wiped the bar with his sleeve then sucked it mostly dry before finishing what was left in the glass. A drink, that's what he needed. A drink and then it would be fine and he'd go home and go to bed and sleep and wake up and it would be fine and where was Cole? What had he done with Cole? Oh, Cole was in the car. Cole could drive. Cole could drive him home. He was already DWI – Dog While Intoxicated – good ol Cole he loved Cole and

Cole loved him and Cole, Cole.

Maybe he'd lie down now on this flat surface. Maybe this was the moon. Yeah, he flew to the moon, but Cole wouldn't be there and he'd be sad without Cole and what would he eat? This was better, this was soft, he was so tired. I'll rest and then I'll find Cole and we'll go get ice cream except ice cream gave Cole stinks and then he'd have to go out and it was so hard to get up and he'd just rest for a bit. On a sofa. He was pretty sure this was a sofa. He hadn't killed her. She wasn't dead. He was dead. He was cold and spinning and dead.

Dash rolled over and instead of falling into the voluptuous arms of love, hit the filthy floor. His body summoned the energy to moan, and received a bit of sympathy. "Poor baby. Worse than usual?" He squinched open his eyes and recognized the legs. Rita! He was with Rita! He didn't remember THAT. Waiting all this time for her: angling, flirting and now he couldn't remember.

Further eye opening brought into focus the grimy floor, encrusted with decades of hard partying at Shady Grove, and he registered the fact that he was lying on it. Spurred on by disgust, he staggered up with the help of Rita. Lovely Rita – the obvious. She gave him a great smile and a fulsome hug, as his mind hit bottom when last night came back to him. Dash moaned again and leaned into Rita. "Well someone got up on the wrong side of the floor this morning." She propped him up against the wall, which wasn't much cleaner than the floor. "Come on Dash. I've gotta get ready for the lunch crowd. Lenny parked your car in the back and he took care of Cole. Just go on home."

"Gah go bafroom first," scraped out of his dry mouth. His tongue clicked against his teeth. He fell into the cloying Airwick of the restroom and gagged at the sight of his father in the mirror but it shocked him awake along with cold water splashed all over his head. Then the memory of Eunice at the mulch site hit him and he threw up into the sink.

22. MURDER IN THE MULCH SITE

The discovery of Eunice's body in the mulch forced a collective gasp followed by small cries and screams that broke the initial silence. Some of the Deer Creek Garden Club ladies stifled these noises with their hands, as if the inward course of air had sucked the hand up to hold it over the mouth. Other hands flew to cover the eyes: instinctive reactions to sudden, unexpected death thrown right in front of you.

Then stronger voices emerged. "No, no, no...."

"Call the police!"

"Call an ambulance!"

"Call the fire department!"

Ivy advanced slowly toward the body shouting, "Stay back," and holding up her hand to Mungo to stop the front loader.

Grace tried to herd the group back, away from this pitiable creature that had once been a person. She wanted to shield them from the sickening sight, protect them from storing too much memory. It was a stupidly vain endeavor, but Grace persisted until everyone had retreated to the refreshment tables that now appeared so wantonly festive.

Mungo had backed the front loader away and turned it off, bringing a new measure of calm. He clambered down jerkily and went over to peer at the remains of Eunice. "Oh no, oh, no, oh no," he kept moaning. Humpty Dumpty, this was bad. He reached toward the body but Ivy pushed his arm back.

"Don't touch anything. There's nothing we can do."

Someone had opened the office trailer and found the telephone to call the Police Department.

After an eternity of gaspy breathing, the stricken garden club ladies could hear the sirens. All sorts of emergency vehicles charged into the mulch site. Police cars, fire engines and ambulances from several surrounding communities surged around the Deer Creek units. Nothing exciting ever happened in this neck of the woods, so everybody wanted a piece of the action.

The Deer Creek police force took charge and Ivy sank onto an old wooden pallet. There were no chairs, not even a bench. This is impossible, unthinkable. No matter how much everyone had disliked the old bat. Was bat short for battle axe? That idea had never occurred to Ivy before. Merit would know. She wished that he was here. He was so solid and comforting and lived in another world. Poor Eunice. She had not deserved this.

Grace was thinking that Olivier would have described the scene in his precise but mellifluous writing. It would be like something that he might encounter in the course of his travels to some brutal, far-off land; a distant but clear picture of death, capturing the fear and ugliness. Oh, how had he died? Why had he died? Grace was shaking a bit but managed to pull herself up. Others needed her.

Gardenia fluttered and mewed, "This is terrible, this is just so terrible," as she tripped around in circles. Grace guided her over to the pallet where Ivy was sitting. "Stay here with Ivy. I'll go get you both some tea."

Grace hurried toward the garden club tables that were still laden with muffins and petit fours, percolators and teapots. They now formed a ready-made canteen for the emergency workers. Rallying the sensible, Grace soon had a smoothly running operation, offering nourishment to the police, fire and ambulance services. It also gave the garden club ladies something to do. She then poured two cups of tea and brought them over to Ivy and Gardenia who both lurched up from the pallet, gratefully grasping the cups.

Gardenia suddenly swayed to starboard and dropped the cup of tea. Grace and Ivy managed to catch her before she hit the ground too. They steadied her, Ivy shouting to an ambulance crew, "We need help here!" while she tried to balance her own teacup as well as Gardenia. Eager rescue men ran over, delighted to have a live victim. Relieved that Gardenia was in professional hands, Grace just wanted ed to go home, make a pot of tea and pat Parsley.

"Listen, I heard that a lotta people woulda bin happy to clobber the old battle axe," a policeman from another town informed his partner about the dead woman.

"She may have been an old battle axe, but she was OUR old battle axe." Ivy glared at the oblivious pair.

Shaking her head, Grace sighed and asked, "Why is Gardenia even here? I assume she knew about the mulch site tour since she's an honorary member of our club but this just isn't a Gardenia type of event."

"Oh, I asked her about it. Apparently there was a meeting here last night. Dash Lethaby had some group of people he's trying to convince to invest in buying the mulch site property from the village and building townhouses. Dash had invited her and she brought the Garden Club of St. James's ceremonial shovel as a sort of encouraging prop. But she left it here so she came back to get it."

"So where is it?"

"She couldn't find it and she was so ridiculously upset about it. Mungo probably just put it away in a shed or something."

Grace and Ivy stood there for a while, mesmerized by the law enforcement procedures. The police cordoned off the area and took statements; well not really statements, rather the monotone recitations of names, addresses and phone numbers so they could contact everyone later. The extraneous vehicles and their staffs left quite reluctantly, finally prompted by the fact that they had eaten all the cakes and muffins.

Ivy sounded oddly expressionless and echoed Grace's wish, "I just want to go home but I can't seem to leave." After a tired silence, she added, "I found myself wishing that Merit was here."

Grace closed her eyes. She didn't think that Merit Wilcoxen would be able to provide much in the way of sensible help, but then Ivy was talking in terms of emotional support, not constructive action. Grace was always wishing that Olivier were here. It hit her with a fiercer pang – those words of Eunice's about Olivier's death, "Well, he should have been more careful. But you've got plenty of money. Somebody will want to marry you."

What would Olivier have said, had he been here? With his wry sense of the absurd, he probably would have observed that only the Deer Creek Garden Club would have refreshments at a murder scene.

23.   DEAD BODIES ARE HARD TO LOSE

Siggy took the call calmly and efficiently, then carefully replaced the receiver. McKnight stopped working on his detective novel, welcoming the interruption because he was kind of stumped: how does one get rid of a dead body? Siggy exhibited atypical signs of suppressed excitement in a higher tone of voice.

"That was police dispatch: a body has been discovered at the mulch site."

"What?" exclaimed McKnight, shoving back his swivel chair with the good lumbar support and leaping to his expensively shod feet.

"All they said was a body was found at the mulch site. I suggest we go over there right away. The media will be all over this one."

"Right." Siggy was already holding his jacket open for him to jam his arms into. Combing his hair, they hustled out the back door of the village hall and got into his dark blue Jaguar XJ6 Series 1 with custom maroon leather. McKnight loved his car and called it "Blueberry Rampant." He frequently spritzed the seats with a bottle of "Old Leather Enhancer," a name that oddly somehow made him think of Pinckney.

Siggy briefed him as he drove well over the speed limit down Hereford Street, which was the main road of Deer Creek. It was only a mile or so, almost a straight shot to the mulch site.

"Roman Messina is the reporter most likely to be there – Channel XI. The young good-looking one." Siggy tittered; the woman actually tittered. McKnight shot a sideways eyeball at her. That was a new sound to come out of her mouth. She started flicking a clothes brush over his right arm and shoulder until he batted it away as they rocketed into the mulch site.

McKnight rolled smoothly out of the car, trying to look mayoral or possibly even senatorial. He strode with officious confidence toward all the action while reminding himself: "I am serious, powerful and in charge." Police Chief Vaughn "Heck" Hequembourg marched up to him looking serious, powerful and in charge. They shook hands solemnly and strongly, McKnight casting about for the television crews.

"So, what's the story?"

"Dead body, female, identified by witnesses as Eunice Kingblade."

"Good God!" McKnight was truly shocked. He had just assumed that it was some transient or worker or something; or a drug dealer drive-by – drive by and fling the body out that is, right before getting on the highway.

Maybe she'd had a heart attack after last night's confrontation. Well, he hadn't said anything to her; hadn't even gone near her. Once again, he thanked his lucky stars for Monday, getting him out of there right away.

"How?"

"Murdered. Probably killed by a blow to the head."

"Oh my God!" Now he was really thrown and even literally stepped back. Cuppy must have finally snapped. Not that he blamed him; that shrew was the limit.

Siggy unobtrusively steadied him and he drew himself back up to a gubernatorial level of cool-headedness.

"Any idea who did it?" wondering if he should say anything about Cuppy.

"We have to question everyone here and whoever must have seen her last."

"Well, there were a lot of people at that meeting last night."

"What meeting?"

"The one that Dash Lethaby had – to talk about his proposed development of the mulch site."

"Including you?" asked Heck in his stainless steely-eyed police chief role.

"Umm, yes, but I left right away."

"You just got there and left right away." The police chief heaved the words out leadenly.

"No, I mean I left right away after Eunice showed up." McKnight was suddenly flustered and summoned his oratorical powers to end the conversation.

"We will bring the perpetrator to justice. You have the full support of the mayor's office to leave no stone unturned." (Or leaf in this case but he stifled that remark with a clearing of his throat and mind.) "But don't let me keep you." He had seen the Channel XI news van pull in. Chief Hequembourg nodded at McKnight sharply then headed back toward the body, but before he could reach the safety of the cordon the reporter Roman Messina and his ace camera crew ambushed him.

"Chief, can you tell us who the victim is?"

"No."

"Murder? Suicide? Natural Causes?" (Oh he hoped not.) "Weapon?"

"No comment." The chief ducked behind the yellow tape into his secure field of command and with his back to the reporter. "Olney – go rustle up Dash Lethaby and get a list of who was here last night."

Roman turned and plunged toward the mayor who eagerly awaited him. Siggy had been running him through appropriate things to say. "Look serious: you are NOT happy to see him." Her still face could enunciate with the skill of a ventriloquist.

"Morning, Roman. This is a sad day for Deer Creek, a sad day."

"Can you tell us the victim's name?"

Now here some native cunning and natural caution snuck in, causing McKnight to pause and actually consider his response. He wanted to project the image of wrought iron resolve, leadership and inside knowledge, so what to divulge and what to hint at? Better remain mysterious but knowing for a while, clearly in the loop and running the show.

"We cannot divulge that at this point in time. The victim's family has not been notified."

"But you do know who it is?"

"Yes, the body has been identified but I am not at liberty to divulge that information at this point in time. The investigation is ongoing at this point in time." Siggy invisibly nudged him at that point in time.

"How was he murdered?" The "he" and the "murdered" were an attempt on Roman's part to jolt some admission out of the slightly dimwitted (in Roman's opinion) mayor by implying more knowledge than he actually had.

"Now no one has said she was murdered." Siggy stepped on his foot. He stopped, mad at himself for being drawn – lousy reporter. But taking the confidential, avuncular approach, "Now Roman, you know I cannot divulge any details at this point in time. But the citizens of Deer Creek can rest assured that we will bring the perpetrator to justice."

So it was murder, YES! and the vic was female. "How old was she?"

"Now Roman," McKnight continued in this melodramatic vein but when he got to, "Truth, justice and the American way," Roman just couldn't stand it anymore so he turned sharply into the camera, "Thank you Mayor Freemantle. This is Roman Messina reporting live at the scene of a gruesome homicide in the exclusive village of Deer Creek."

As the reporter marched off, Siggy started issuing stern, calming instructions to McKnight. "Remain mayoral and formal. Don't get friendly with the reporters. Don't keep using the phrase 'this point in time.' Keep it short and clear. We cannot release the identity of the deceased until family members have been notified. Cause of death has not been determined."

"I know, I know," he answered impatiently, looking around for someone to impress but there was only Grace Mere and Ivy Wilcoxen and a bunch of those faded old garden club gals. Good God, was that Thyra Tillotson? They used to call her Thyroid Tillotson. Hadn't she married somebody and moved away? Well, he couldn't keep up with everyone.

McKnight breathed in deeply and advanced toward the huddled masses of his constituents. He would bring comfort to the poor dears.

24. INVESTIGATIVE REPORTING

Grace and Ivy had witnessed McKnight triumphantly enter the mulch site, exuding authority and good taste. They had both known him for years and held him in somewhat irritated affection for his silly but harmless pomposity. Too far away to hear his conversation with the police chief, they observed the exaggerated pantomime with increasing impatience.

"Oh, good grief," muttered Ivy as the Channel XI News van hurtled into the mulch site, causing the garden club ladies who were packing up the percolators and card tables to scatter like potpourri in a hurricane.

"How do these people find out about these things?" asked Grace.

"By listening to the police scanner. There's some gizmo

you can get that'll pick it up. Merit and the twins wanted one but I said no."

This was not the first time that Grace had tried to assess Merit Wilcoxen's mental age. How old were the twins? 12? 14?

They recognized the television reporter Roman Messina – a newcomer, young, gung ho, quite good-looking and surprisingly well-spoken. Merit actually approved, which was most unusual. It drove him crazy when those idiots mixed up "he" and "him" and "I" and "me"; and they were allegedly well-educated people. Education had nothing to do with it. Background was what counted. In Merit's opinion, he had spent his entire career as a university professor trying to educate the un-educatable.

Grace and Ivy slowly drifted toward their cars. The reporter and crew had attempted to surround the police chief who easily escaped into the sanctuary around the body. Dismissed by the police chief and acting like a wolf pack that had just lost its prey, the news vultures turned eagerly toward their next victim: the mayor of Deer Creek.

McKnight graciously sought their attention and Grace and Ivy could hear portions of his speech: "Blah blah blah this point in time something something closure for grieving loved ones blither blither pillar of the community." Ivy moaned at that one and shook her head. "That's pretty bad even for McKnight."

As soon as Roman had brought the interview with McKnight to an abrupt end, the relentless newshound pivoted toward the few remaining garden club members who were putting the bouquets from the refreshment tables at the edge of the yellow police tape. Who in God's name were these people? Instant mourners? How had they gotten flowers here so fast? They were clearly some sort of group or organization of nicely dressed middle-aged women. Maybe the victim had been one of them. Roman beetled in their direction.

Grace and Ivy moved toward their friends to try to ward off the media onslaught but they were too late.

"Excuse me ladies. Did any of you know Mrs. Umm...," here he pretended to consult his notes.

"Oh we all knew Eunice," Beatrice piped up like a teacher's pet.

Bingo! Roman had his source. Despite Ivy's cautions and Grace's entreaties to her, Beatrice was unstoppable and indignant. "Dear Eunice was my next door neighbor for almost ten years and I want to talk about her." And talk she did. That ended it for Grace and Ivy. The exhaustion of strained nerves and shock and distress had finally hit home. Ivy patted Grace on the arm and they parted to go to their cars. Grace suddenly didn't want to be alone.

"Ivy – would you like to come back to the shop for tea?"

"Oh, that'd be great. I'll be right behind you."

25. *MCKNIGHT HAS LUNCH*

McKnight wanted to hang around the mulch site for as long as possible to snag more interviews as additional news crews showed up. This could also provide him with

material for his novel. But activity leveled off and a lot of
the mulch site was out of bounds and there was no bathroom and it was past lunchtime, so Monday was able to
convince him to leave.

He dropped her off at the village hall then proceeded
to Shady Grove to see who was there. His father-in-law
Bonn Hagensieker was there with his usual crony, a former sportswriter. It had long been a matter of village con-
jecture as to whether the duo was holding up the bar or
the bar was holding up them. Bets had been placed on a
number of probabilities. Then old Mr. Griffin came in,
carrying his jar of cranberry sauce to go with the chick-
en pot pie that he always had for lunch. McKnight filled
them in on all the details while putting away a couple of
scotches and a hamburger.

"So I activated the Major Case Squad right away. Told
those guys in no uncertain terms that I wanted this solved
fast – high profile murder like this – pull out all the stops.
I want an arrest pronto."

Monday had impressed upon him the need to be in
the office in order to be readily available for interviews and
police updates so he did not linger too much at the bar.

"Well, duty calls, gotta go. Major Case Squad wants
me to keep them in the loop as well as handling all the media. All part of leadership I guess." McKnight shouldered
his burden and gave a world-weary wave to the masses.
Bonn lifted a glass toward his son-in-law, then turned
back to the sportswriter.

There was not much going on at the mayoral office
though.

"Oh, there you are – Monday – listen – I want you

to prepare a bunch of statements for me. Anticipate what questions they might ask – that kind of thing – you know what to do. I'm going to go home to shave and shower and change then I'll come back here so we can go over what you've come up with. Want to be prepped for any possible evening news appearances."

This was a bit aggravating because Monday wanted to go to the car wash as soon as possible. Her nice white car was all muddy from the mulch site and she hated having a dirty car. Oh well, Monday sighed and got to work. For McKnight, she'd do anything and he didn't have to know. She was the power behind, if not the throne, then at least the swivel chair with the good lumbar support.

26.   *CUPPY AT THE LODGE*

He had actually told Eunice to shut up; had even shouted it in front of all those people. Well, a lot of them had left by then. Or so he hoped. It had been embarrassing and he didn't want crowds of witnesses to his anger. But even if they had – so what? Relief was kicking in, making him feel better already.

As soon as he got to The Lodge, he unplugged the telephone that still had the good ol' rotary dial (his kids didn't even know how to use it, which was another reason for keeping it) and poured himself a large brandy. Cuppy sighed in relief and his hands stopped shaking as he sat out on the terrace, although it had gotten chilly.

Beautiful stars! You could see them so much better in the country. It was as if you were on another planet. The planet of quiet and solitude and peace of mind. Peace of mind, all passion spent – that was from somewhere, probably Shakespeare. Shakespeare was always saying something: must have been a tiresome neighbor, constantly quothing over the fence.

Have I spent all my passion? Cuppy asked himself. He had certainly spent a lot ON passion. Kimberley sizzled into his mind. He was going to rev that relationship up now. Eunice was not going to bother him anymore. Cuppy treated himself to another drink and went to bed a New Man.

The New Man got up feeling like an Old Man, but he attributed this to alcohol not age and resolved to avoid both in the future. Cuppy needed a restorative breakfast so he fixed himself bacon and sausages and scrambled eggs and English muffins. He brewed an entire pot of super strong coffee. His part-time housekeeper kept the fridge and pantry freshly stocked.

"Nothing could be fina than to be in Carolina in the maw aw orning," sang Cuppy. "Good morning, good morning, I slept the whole night through. Zip-a-Dee-Doo-Dah." Calm of mind, that's what it was, calm not peace. Yes, he was calm now. Here at his beloved Lodge he could even think about Eunice calmly. But not for long, as a more petty memory churned up the murky waters of resentment. She had never even needlepointed a belt for him. Calmness fled.

Eunice's drill bits of scorn and contempt pierced hope, dreams and the soul. Really, it was a gift. All he wanted was just to be left alone with a beat-up saggy sofa that he could lie on to watch football and baseball and fall asleep. He wanted to leave the windows open so he could hear the rain. What did it matter if things got a bit damp? He wanted to eat stuff that ended in "o" like Frito, Ho Ho, Oreo. He wanted to be able to park in his own garage. He never wanted to see another kink free hose. He didn't care if all the plants died. In fact, he would like to watch them die. He would rejoice in the midsummer burnout of the lawn and dance on it in the light of a pink sky and a crescent moon.

How can Eunice cause instant depression just like that? She infuses everything with defeat. There is always, always, always something to complain about and she always does. It just wears you down over the years, right into the Grand Canyon of depression; and he was on the north rim staring into the abyss.

Disheartening and discouraging, the poisoned air of constant grievance wafted before her and trailed behind her. Constant Grievance: it sounded like a Puritan, one of those witches. If those Puritans had seen Eunice when she was brewing her herbal tea in vats steaming away on the stove, they would have burned her at the stake. She could drop the sunniest of optimists at fifty paces. Cheerfulness dissipated like dew in the morning. No, that was too positive an analogy. Cheerfulness dropped dead. The glass wasn't half empty, it had never been filled. She would sometimes give grudging approval but it was so obviously suspicious, as if the object or project in question would ultimately prove faulty as usual, and the person unreliable.

Would he ever have the courage of a Fletcher Christian,

say, or...? Well, he couldn't think of anyone else at the moment. He would have to ask Father Wedgewood about some suitable martyr. How could you survive without going crazy, knowing that you would never leave that pitiless island – Pitcairn? It sounded appropriately doomed. Thank God he had The Lodge. Maybe he would rename it The Sanctuary; and his house, Durance Vile.

Some police vehicles pulled into the circle drive in front of The Lodge. A granite-faced State Trooper informed him that his wife Eunice Kingblade had been found dead. Would he please come with them to Deer Creek so he could formally identify her?

The shock it encircled his head like a wreath. No. That was from *The Night Before Christmas*. He was going crazy. Cuppy shuddered onto the sofa. Oh, oh, yes he had so wanted her dead. Agonized over it; raged for it. If I saw her keel over while she was out hacking away at the bush honeysuckle I would just go take a nice long shower. No, of course I didn't see her, I'd say. She would die and it would not be his fault (well, not directly). Ah, ah, his head hit his hands. He had to call the kids. Oh Eunice... I didn't think that it would feel like this. Who could have done this? Had to be a hobo or something. Wait, there haven't been hoboes since the thirties. People didn't like her but they wouldn't kill her. Dash wouldn't kill her, would he? What about those whacking motions that Dash had made with the shovel? If only I'd gone back. I wouldn't really let her die, would I? I could have gone back. If I had gone back and if I had seen her lying on the ground, would I have hesitated to call for help? Cuppy didn't want to answer that question.

27. IVY'S STATEMENT (SUCH AS IT WAS)

After tea at Grace's house, Ivy came home and parked carefully in the ramshackle garage. She didn't want to hit the front wall, which was a bit wavy. Plaster the size of dinner plates had randomly cracked and threatened to fall away from the lath. Imagine lath and plaster walls in a garage these days. They didn't even put them in houses any more. What a day it had been; a murder in Deer Creek. It was unthinkable, but all she could do was think about it.

Ivy wended her way through the old back entrance. The covered area had once been a place to unload groceries and supplies into the pantry and kitchen. Just inside the door was another door, behind which stone steps led to the basement. But out here was the debris of family life: a jumble of old wooden crates, oil stricken coils of frayed rope, the handle of an ancient rake, other broken tools, falling apart baskets, the inevitable old bicycle on withered tires, banged up dog bowls, raggedy old dog beds, the prong portion of an ancient rake that did not match the handle of the other ancient rake, and flowerpots – oh flowerpots galore (chipped, broken, terra cotta, stone, plastic, unidentifiable, possibly from some ancient civilization), a rusted wheelbarrow, several old gas cans, a begrimed kerosene lantern and swaying stacks of damp National Geographics.

If one were to put together the stockpiles of National

Geographics that languished in American garages, basements and attics, surely the result would dwarf the Great Wall of China. A National Geographic correspondent could write an article about it. Olivier Mere could have turned it into a Shouts and Murmurs column for the New Yorker. Speaking of which, Grace had about a million old New Yorkers. Although with Grace, of course, the magazines were in order, year by year, in carefully labeled archival boxes on dry shelves.

Ivy tiredly picked up one of the old cans of paint. The faint letters proclaimed it to be the color "Brazen Landscape." What on earth could anyone have possibly painted Brazen Landscape? What did it look like? Who thought up these names? There were so many cans stockpiled here – they had to be a fire hazard. They probably contained enough paint to cover the National Geographic Great Wall of China. It was hard to believe that those deflated footballs had ever been used athletically and the poor old lacrosse stick was propping up a screenless screen door. The only new items were half a dozen chaotic miles of kink free hose that were even more tangled than usual.

Lingo and Wooly burst out of the house to greet her with overwhelming joy. She'd been gone for months and months! Ivy hugged them to her, putting her face into their fluffy fur. What magnificent comfort dogs give to humans.

Two impossibly young officers, very serious and earnest came to the house that afternoon to take Ivy's statement, such as it was, which was not much.

"Mrs. Wilcoxen, why were you at the mulch site?"

They were politely incredulous that anyone would

actually want to tour a mulch site. Ivy started to explain the advantages of the system and describe the process of mulching, from the collection of leaves, the function of the windrows, the scarab, the – but she was cut short.

"When did you last see the deceased?"

The Deceased, that is what Eunice had become.

"The last time I saw Eunice, Mrs. Kingblade," slightly emphasizing the name, "was a couple of days ago. I ran into her at the hardware store. She was trying to get them to buy some of her excess kink free hoses but they knew that the hoses were defective."

"Did you speak to her?"

"Just a quick as possible hi and bye. I did not want to get dragged into another fight about the hoses."

"What fight about the hoses?" The officers exchanged blinks: could this be a motive?

It all sounded so silly and petty to Ivy as she related the story of the kink free hoses. These policemen were supposed to be investigating a murder! Surely this garden club squabble couldn't be relevant but they pressed Ivy for details and took lots of notes. If it hadn't been so grim an occasion, Ivy would have laughed at the idea of killing over some leaky hoses.

After exhausting that topic, the usual litany of questions followed, eliciting nothing really but making Ivy think about what her relationship with Eunice had been. Had it meant anything? She was a fellow traveller in life. Similar to sitting next to someone on a plane maybe, but on a grander scale? From having grown up in the same town they necessarily had some general things in common. Had she ever really tried with Eunice or had she just impatiently dismissed her? Eunice had been difficult and at times unpleasant, but death had earned her compassion and Ivy finished with the simple, "She was a friend."

The policemen were walking somewhat erratically to their patrol car and slapping at their uniforms in a rather violent fashion. Then one started banging his notebook against his leg. Puzzled by their behavior, she, Lingo and Wooly continued to observe the men flapping and batting at themselves. Were they being attacked by an unseen swarm of insects? As Ivy stroked the fluffy dogs, puffs and clouds of fur swirled gently into the atmosphere, alighting on furniture and clothing.

28.   REAVIS AND DOG SWEATER LADY

That Mean Lady was dead but he hadn't killed her. Reavis told Mungo that he knew who did it, but Mungo told him to shut up and never say anything, and to stay away from the Compound until all the people left. Maybe he should tell somebody else. But who? There must be some nice ladies in the garden club – maybe that one that made the dog sweaters – anyone that made sweaters for dogs must be nice. He could ask her about snake sweaters to see what she was like. Reavis was cautious about other folks.

After Mungo had told him to stay away from the Compound, he had followed the faint trail through the woods to the tunnel that went under the highway. Hardly anybody used the tunnel except the horse people. It was a really good place to hide but he was getting tired of hanging around in the damp tunnel and he was feeling hungry too. By now it must be safe to go back to the Compound and he could stop by Deer Creek Yarns on the way. That's where the Dog Sweater Lady lived.

The jingling bell startled Reavis as he carefully opened the door of Deer Creek Yarns. He held his slender body still and stared around at the shelves of brightly colored wool. From his hiding place under the pale yellow boudoir chair, Parsley examined the unfamiliar creature. Parsley kept quiet but was ready for action. He could sense that this guy was afraid and a frightened human could be dangerous and unpredictable.

Grace wished that she could ignore the bell. She just did not want to get up and have to deal with someone. Ivy had left a few minutes ago and Grace had hoped to have a nap or at least lie down for a while. The tiredness enveloped her, but of course she did get up and go out into the front hall.

"Hello – oh it's Reavis isn't it?" Grace had seen him many a time around town but had never met him. Reavis blinked hard then slowly swiveled the filthy baseball cap around on his head a few times. He paused, still looking around as if trying to figure out which way was north.

"Can I help you with something, Reavis?"

"Are you the dog sweater lady?"

"Ah, yes, I make sweaters for small dogs," Grace admitted slowly, not sure where this was going. She had never seen Reavis with a dog.

"Do you make snake sweaters?"

"Ah, no... I must say that I have never had that request before." Grace regarded him wide-eyed. "I'm not sure that snakes would like sweaters somehow. They might find them kind of scratchy."

"Oh." That hadn't occurred to Reavis.

Clearly he was now searching for words and Grace's kind nature wanted to help him out.

"Would you like a cup of tea or a cookie?"

Dog Sweater Lady was so pretty and nice. Except for Mungo and Rita, people usually weren't nice to him. "Oh, I like cookies."

Grace went into the dining room and put several cookies on a plate and took them out to him. Parsley erupted from under the chair and ran to greet the stranger, who gobbled the cookies all up just standing there. Humph, thought Parsley. An aggrieved dog stared at Reavis hoping for eye contact or better yet cookie contact.

"Would you like some more cookies?"

"Oh yes, more cookies. Please. Rita said I should say please. And thank you. Please and thank you."

While he crammed more cookies into his mouth, Parsley hopping hopefully at his side, Grace wrapped up the rest of that morning's batch for him to take home. Reavis knelt to give a bite to Parsley but Grace stopped him.

"No, wait. Chocolate is poisonous for dogs and he doesn't like cranberries so he spits them out all over the floor. Here, you can give him some of these."

She held out a canister of bone shaped dog treats that she made out of wheat germ, powdered milk and baby food. Reavis gave one to Parsley, then ate one himself.

"These are good too!" Grace added some of them to the other cookies that she had packed up for him.

Reavis studied the chairs with pretty flower pillows on them. He wished he had a chair with flower pillows and he walked over to stare at a really comfy looking one. Maybe he would sit down for a little while but not on a chair. He might get it dirty. The Dog Sweater Lady smiled at him so Reavis smiled too. He would trust Dog Sweater Lady to know what to do. He sat down on the floor next to Parsley who immediately climbed into his lap and started sniffing him. He had the same scents as the path along the creek where Parsley walked with Grace sometimes. Stroking the wiry little dog that was licking his trousers, Reavis told Grace all about the ghost that stole the silver pirate shovel.

29. MCKNIGHT TALKS TO THE POLICE

"So Mayor Freemantle, when did you last see Mrs. Kingblade?"

McKnight was nervous even though he and Monday had gone over the best way to say things to the police. You should always talk to the police in their own language: that euphemistically laden and stilted vocabulary which referred to a mass murderer as a "gentleman," and a "getaway car" as a "vehicle," and when the bad guy slugs you he "became increasingly physically uncooperative."

Unfortunately, Monday was not in the room with him

and they had not had a lot of time to prepare. Also unfortunate was the fact that these were Major Case Squad officers, not the familiar local guys Heck and Olney. The Deer Creek police had been removed from the case almost immediately because they were friendly with everyone involved. Heck and McKnight also suspected that the Major Case Squad wanted the glory for themselves in what appeared to be a juicy high society murder.

"I last saw the victim on the evening that she died, prior to her death at the Deer Creek Mulch Site where Mr. Dash Lethaby was holding an informational gathering about his proposed residential development of said mulch site."

"Can you describe what happened, please?"

"The deceased, who was still alive at the time, interrupted the informational gathering organized by Mr. Dash Lethaby. She appeared to be highly agitated and became increasingly verbally abusive. My administrative assistant and I exited the scene with all due velocity while practicing approved safety measures with respect to the public well-being."

Officer Burgess fought the urge to break into hoots of laughter. This guy could write screenplays for TV cop shows.

Officer Nichols continued coolly, "Then what did you do?"

"I returned to my primary place of residence at 24 Outer Hebrides Drive where I remained until 9AM this morning."

"So you didn't go to Shady Grove for drinks with a bunch of the other folks?"

"No. Monday said...." McKnight stopped. He didn't want to admit that he had meekly followed his assistant's order to go straight home.

"No, I just went home."

"And what time was that?"

"Um I think around 6:30 maybe."

"Was there anyone else in your home who can verify your presence there?"

"My wife, Pinckney Hagensieker Freemantle."

"Had she been at the mulch site?"

"No, she doesn't care much for mulch sites." From what Officer Burgess had seen of Mrs. Freemantle he would not think so. She was a real piece of work.

"So she was at home when you returned?"

"Well, no, not then. She came in just a bit later." McKnight was starting to feel hot and a trickle of sweat rolled down his side. Actually Pinckney hadn't come home until a lot later – maybe around eleven; and she'd been completely sloshed. Now he was getting flustered. Loads of people would have seen her at Shady Grove and some would have clocked her departure.

"So what time did she get home?"

"Well, now that you bring it up, I'm not really sure. I had gone to bed."

"So she can't verify that you were at home all evening?"

"Not in so many words exactly, but she can verify that I was at home when she got home." Christ, he hoped she could remember that.

The inquisition finally ended with Detective Nichols saying that they would be interviewing Mrs. Freemantle soon.

Officer Burgess had observed that the mayor had been starting to sweat and get somewhat vague in his answers, but that could be due to many things other than being guilty of murder. Freemantle had some motives similar to Lethaby's. He wanted this project to go through too, not only as an investment, but as a mayoral achievement during his term in office. This guy warranted closer scrutiny.

Officers Burgess and Nichols nodded at the mayor's assistant – weird name – who was standing right outside the mayor's office. They had questioned her earlier, but she had not had anything substantive to contribute. But if her boss needed an extra look, then she probably did too. He'd get somebody to see if she had any kind of record. There was something about that name that faintly rang a bell. She was one cool customer though. Nothing would rattle her. The polar opposite of that St. Cyr woman. Jesus. Goofiest witness he'd ever had to question.

Monday didn't care if the police were wondering about her. Well, let them. She had nothing to worry about except keeping McKnight calm. She would have to tell him that Eunice had known about Kimberley. How had she found out? That baffled Monday. What if McKnight had somehow let it slip to Cuppy when he'd asked him to get Kimberley a job at Tirano and that evil witch had wormed it out of him? That had to be it. What if Cuppy had told the police about Kimberley to throw suspicion off himself? It was critical to prepare McKnight for this contingency.

Monday waited until the policemen were out of sight. Officer Burgess had turned to look back right before he and Nichols went around the corner. That assistant was staring in their direction, but as if she could see into the future, not at them. He gave a bit of a mental shudder and went on. That name, that name....

Monday filtered into McKnight's office. "Oh there you are," he gruffed at her impatiently. The policemen had unsettled him more than he could have imagined. They could make a saint feel guilty. And while he hadn't exactly been grilled by the police, he had certainly been lightly sautéed.

"We need to prepare for another scenario."

Startled and apprehensive, McKnight peered up at her in confusion. "Now what?"

"Mrs. Kingblade knew about Kimberley."

Aghast and incredulous, McKnight flung himself back so hard into his swivel chair with the good lumbar support that it rolled into the wall.

"That's impossible. I didn't tell anyone except you."

"You didn't let it slip by accident to Mr. Kingblade?"

"My God, no. I only asked him to give her a job. They're always hiring girls over at Tirano. I asked him to keep my name out of it, but that's all. She couldn't have known. What makes you think that she knew?"

"She told me so. The day she died."

McKnight's fingers started to rant and rave through his diminishing hair as his heels clawed the chair's way back to his desk. He wrenched open the lower left-hand drawer: empty! How had that happened? Monday was holding a fresh bottle of scotch. Thank God. The woman was prescient. He lurched upward to grab it but, without expression, she held it out of his reach. Well she never had any expression so that didn't mean anything, but she'd certainly never withheld scotch before. This must be fatally serious.

Standing like a frozen statue she monotoned, "Mc-Knight."

This was ominous. She never called him McKnight. She never called him anything come to think of it. What was going on? He slumped back like a sulky schoolboy and waited.

"She… Knew… Something." Monday deliberately separated and capitalized the words. "She threatened to tell Pinckney. The police will question Mr. Kingblade relentlessly. They will get it out of him."

"And I tell you that there is nothing to get out of him." McKnight was fired up now.

"The only thing I said to him was to ask him to give her a job. Nothing else – zip-nada-zero-zilch. And he never asked for an explanation. Only thing he ever said was that she had worked out really well. Great, as a matter of fact."

McKnight was pacing around his desk by now. He considered grabbing the scotch bottle away from Monday but caution stayed his hand. Instead he cast his eyes out the window to contemplate his beautiful blue Jaguar sitting there waiting for him in the smoothly paved parking lot. The sight of his car always soothed him. His first act as mayor was to have the village hall parking lot repaved. The spot reserved for him was the size of two spaces, defined by extra wide stripes. His "double-wide" he joked. "Blueberry Rampant": the classic car glistened regally in the sun. What a magnificent color! He had Mungo wash it every day at the Hose and Elbow, the illicit car wash that Mungo ran behind the Department of Public Works building.

McKnight sighed and turned back toward Monday.

"So what are you suggesting we do?"

"We prepare some statements in case it comes up. Why would you ask him to give her a job but say nothing about it? Mr. Kingblade had to suspect something. He might have mentioned it to his wife. She's suspicious and nosy. Pokes around. Makes assumptions. Sees if she can use it against you to make you change your mind about the mulch site."

Horror was dawning in McKnight's mind: Pinckney finding out; people snickering; his career gone; his political ambitions shot down; his entire future ruined; he'd never eat dinner at the country club again. "I'd kill her!"

"Exactly what the police will think."

Although the enormity of the situation was sinking in, McKnight was not going to give up.

"Just tell me what to say and give me that goddamned bottle of scotch!"

The alcohol soothed his jangled nerves and made his back, where he had hit the wall, feel better too. McKnight started thinking a bit more calmly and analytically. What exactly had Cuppy said about Kimberley? That she was really great. Really Great! REALLY GREAT WHAT? McKnight imagined the worst. That bastard Kingblade must have taken advantage of her! Played on her obligation to him for the job. But McKnight himself had put her in that position. Aghhh! Monday would think of something. She always did.

❦

30. PIZZA

That evening Ivy was very subdued and just sat there in the living room, gazing blankly around. She loved her messy, well-lived-in old house. The saggy sofas were covered in faded cabbage rose chintz and the unmatched wing chairs sprawled around in varying stages of shabbiness. The fraying edges of the arm covers hung in uneven lines. There was a jigsaw puzzle partly put together on a card table off to the side of a huge fireplace. God knows when they last had the chimney swept.

Ivy's mother's needlepoint fire screen tilted a bit to the right. Old paintings of English landscapes with cows and sheep hung next to oils of ships in peril on the sea, above shelves stuffed with well read books. Even the staircase was piled with books, narrowing the steps up to the landing, filling the landing and continuing up to the second floor and the attic. The stacks of books in the basement fortified the floor under the Steinway baby grand piano. It was the soothing, comfortable house of old family money that had been spent wisely. The worn oriental rugs had absorbed plenty of wine over the years. "Adds to the ancient look," Ivy had rationalized. "Probably preserves them too."

After a while she got up and wandered around, sitting in one chair then moving to another. At one point, she sat on a splayed open copy of a Ngaio Marsh book that she'd been looking for. Lingo and Wooly trailed mournfully after her, putting their heads in her lap whenever she sat down. Dogs always know when something is wrong.

Merit, sensing no dinner in the offing announced,

"I'll just rustle something up." Ben started making frantic throat slashing motions at his mother while Trevor mimed throwing up. Their antics knocked Ivy into awareness.

"The last time you 'rustled something up,' the Christmas tree caught fire."

"That was sheer coincidence," said Merit, "and besides, the Christmas tree isn't up now."

"Dad – let's just get pizza."

"Carry out, what a concept!" What a relief. Now he wouldn't have to cook or wash up. Not that he ever did anyway. How handy teenagers could be, especially teenagers with drivers licenses. Although usually nocturnal, they did sometimes appear in the daytime when they came out to forage for food. And his boys were experts as pizzologists, pizzaphiles. Maybe he could write an article about it or a letter to the editor.

"Okay. Get lots of stuff on it, all the stuff your mother likes." Merit could not really remember what Ivy liked on pizza. "Vegetables – you know – toppings. She needs sustenance." Did eggplant ring a bell?

"Yeah, Dad, we know. One large Sustenance pizza coming up." Trevor grabbed the keys and they made a break for it.

"Lots of meat and extra cheese for me." Merit hurled after them.

"WE KNOW!" The boys shouted away in the car and the house was suddenly quiet.

Merit recalled the pizza of his youth. Oh, what his boys were missing: those gargantuan slices with heavy slathers of cheese and blobs of tomato sauce and hunks of meat swimming in orange grease. The stuff these days was much thinner, more healthy allegedly; even had things like spinach on it sometimes, which wasn't bad but that old stuff had sure hit the spot. Maybe his spot had moved. Merit worriedly poked his stomach then glanced over at Ivy, who had been still for a while now.

Ivy usually started the evening with a cocktail but Merit preferred and opened an appropriately somber cabernet sauvignon. Maybe he should give it to her in a mug. One of those comforting mugs from her childhood that had the little animals in the bottom to encourage a child to drink all the milk. There was a frog, a duck, a cow and a stump. No one could remember what the stump had been. The frog and the duck made sense, but a cow? Why would a cow be in a pond? Maybe the stump had been a fish. Merit got her the frog mug and filled it to the brim. He poured himself the duck mug and sat beside her on the sofa. Ivy, unable to get the sight of Eunice out of her mind's eye, drank automatically and soon the frog appeared.

31.   MADELEINE AND DASH

Madeleine opened the front door with the same old key. She stepped into the quiet hall and stared at the wall where the mirror had been. Dash had really scared her when he smashed up the kitchen and then sent that box of broken mirrors to her. The place was unkempt and abandoned looking. A thump told her that Cole had just jumped off a sofa and was coming to greet her. His nails clicked along the floor as he ran toward her, making those roo noises and dancing around and licking her face when she bent down to hug and pat him. She'd been gone for years and years!

"Oh, Cole, I miss you, you sweet sweet doggy woggy yes I do yes I do; oh what a good doggy; yes I love you too! Where's Dash? Where is he? Is he in the den? Let's go see." She followed the deliriously happy tail down the hall to the den where Dash was struggling to push himself up from the sofa.

"Mad, what are you doing here?"

He was hungover, rumpled, bristly faced with heavy bags under his bloodshot eyes, and older, definitely older. Although she had caught glimpses of him around town now and then, she had not been close since they started their trial separation. Sad and lonely would also describe him. A wave of pity swept her toward him but caution detoured her in the direction of the wing chair.

"Christie called me to tell me what happened so I came back to see how you are."

"Huh." Dash pushed up to his feet and stood over her, staring, forcing her to lean back. Then he turned away and went over to the window, to rest his face against the cool pane. "I didn't kill her, if that's what you want to know."

"I never thought you did. That's why I thought you might want some – oh, I don't know, a friend or something."

"I'm fine. I've got Cole. And your Father Wedgewood came to call. Actually made me feel like going to church but this was the one time I had a genuine excuse not to: house arrest." He continued to stand with his back toward her.

By now Cole was half in her lap and they were rubbing noses. "Eskimo," she cooed. That made Dash turn with a hint of a smile, remembering how they used to do that, an Eskimo kiss. He and Mad that is. He loved Cole, but not for an Eskimo kiss.

It was good to see her. Who was he kidding? It was wonderful to see her. That glorious face and graceful body: just as fabulous and fresh as ever. "Would you like something to drink?" He gestured sort of vaguely with his hands.

"No, umm, no thanks, Dash. If you're sure you're all right, I'll go." She gently pushed Cole off her lap and got up. The violet eyes almost level with his own captured him again.

"Please stay; just for a little. I – frankly, it's been hell."

He walked around and sat on the edge of his desk, knocking a bunch of stuff off, but he ignored it. Madeleine restrained herself from picking it up and straightening it out and sat down on the sofa, much to Cole's delight. He wriggled up next to her, sighed contentedly and started chewing on his foot.

"They think I did it. The police. They found the shovel in my car. Of course the shovel was in my car I said. I put it there. Gardenia left it at the mulch site and I took it to give it back to her. Do you think I would leave it in there if I HAD killed her? I swear I did not kill Eunice. The police said blows from the shovel killed her. I did not kill her by hitting her with the car."

"Wait, you hit her with the car? What do you mean?" Madeleine straightened up in surprise.

"I didn't mean to. I was mad and she tried to stop me

and I just hit the gas and kept going and I tried to miss her but I think I hit her. But that is not what killed her."

"Good grief, this sounds crazy! Where were you? How did this all happen?"

"Urhhh," Dash moaned and deflated onto the sofa next to Cole who stopped chewing his foot long enough to give Dash a sympathetic lick. "Wait," getting up again, "I need a drink, then I'll tell you the whole story. Sure you don't want anything?" Madeleine shook her head.

Fortified with scotch, he settled back into one of the old wing chairs. "You know, everybody knows, that I want to develop the mulch site. It's my last chance, Mad, to save the business."

Terrible guilt struck Madeleine about all the money she had spent on redecorating the house, but she hadn't known. If ONLY she'd known. Why hadn't Dash trusted her enough to tell her?

"And Eunice kept causing trouble and raising hell and organizing all these people to try to stop it. I swear, that woman was seriously deranged. But I thought I could still get it through. The mayor was for it, even her husband Cuppy, and a bunch of other heavy hitters. Most of the village council was on board, but I needed more money. So I invited some folks to a presentation at the mulch site to show them how much better it would be for everybody. With the architects' drawings and views up on big easels – very swell, that sort of thing. The meeting was supposed to be hush-hush, but someone blabbed or tipped off Eunice on purpose. So she shows up and starts yelling and accusing everybody of conspiring against her. So people start leaving and I'm trying to get her to calm down. By now everyone's gone I guess, so I give up and get in the car and drive out, but she jumps in the way – she actually jumps in front of me! So I swerve, but I think I may have slightly bumped her, but I just left anyway and drove around for a while. I went back to check on her, but nobody was there so I figured that she was okay. I saw the shovel and put it in my car. Then I went to Shady Grove. Next thing I know it's morning and later I find out she's dead."

Madeleine sighed and leaned back, rolling her head around and rubbing her neck.

"I've changed my mind. Do you have any wine?"

Dash perked up a bit and went to forage in the kitchen, coming back with a very nice Pouilly Fuissé, which had been one of her favorites. It was already open and she hoped that it had not been in the refrigerator for the last three months. He poured it heavily into an old grape jelly jar that had a faded Wizard of Oz design on it. "All the wine glasses are dirty because you said not to put them in the dishwasher."

All those dozens of lovely old crystal glasses that she had sorted and washed and dried so carefully and arranged in proper rows in the freshly painted pantry cabinets: they were ALL dirty? Dear God, there couldn't be an inch of counter space left. The whole kitchen must be a toxic waste site. What had happened to the housekeeper? Dash must have read her mind.

"Glinda quit. I think that the glasses put her over the edge; or it could have been the towel situation."

Madeleine did not want to know, which was just as well because it had been finding a towel wrapped around Misty Tallois that had been the deciding moment for

Glinda. Dash could have kicked himself: why hadn't he found out in time that Misty was a real estate agent? She'd gone on and on about listings and went around flushing toilets all over the house. Jesus. It was all he could do to....

"So how did you find out she was dead?"

"The police showed up at the door that afternoon. Heck and a couple of county guys. At first they just said that they had some questions about the meeting last night. I thought that was a bit odd, but I said okay sure come in. But then it hits me: oh God – Eunice has lodged a complaint about me running into her." Dash was thumping around, flinging his non-drink hand out for emphasis. "Well I wasn't thinking too clearly, and I felt and probably looked horrible because I'd sort of inadvertently spent the night at Shady Grove."

"Oh Dashley: One sofa."

"Right. One sofa." Thus did Shady Grove bill him for his drunken overnight stays. Dashley half smiled. Things were looking up if she was calling him Dashley again.

"So I said, look, if this is about Eunice I'm sorry but she started it and then jumped in front of my car. It wasn't my fault if I might have possibly slightly hit her and knocked her down. I drove by the mulch site later and she wasn't there so I figured that she was fine. Is she pressing charges against me? And there was this silence while I was pouring myself a drink. I offered them some but they said no."

Dash paused to top up his scotch then automatically spilled more wine into her glass. "So that's when they said that she'd been found dead at the mulch site. My first thought was that Cuppy had killed her. He just couldn't take it any longer. But I didn't say so. And I told them about going to Shady Grove and spending the night there. So they ask me if they can search my car so I say sure. I figured they're looking for damage that hitting a body would cause. But they find the shovel in there and they say it's the murder weapon. Now they're running all these tests on it. They put it in this big plastic bag and everything. I told them all about it but they went on and on that it was the murder weapon and forensic tests would find hair and blood etc etc. I finally said look I may, emphasize may, have hit her with my car, but I never hit her with the shovel."

"But Dash, that doesn't sound like a very good defense. Golly gee your Honor, I didn't hit her with the shovel, I only hit her with my five ton Jeep Wagoneer."

"I would never say golly gee. And I think they're only two tons."

"For heaven's sake, have you talked to Hoover?" Hoover was Dash's attorney.

"Yes, but it's not really his area of expertise, so another guy from his firm is handling everything."

"So what happens next?"

"The police said not to leave town blah blah blah and I had to surrender my passport, but I said I didn't know where it was. So they said they would have to search the house and the safe deposit box, but I couldn't find the key – the key to the safe deposit box that is. And I wasn't entirely sure what bank it is in anyway. So the judge decided that I did not pose a flight risk because I was too disorganized." He flung out his arms to make aggrieved quotation marks. "So then the damn prosecutor asks for at least an ankle bracelet but the judge said that I would probably lose it and they're expensive."

"The brute." Madeleine blinked at him with faux seriousness.

"Plus," in an increasingly annoyed tone, "no wheels: they took the Wagoneer as evidence. So I can't go anywhere anyway. I told 'em to make sure they bring it back with a full tank."

"But you weren't actually in jail were you?"

"Oh yeah I was. Overnight. With Reavis Huckstep and two ferrets."

"What?!"

"They had arrested Reavis too – before they found the shovel in my car I guess, or lack of communication or something. Police from all these different jurisdictions just screwed up the whole process. Huh. And they think I'M disorganized. And..."

Madeleine interrupted him. "Well wait, why did they arrest Reavis?"

"I think because the poor guy is an obvious scapegoat. Weirdo loner who hangs out at the mulch site – in fact he may live there. Then, Mungo Gummers – the mulch guy – has these ferrets; claims they're a Special Breed of Racing Ferret, although that sounds bogus to me. At any rate, he kept them at the mulch site where Reavis took care of them. Somehow Eunice finds them and tells Mungo to get rid of them or she will. So he brings 'em to the jail for protective custody. Heck probably went along just to aggravate Eunice."

"Oh, Dashley," Madeleine started laughing. "That really is carrying small town eccentricity too far." He laughed too and they sat there for a while quietly contemplating ferrets. Then Madeleine said what Dash had kind of been wondering too. "Do you think Mungo or Reavis killed Eunice to protect the ferrets?"

"Oh, I don't know. It's as good a reason as any, I suppose. And neither one of them has an alibi. Plus there's something wrong with Reavis to begin with. Oh God, what a mess. Man, I'm tired."

Dash smiled as she got up and came toward him. "Listen, why don't you go take a shower…" (not what he'd been hoping for) "and I'll wash some wine glasses. Then we'll figure out dinner. I can go get something."

Cole happily accompanied Madeleine into the kitchen. She had been dreading what she might find there and it WAS a mess, but a regular bachelor type mess, not something that would qualify for Federal disaster aid or require a call to the Health Department. The dishwasher was crammed full, but by surgically precise rearrangement, Madeleine managed to fit in three more plates, two cups and four saucers. She regarded loading a dishwasher as akin to putting together a jigsaw puzzle. Oh, it was so gratifying to get everything in! If there had only been some dishwasher detergent, she would have triumphantly run the cleverly loaded appliance.

The cupboards had been replaced with ones identical to the old ones and the walls had been repainted. The refrigerator still bore a couple of hack marks across the cherry wood front though. He had been drunk and flailing the axe.

"I want a plain white refrigerator that hums!" WHACK "And you can put magnets on it!" WHACK "And you even have to defrost it!" No whack. Maybe frost free was good? No! Defrosting it meant you had to eat up all the ice cream. One of many happy childhood memories. And there was that time when he and his father had gone to Baskin Robbins and their power was out and they were selling those big tubs of ice cream really cheap so they bought six and brought them home and his mother pointed out that they would not fit in the freezer so they had to call all their friends and relations to come over right away to eat ice cream. The axe had gotten kind of heavy by then though, so he put it down and slumped after it just as she'd slammed the door behind her.

Dash came into the kitchen, both man and room looking and smelling a lot better. He opened another bottle of wine and poured some into the proper clean wine glasses. Handing her one, he leaned back against the counter. "Like I said earlier, the first thing I thought when I heard Eunice was dead was that Cuppy had killed her. He just couldn't take it any longer. At the presentation she lit into him right in front of everybody. Although he did actually tell her to shut up."

32.   *CUPPY PONDERS*

Still brooding over the fact that one of the last things that he had said to Eunice was shut up (although it could have been worse he told himself consolingly), Cuppy was joltingly stunned when the police told him that Dash had been arrested for the murder and that Reavis was being held on suspicion.

"Dash? Dash Lethaby? Are you sure? No, that can't be right." Cuppy wasn't thinking too clearly, but Dash? "And Reavis? On suspicion of what?" He really could not see Dash and Reavis as in cahoots. A gleaming model of money and charm paired with a retarded hillbilly? "No, that's impossible."

The police hadn't been too forthcoming on details. Plus there was all this disagreement on motives and ominous muttering about ferrets. He must be hallucinating. Ferrets? Well, Dash had just cause and all that, but you still can't believe that someone you've known forever could kill someone else you'd known forever. Maybe Dash was more desperate than people could have imagined. But, barring strangers, who else could it be? Reavis made much more sense than Dash. And Reavis wouldn't even need a reason. He was just plain old crazy.

One of the officers from the Major Case Squad was watching Cuppy closely. They always suspected the husband, didn't they? And he did not have an alibi that he could prove. No one had seen him arrive at The Lodge and he hadn't stopped anywhere for gas. Stop protesting that it couldn't be Dash or Reavis, you idiot. Not that he wanted it to be Dash. Reavis was expendable though.

33. *MADELEINE AT HOME*

As soon as Madeleine got back to the carriage house, she started looking for Dash's passport. Exactement! There it was – right next to hers in the pigeonhole directly to the left of the center compartment in her desk. Inevitably, it was about to expire. Unlike most people, his passport photo was of Hollywood leading man or fashion model quality; a more civilized and better dressed Marlborough Man. Any country would happily welcome him and sigh regretfully at his departure – well the female half of the population at any rate.

Maybe they should just leave the country and disappear to some island. Why do islands entice with the idea of freedom? In a way, an island would not be a good place to go if you were on the run. They were usually (A) on the small side so it would be hard to keep your presence a secret, (B) for the same reason, there would be a lack of successful hiding places and (C) they offered a limited number of escape routes. Ditch that idea.

Madeleine held dual Canadian and French citizenship, but Dash had only U.S. Did marriage to her bestow either on him? Even if it did, it would be a long bureaucratic fumble to acquire a passport.

What countries or islands do not have extradition treaties with the U.S.? Probably places where no one would want to live anyway. Besides, Dash was innocent. There was no need to run. That would look like an admission of guilt.

Ballet had given her life structure with guidelines and goals, deadlines, rules of behavior, dress and personal appearance. Your hair had to be the right length and your nail polish had to be color coordinated with other dancers or eliminated. Now she was confused and drifting through life. She needed a new project. Dash would be her new project! Instead of divorcing him, she would prove him innocent and renew their love along with his passport.

With enthusiastic optimism, Madeleine took a shower and got into her pajamas. In typical fashion, she proceeded to then stub her toe and fall into bed. (Dash had always loved the falling into bed part.) Soon, however, she was all comfy and snuggly with four mechanical pencils and a yellow annotation ¼ inch ruled acid free 90 gsm paper stock pad with a firm backing. At the top she had put "Restructure Life." That should still cover it.

She had started the list right after she left Dash, vowing that unlike Anna Karenina, she would not throw herself under a train. She would (A) go to grad school, (B) start a wedding planning business, (C) join the garden club or (D) even take up needlepoint. Before things had gotten that dire, however, she had gone back to Canada to see about resuming her ballet career. That is where she had been when Dash's sister Christie had called her about Dash's arrest. So the abandoned list now took on new, essential meaning: it gave her Purpose! First she had to establish the facts that were working against Dash's claim of innocence.

RESTRUCTURE LIFE

POINTS AGAINST DASH

1. Well-known, long-running animosity with Eunice (not good).
2. Very public argument with same right before murder (not good at all).

3. Murder weapon found in his car (that was a tough one).
4. His fingerprints are on the murder weapon (ditto).
5. He was the last person known to have seen her ("known" being the operative word).

All of which added up to motive, means and opportunity. Maybe she would have to add to the list (E) go to law school.

In the meantime she could develop a

SUSPECT LIST

1. Anyone who invested in Dash's development project.
2. Anyone who hated mulch piles.
3. Anyone who hated Eunice.
4. Anyone who purchased the defective kink free hoses.
5. Anyone who liked ferrets.

There were so many anyones that it became almost everyone. So she had to devise a

PLAN OF ACTION

1. Get names of investors from Dash.
2. Call the village hall to see if they have statistics on the citizenry's opinion of the mulch site. If not, conduct survey to determine popularity of mulch site.
3. Go through village directory.
4. Ask garden clubs who had purchased kink free hoses.

5. Contact local veterinarians.

Madeleine double-checked her PLAN OF ACTION with growing excitement. Organization was so wonderful.

Then it hit her: Cuppy! Of course, the husband is always the first to be suspected. So why wasn't he in this case? He fit into the first four categories: he was an investor, so by definition he did not like the mulch pile, despite the botanical benefits of mulch. He was in the village directory. It was well known that he had a garage full of defective and unsold kink free hoses. The only question was his position on ferrets, but that did not really matter. He was Suspect Number One.

It was getting pretty late so Madeleine made sleep the next priority. First thing in the morning, she would stop by the Badger Tearoom to pick up some of their scrumptious Butter Rum muffins, then take them over to Dash's house and get the list of investors. Even with Cuppy as SN1, she and Dash could go through the list and the village directory together. He could identify some other possibilities in case Cuppy did not work out. Blissfully, she turned out the light, so happy to have a Plan.

Her brain wanted to stay up however. Should she go talk to Cuppy in person? She had met and chatted with him at various cocktail and dinner parties. She would make a condolence call: that was it.

Madeleine sat up and turned the lamp back on. She grabbed the RESTRUCTURE LIFE writing pad from the second shelf of her bedside table. It was right on top of the book *Cooking With Can Openers*. She started a new category:

REASONS FOR CUPPY (SN1) TO KILL EUNICE

1. Hated her (good reason).
2. Met someone else (who?).
3. Needed money (what would he inherit or make from investment in mulch site?).

Another book on the second shelf gave her the idea of how she would orchestrate her call on Cuppy. *Casserole Cookery* had been a housewarming gift from the Kingblades. Oh perfect: he probably loved casseroles. She would be a ministering angel and bring him a casserole. Casseroles couldn't be that hard to make could they?

34.   HECK AND THE JAIL

Police Chief Vaughn "Heck" Hequembourg heaved a sigh of relief when the last of the Major Case Squad guys left. They had been very professional and for the most part polite but there had been that underlying air of superiority and an occasional spurt of outright smugness. He hadn't been insulted that the case had been taken away from the Deer Creek Police Department because they were all friends of those involved. It was a relief and a lot less work. Dash hadn't killed that old termagant anymore than he had. Only an idiot would keep the murder weapon in his vehicle and let the police search it. Even when falling down drunk, Dash wouldn't be that stupid. No, there was less here than met the eye.

Heck longed for the good old days – back when the Police Department had first started. In nice weather the "office" had been a tasteful white lattice shelter with an old card table and two cars in the parking lot of the country club. If cold or wet, the "office" moved indoors, right outside the entrance to the men's locker room. When somebody needed the police, they simply called the country club. On Mondays, when the club was closed, you had to go up there yourself, although that was also the day when the policemen were allowed to play golf. A domestic disturbance was usually raccoons in the garbage pails. Once they had to break into a house to get a wedding dress out of the attic.

Initially, Heck hadn't wanted to arrest Reavis and the poor kid had gone berserk when they had – screaming and crying and swirling that cap around until they handcuffed him. Then he just howled and sobbed. It had been horrible. "The Imports," aka the Major Case Squad guys, had offered to haul Reavis off to the county booby hatch, but Heck had convinced them to leave him here. The Major Case Squad guys were only too happy to let him have Reavis. They didn't care about the marijuana and they certainly did not want the ferrets.

It was also a bit devious on Heck's part. He was now convinced that Reavis had killed Eunice Kingblade. The truth would come out eventually and he, Chief Hequembourg, not the Major Case Squad, would be the one to have been right all along.

"Listen," he told his troops, "none of us is looking for work. It's enough just to patrol Deer Creek. So let the

Major Case Squad guys think they've got it all wrapped up. Things'll slowly unravel and we will be the ones who end up with the killer in custody. So in the meantime, hands off – just go about business as usual."

He did tell his suspicions to Mungo though, who could understand Heck's way of thinking. It was the way everybody judged Reavis. "Look, Mungo, I sympathize, I really do and you and Rita are so good to take care of him. But you know he isn't right in the head – he killed her to protect the ferrets or the marijuana or just his camp there by the creek. Something like this has just been waiting to happen. What did you do with the marijuana by the way? I'm asking as a friend, Mungo."

"The police have the whole place taped off. What could I do?" Heck speculated silently that Mungo could have done a lot of things.

Indeed, he had worked feverishly through the night, digging up all the plants and lugging them back to the Department of Public Works. Then he raided the garden clubs' closets for flowerpots and found enough to trans-plant almost all the seedlings. He would be planting the village flowerpots soon – the big urns that sat on Deer Creek street corners, and he would just tuck a marijuana plant or two in with the flowers. Nobody paid any atten-tion to those things – just drove past them and took them for granted. He was in charge of watering the flowerpots so he could easily tend and harvest his little crop.

Reunited with the ferrets, Reavis calmed down and just huddled there next to their portable cage, which was a cat carry box. A lunatic and two ferrets were the sum total of Heck's prisoners. Earlier that day, they'd had a stray dog in one of the cells. Retirement could not come soon enough. Of course the ferrets weren't really prisoners. They were in protective custody. That was a concept seemingly lost on the Major Case Squad boys. Even though it was safe for them now, what with Mrs. Kingblade dead, if the ferrets kept Reavis quiet, Heck intended to keep them as long as he did Reavis. Sit tight, he told himself. That's right, soon he'd be fishing with his dog Felon and trying to overcome his addiction to Tums. All he had to do now was nothing.

35.   DOING NOTHING
OR NOTHING DOING

"Nothing! Nothing, nothing, nothing! The police are doing nothing! Even Heck – and he's friends with Dash – sort of." Ivy was incensed.

Merit, who held the concept of doing nothing in high regard, did nothing and waited for Ivy to subside. Sometimes doing nothing was a positive action. Maybe he could write a letter to the editor about it. Certainly the Deer Creek Crier could benefit by not publishing a lot of that nonsense people were always whining about. After Ivy had stopped flailing her glass around and was holding it in a more or less stable manner, Merit poured more wine into it.

Ivy inhaled a gulp. "The police are closing the case without investigating all the possibilities. I think it's just plain old easier for them to arrest Dash and call it quits."

Ivy had gotten up and was pacing around on the blue-stone terrace, gesturing increasingly wildly with her wine glass, slopping and flinging wine like some obscure religious rite. Good thing we're outside, thought Merit, although I better go in soon to put another bottle in the fridge. It was a nice dry rosé – French – pas de Californie! Now that would be an interesting article: casual foreign words that were in common use. What were some others...? This might warrant a trip to Provence this summer.

Merit re-entered the atmosphere to hear Ivy say, "So Grace and I are going to investigate Eunice's murder."

"WHAT?! WHOA WHOA WHOA Wait a minute! Let's talk about this." What had he missed while in the South of France?

"Ivy, I'm sure the police know what they're doing. Stay out of it."

Ivy pulled up a few little weeds in the garden path, spilling more wine. "Too bad wine isn't an herbicide. Dash couldn't have killed her. I just know it."

"Oh how can you know it? The guy hacked up his kitchen with an axe!"

"Well, maybe so, but he didn't hack up Madeleine!"

"Fine. He didn't hack up Madeleine. That clearly lets him out as a killer. In which case that's all the more reason to stay out of it. There could be a murderer still out there! Don't get involved! The police will figure it out eventually."

"But that's exactly why I need to get involved. The police don't care, so they'll never figure it out."

"Well, I care – about you – about the boys! I do not want you putting you or them in any kind of danger."

"Oh, it will not ever remotely be like that."

"Oh really, what will it be like?" Merit was breathing heavily. This could be a three bottle night. Sounded like a song. Maybe that could be an article: the daily phrases that were musical. Like "Your plate is singing!" He had said that recently to Ivy. What was it that they had been having?

"What's for dinner?"

Ivy ignored this non sequitur.

"I feel obligated to investigate Eunice's murder."

"Why? Why on earth would you?" Merit stomped inside to open another bottle of the dry rosé, so hard to find. Rosé had such an undeservedly bad reputation.

"Merit, this is a friend, wrongly accused. How would you feel if it were you?" Ivy followed him inside.

"But it isn't me! I'm sure the police know what they're doing. Don't get involved. Nothing doing!"

Bottle in hand, he barged out the back door into the cool spring evening. His anger made him unwary and he tripped over the kink free hose that had been hiding in the dark grass. His determination not to drop the wine bottle enabled him to stay upright. Merit then vented his frustration by kicking the damn hose around the yard. Lingo and Wooly burst out to join him in this fun new game that called for lots of barking and running around in circles then ending with a magnificent clash of tug-of-war.

The topic was not referred to again, Ivy silently affirming to herself her determination to investigate and Merit considering the case closed. Ivy did more than mull: she was getting revved up over this. It was intriguing and unusual to say the least: flabby neurons were firing up lethargic brain cells. I am going to figure this out, she shouted inside her mind.

"What did you say was for dinner?"

Ivy didn't reply and just clanked some pots around but Merit took pride in his commanding ability that had forced her mind off the murder. She would stay out of it now. He could always make her see reason.

36. NEVER UNDERESTIMATE THE POWER OF COOKIES

Ivy took off into the wind in her new role as caped crusader and Investigator Extraordinaire. "Reavis obviously feels comfortable with you, so if we take him some cookies, maybe we can get more details out of him and we can go from there. The problem will be to keep the police out of it."

Grace sounded doubtful. "Might that not be construed as obstruction of justice?"

"Justice schmustice. It isn't justice to arrest that poor soul Reavis for killing Eunice. He's just the obvious scapegoat because he's mentally challenged and seems kind of weird to people who don't know him."

"I'm afraid that Reavis seems kind of weird to people who do know him."

"Grace, let's just give this a try. We'll bring a whole bunch of cookies for the police and Reavis. Then I'll distract Heck or Olney or whoever it is, while you talk to Reavis. If it goes wrong, well then, we're just a pair of interfering old biddies."

Grace bridled mentally at that classification. Would an old biddy even be capable of distracting the police? Lawmen must face many temptations far more irresistible than a middle-aged garden club member; even one armed with homemade cookies. "Well, my mother often says, 'Never underestimate the power of cookies,' but that's usually in the context of car mechanics and yardmen. Surely policemen are far less susceptible and more suspicious."

"Don't you believe it. They are mere men after all. They'll probably pooh-pooh anything we get from Reavis anyway, so we have no choice. They have forced us into it."

"But if the police are going to dismiss anything he says, does it matter if they overhear?"

"Yes, because we don't want them to know what we are up to. I'll make some of my special extra chocolate chocolate chip cookies and you make your cranberry date oatmeal ones. They'll never know what hit 'em."

Grace thought that Ivy was being a bit silly with all this imagined intrigue and she truly did not see what else they could possibly discover, but she silently went along with the plan. You always have lacked gumption she told herself sadly. Olivier had once teased her, saying that for her an act of defiance would be not following the washing instructions on the garment label.

37.   THE PISTOL RANGE

"Grace! I had a brain wave!" Ivy leaped into Grace's little old two-seater Mercedes. Olivier had given it to her and although it wasn't something that she would have bought for herself, she loved it dearly. Now that he was dead, she would keep it forever. Ivy was sporting an outfit that brought Annie Oakley to mind. As if this weren't alarming enough, she had a real gun in the holster that she was holding. "I'll put this on when we get there."

"What on earth is going on?" Could Ivy possibly be planning an assault on the Deer Creek Police Department? Would she run in there shouting, "Free Reavis"?

"The old pistol range! I'd forgotten all about it. It's in the basement of the Police Department. I'll tell Heck or Olney that I need to practice. That'll distract them more than cookies, but I brought those too."

Grace just sat there and rubbed her forehead. "I've never heard anything about a pistol range."

"Ha! That's because they try to keep it quiet."

"How can you possibly keep a pistol range quiet?"

"Very funny. C'mon, let's go before Merit gets back."

Grace drove slowly and with definite misgivings, trying to think of some way to circumvent potholes and Ivy's increasingly preposterous schemes.

When Grace had called Heck to find out about visiting Reavis (she had certainly never visited anyone in jail before, so she was not familiar with the procedure), he told her the story of Reavis's arrest.

"Poor kid. Major Case Squad guys just wanted to

question him – somebody told them he lived at the mulch site but he got scared and tried to run away. So they grab him and throw him down, trying to cuff him. Kid goes berserk and in the tussle his book gets lost. He keeps asking for it. *The Happy Man and His Dump Truck*. Do you think that you could find another copy and bring it to him?"

Ivy sauntered into the Police Department like a gunslinger going into a saloon. "Hey there, Heck, Olney. Been a while since I've had any practice. Any chance the range is open?"

"Always open for armed ladies, Ivy. Are you shooting too, Grace?" Heck asked with a bit of surprise.

"No, I'm here to visit Reavis. I brought him a new book."

"Hallelujah! That should make him happier." Reavis was starting to get on his nerves. "Are those cookies? Thanks so much. Olney, why don't you take Mrs. Wilcoxen down to the range? You could use a bit of practice yourself. I don't need to keep up my qualifying anymore so I'll keep an eye on things up here. You can unlock Reavis's cell on the way for Mrs. Mere. Remember to sign in on the pistol range sheet."

Grace followed Ivy and Olney downstairs. They had to pass the two cells to get to the pistol range and Olney menacingly whacked the bars with his baton. To Grace's relief, Reavis and the ferrets were the only occupants. Olney unlocked Reavis's cell for Grace. "I won't lock you in. Just holler if you need any help."

When Grace gave Reavis the new copy of *The Happy Man and His Dump Truck*, he cried and cried. After she read it to him several times, he finally calmed down and even stopped twirling his cap around on his head.

Talking very slowly and gently, Grace started by reminding Reavis of the basic facts. Mrs. Kingblade had been found dead in the mulch pile. Someone had killed her. "Reavis, I need your help to solve this case and prove that you and Mr. Lethaby are innocent. Now I know that you've already told me all about it but let's go through it again. Maybe there are some more details that you can remember about the ghost and the silver pirate shovel."

Reavis ate cookie after cookie, carefully alternating between chocolate chip and oatmeal date cranberry and making tidy little piles of crumbs for the ferrets while he told Grace about the evening at the mulch site.

After listening to a lengthy account, which was an odd combination of obsessive observation and vague fairy tale, Grace left Reavis in his cell. He hunched happily over his book, which he was now reading to Lightning and Superman.

Grace continued down the hall in the direction of the muffled shots of the pistol range. There was a small glass window in the door so she took a peek in and knocked. Olney opened the door and she stepped into a room that had a ceiling pockmarked with bullet holes. At least, she had to assume that they were bullet holes, never having seen a bullet hole before. There were also what appeared to be mysterious scorch marks along the walls.

Ivy was quite flushed and breathing hard. "Whoosh, been some time since I've done this. Used to be a lot better. I need to come over here more often. Want to give it a try, Grace?"

"Oh, no thank you. Are those bullet holes in the ceiling?"

"Yup," said Olney. "Some folks aren't very good shots. And those burn marks are from really bad shots who need to steady their gun against the wall. Of course, this is after they've had a few."

Grace hoped that he was referring to private citizens and not Deer Creek police. Although that alternative was scarcely reassuring. They trooped back past the cells, Olney locking Reavis in. Heck had saved some cookies for Olney, although not very many.

Ivy sat down heavily in the little car and turned to Grace. "Well, guess what I learned from Olney?" She immediately continued, "Heck is convinced that Reavis killed her. That's why he's keeping him in jail."

Grace stared at her. "Good heavens! So the Deer Creek police think it's Reavis and the Major Case Squad thinks it's Dash!"

"And we know it's neither one of them!" Ivy sighed. "Well, did you get anything new from Reavis?"

"Not really. He gave me a minute by minute account of the evening with more details than he originally told me, but.... He seems to remember lots of specific things and he knew what was going on because he said that he spied on the people. So the basic points are that Eunice discovered the Compound, that's what he and Mungo call their camp by the creek, and jumped out and scared them so Mungo took the ferrets to the jail to be safe."

Ivy broke in impatiently, "Right, we know that already; and the police are saying that that was Reavis's motive: to protect the ferrets and the marijuana."

"Yes, but Reavis says he knew that the ferrets were safe because Mungo had taken them to jail."

"Well, what about the marijuana then?"

"Mungo had told him when they first started growing the marijuana that if it got discovered, Reavis didn't have to worry about it, the crop belonged to Mungo."

"Okay, then what?"

"That he stayed in the Compound during the meeting but when he heard cars leaving he came closer to spy on what was going on. He'd peek out, then hide and make his way a bit farther around the perimeter, then peek out again. He thought they had all left so he started out into the main part of the mulch site, to cut across back to the Compound, when he saw a ghost. He said it was a white shape and it was carrying a silver pirate shovel."

"Yeah, that's the part that worries me – the ghost carrying a pirate shovel." Ivy rolled her eyes. "Oh brother, there goes Reavis as a witness. But, wait, what time was it by then? Wouldn't it be dark?"

"He said it was mostly dark but that he could see okay. But he was so scared by the ghost that he ran back into the bushes. Then he heard a car start up and leave. He waited a while, went back out into the mulch site. He saw a hose lying there so he picked it up and took it back to the Compound. And about the ghost, I don't know. Could it have been a person or was he just imagining things?"

Grace suggested that they go back to her house for tea or something stronger and continue the discussion there. Parsley galloped up to Grace, wagging his tail frantically. She'd been gone for months and months! Once he had calmed down with a treat, Grace was allowed to make a pot of tea. Soon they were all settled comfortably in the living room with cups of tea, a bowl of water, lemon shortbread cookies and a chicken chewy. The investigative campaign could continue.

"So where were we? Did you ask him about the next morning?"

"Yes. He said that Mungo got there a little bit before the garden club ladies did. He told Reavis to stay in the Compound and he would bring him some cakes when the ladies went home. Then he heard all the sirens and saw all the ambulances and fire engines so he was spying on that. At some point Mungo rushed toward the Compound so Reavis met him on the trail. Mungo told him that somebody killed Mrs. Kingblade. Reavis told him about the ghost. Mungo told him not to say anything and to go hide and stay away from the Compound until everybody was gone."

"Hmpp…" emerged from Ivy. Since she didn't appear to have anything else to say at the moment, Grace went on.

"Why was Eunice there in the first place? Maybe it isn't relevant but it keeps nagging at me. Apparently you really have to search to find that Compound. Would she really do that just to ferret out the ferrets, so to speak?"

"I don't know, but she was a pretty malicious old snoop," said Ivy. "It seems clear that she did not know about the meeting."

Grace and Ivy sat there in collective detective's block.

"Well, I'm afraid that doesn't take us any farther. So, we are going to have to go over to the mulch site and search for ourselves," declared Ivy, getting up and whacking her handbag decisively. Parsley jumped up and emitted a sharp bark of surprise. Was this a new game? Attack the Sack?

"Shhhs, shhhs, Parsley. It's all right. Search for what?" Grace sounded skeptical.

"Clues of course. Clues that the police missed."

38.   MELODY MCCULLOUGH GOES ROGUE

"If he calls me 'Hon' one more time, I'll, I'll...." In truth, Officer Melody McCullough did not know what she would do if Chief Hequembourg continued to call her that. She was a recent addition to the once all male Deer Creek police force and it had been tough going, but never did she think that they would be told NOT to investigate a murder. The first murder in thirty two years! And they were supposed to do nothing!?!

The discovery of the body had taken place on her day off, so she had no firsthand knowledge of the crime or the evidence. When she came in the next morning, Chief Hequembourg told her that the Deer Creek Police Department was off the case and that the Major Case Squad was handling it. Due to the important people involved, the Major Case Squad was releasing very little information. Obviously Dash Lethaby had been arrested, but no one gave her any details at all. This was even more galling than being called "Hon."

Deer Creek had not been Melody McCullough's first

choice of police departments in which to work. It was much too rural. At night there were all those creepy animal noises and hooting and bugs that could deafen you. She hated night patrol and always kept her car windows rolled up.

Some people even rode horses. It wasn't a one horse town, it was a dozen or more horse town, which by the way, did not improve it at all. Horses had great big eyes and kept staring at you and there was that time a whole bunch of them got loose and galloped down Field Street. Sometimes one would go missing and the owner expected the police to find it! The Police Academy didn't teach horse tracking, for Pete's sake! Plus horses were supposed to be able to find their own way home. Why bother the police who had much more important things to handle? Not that many ever cropped up she had to admit. Until now!

Well, Melody McCullough was not going to take this lying down. Not even sitting down. No sirree Bob. She was going to launch her own investigation and solve the case herself. This meant stealthily finding out the names and addresses of people to interview and using her own car instead of a patrol car. Then she had to interview the witnesses (suspects?) and search the crime scene. Her keen powers of observation would find clues that too many others had missed in the initial frenzy and subsequent assumptions of guilt.

Searching through the files and papers that Olney left lying all over the Police Department, Melody McCullough found two lists of people: those who had attended Dash Lethaby's presentation and those who had been at the mulch site when the body came to light. Comparing the lists revealed that Mrs. St. Cyr was the only person who had been at the meeting the night before the murder and at the mulch site when the body was discovered. Officer Melody McCullough grinned: she had the starting point for her own investigation of the murder of Eunice Kingblade.

39. GARDENIA'S POLICE INTERVIEW

Getting fingerprinted had been so messy! Really, it had been most provoking; and now this. She had already answered a million questions. It had been exhausting and so upsetting and just because they'd found that silly shovel in Dash's car. And it said Garden Club of St. James on it – on the shovel, not Dash's car, so the police had called her right away. Herbert had been at the office and was no help at all. He hadn't killed Eunice. That was ridiculous. Dash not Herbert. Of course Herbert hadn't killed her. How could he when he was playing tournament Monopoly with umpteen other people?

The investigative officer or detective, and she was the second or third one to bother Gardenia – whatever the proper title was – was an exceptionally hefty young woman who probably drove a very untidy car of indistinct color. Gardenia imagined crumpled candy bar wrappers and coffee stained Styrofoam cups all rustling and rolling around amidst stale Froot Loops and dirty laundry. Although why she would have dirty laundry in her car....

Gardenia pulled herself up when the police officer asked her age.

"My age?" Gardenia's life flashed before her eyes. "Is that really necessary?"

"A matter of procedure, Ma'am, for the record."

"Oh, I don't know…" Gardenia sort of trailed off.

"You don't know your age?"

"Of course I know it!" Gardenia was quite short with the girl. "All too well as a matter of fact. Will this be kept confidential?"

"The Bovine Ilk," as Gardenia had privately dubbed her (thank goodness for Ogden Nash – the man rose to any occasion), answered with a monotone of placidity and patience.

"I can't promise that Ma'am but I do need an answer. Lack of cooperation could be construed as at least obstruction of justice or at most complicity." Not that refusal to admit one's age would rise to those standards but you needed to take a firm line with these garden club types.

"Oh all right." Gardenia whispered the shameful truth, subconsciously feeling it less likely to leak out to the world if muttered "sotto voce." That sounded legal, but maybe it was only Italian.

"Thank you Mrs. St. Cyr." Officer Melody McCullough sighed internally and tried not to think about all the candy wrappers and Styrofoam cups and dirty laundry in her car.

Interviewing Mrs. St. Cyr was going to take forever and yield nothing. Melody could not imagine this silly woman bashing anyone over the head. Made more sense the other way around. If they were all like this, it was a wonder there had not been an epidemic of garden club murders. Thinking that this might be the first strike of a serial killer, Melody perked up a bit.

Then again, the woman had driven through the tea-room window, right where Kingblade had been sitting. Maybe there was something here after all. She tried to sum up Gardenia St. Cyr and concluded that she did indeed look worried.

Gardenia was scrutinizing her fingers. Thank goodness all that horrible ink was gone. "Do you think I should have a lawyer here? Although maybe that's just if you've killed someone."

"DID you kill someone?"

"Good heavens, no! What sort of a question is that?"

"The sort I have to ask, Ma'am," lowed the Bovine Ilk, hope fading. "Now, why don't you just tell me what happened at the mulch site, the night Mrs. Kingblade was killed."

"Oh dear, so much happened. I got there a little after five, I think and Dash Lethaby my cousin was already there." Gardenia babbled away, revealing mind-numbingly excessive and inconsequential detail.

As soon as this case was over, Melody decided that she would try Gain detergent instead of Tide. It was supposed to have the best, the freshest scent. Maybe she could sprinkle some in the car then run it through the car wash with the windows down.

"And Eunice was yelling at Cuppy and Dash and people were leaving and oh it was just awful and she called me a traitor so I ran to my car and drove home and when I pulled into the garage I hit two large flowerpots, one was a lovely dark blue one that I had just bought and I was so upset and I ran into the house and Herbert wasn't even here when I needed him he was out at a Monopoly tournament. He's in the ages 5 – 104 division."

Gardenia stopped abruptly, bug-eyed and breathless, wondering why the officer wasn't writing this all down. Maybe she was taping it – "wearing a wire" they called it on those television crime programs and in detective thrillers. But perhaps the Deer Creek police did not stoop to that sort of sordid subterfuge. They had to be uncomfortable, just think of underwire bras, and Gardenia studied the earnest young policewoman for signs of the suppressed need to scratch: shifting about in the chair perhaps or pulling at her uniform.

Melody straightened up and tucked her shirt in more firmly. She had voluntarily left teaching to enter law enforcement. It had to be easier and more rewarding to deal with criminals than school children. Weapons and handcuffs were so handy in that regard. But they were useless in the extraction of intelligent information from garden club ladies.

"You say that Mrs. Kingblade called you a traitor. What did she mean by that?"

Gardenia was now convinced that the detective was "wearing a wire" so the whole interrogation took on a markedly sinister tone. This made her even more nervous so she blithered and blathered at an Olympic level.

"Oh, well, she was referring to my support of the mulch site development but I was there to support Dash of course he's my cousin you know and I'm not really sure about the development although Dash's plans looked lovely and I'm sure he would do a good job and it does look like a nice place to live, why Herbert and I might even consider it well maybe not I'm not sure but because I'm in the garden club Eunice thought that I should support the mulch site would you like some tea?"

The question came so suddenly that it took a few seconds to register and Gardenia had taken advantage of the lapse and was already pattering toward the kitchen.

"I'll make some Earl Grey. That's what I like in the afternoon. With ginger snaps. I make them myself. Everyone calls them my 'signature' cookies. Oh but it's still morning isn't it? Maybe I should serve English Breakfast Tea instead. How worrisome these rituals can be."

Melody followed her out to the kitchen to try to conclude the interview.

"Let's move on to the next morning at the mulch site. You were there for a tour?"

"Oh, no, that was the Deer Creek Garden Club doing the tour. I belong to the Garden Club of St. James. I am the current President as a matter of fact, so be sure to include that in your notes or report. I don't think that it would have occurred to us to tour the mulch site. Oh dear, we seem to be out of lemons." Earl Grey had won out in the tea stakes.

"I wonder why that is." Gardenia went on clattering and rummaging and thinking (in her fashion) out loud. "Not tour the mulch site I mean, not out of lemons. I mean we use just as much mulch as anyone else and probably even more lemons. That must be why I'm out."

"So why were you there?" Could this possibly be a case of returning to the scene of the crime? How many lemons could the woman possibly use? This was such a confusing case.

"I had to go back to get the shovel of course."

Melody's mental bloodhound howled into high alert. She did know that the victim had been bashed in the head so the murder weapon might be a shovel.

"What shovel?"

"Oh, here they are! These wonderful Meyer lemons. They were under the parsnips. Don't you just love them? Meyer lemons that is, not parsnips. Although maybe you like parsnips. Do you like parsnips?" Gardenia peered worriedly at the nearly defeated detective. Someone that hefty probably did not care for parsnips. More of a potato chip kind of person and what about those Froot Loops in the detective's car, or had she imagined them? "In general I mean, not with your tea."

"If you could just tell me about the shovel, Mrs. St. Cyr."

"Yes, of course. Let's take our tea out onto the porch. Here, you carry the cookies."

Once settled in the spring sunshine on the beautifully furnished and comfortable porch, Melody stared expectantly at Gardenia who gazed expectantly back at her. Several ginger snaps later, Melody had had enough of Mrs. St. Cyr. Stuffing some ginger snaps into her pocket, the policewoman bolted from the house.

Gardenia was a bit miffed at the hasty exit of the young woman officer. There was so much more to tell her. She hadn't even asked about the tearoom window incident, which Gardenia had come to regard as her property in terms of turning it into light cocktail chatter. Eunice's death certainly scotched that. Clearly the girl was in the wrong line of work. Would have been better off teaching school children and worst of all, she had eaten all the ginger snaps.

Melody McCullough had narrowly escaped disaster. Her brilliant ruse had worked! She could see it all so clearly now: SWAT Team Leader Melody McCullough charged toward the stolen red Lamborghini, ripped open the door and tackled the empty driver's seat. Revving the engine to racing pitch, she tore down the steep, winding mountain road that clung to the cliff face, scattering gravel and peasants who screamed ancient curses as they fell to their deaths in the sea a thousand feet below. Collateral damage: regrettable but unavoidable. She was beginning to understand the criminal mind and had to get to the mulch site as soon as possible.

The crunching noise assured her that the gas pedal was all the way to the floor. Crushed Froot Loops exploded upward and outward in a rainbow mushroom cloud. Melody McCullough, cereal killer, ha-ha. Once she was promoted she could buy a new car, which she would keep scrupulously Froot Loop-free. Rainbow patterned floor mats might help in the meantime, until she solved the murder and rocketed to the top (or close to it) of her profession.

40. *MELODY MCCULLOUGH AT THE MULCH SITE*

Melody McCullough did not want to call attention to her mission, so she eased off on the gas until she was going exactly the speed limit and hit that stupid pothole in front of St. Melchior's. She stopped ponderously at every stop sign, counting six of them between Mrs. St. Cyr's house and the mulch site. The missing garden club shovel had to be the murder weapon and SHE was going to find it, even if it meant defying that old goop Chief Hequembourg. He had never even asked her to call him Heck like everybody else did.

Now Melody McCullough was not a mean person but she could be somewhat abrupt and abrasive. "Needs work on interpersonal skills" her last evaluation had stated. That was unfair and probably sexist or non-feminist. Was she supposed to be "nicer" than male cops? And as if that weren't enough the stupid gate to the mulch site was closed. How high, or maybe more accurately, how low did you have to be on the village food chain of command to get a gate clicker to the mulch site?

Careful now, McCullough. She did not want to alert others to her newly energized ambitions. Not that there was anyone around – who in their right mind would be hanging around a mulch site? So Melody McCullough slowed into nonchalance as she cruised past the entrance gate. The police tape was still strung across it. She briefly considered ramming the gate but figured that her car might not survive the impact. How the heck was she going to get in? There had to be a back way known only to locals, of which she was not one.

So she kept on driving to make a leisurely tour of the neighborhood. If only there was somewhere she could park out of sight then backtrack to the mulch site. The Racquet Club parking lot appeared on the right and she turned into its main entrance. Then she headed toward the back where her car would blend in with those of the help, not the Jaguars and Mercedes of the members.

The back of the lot abutted a wide swath of woods that led to the creek. An old horse trail, one of the many that rambled and twisted through Deer Creek, roughly paralleled the creek.

Melody McCullough struck out on the trail in the direction of the mulch site. In some places deeply indented by horses' hooves, in others barely discernable, the path curved and angled and turned back on itself. It made the distance to the mulch site probably three or four times its actual length as the crow flies. Although she would bet that crows did not fly in a straight line.

Down into gullies, over downed trees, through tiny tributaries of the creek, Melody McCullough pressed relentlessly onward. Huffing and puffing, shedding her police jacket, undoing the top button of her shirt (strictly forbidden), she slapped away at the branches on either side of her.

The spring explosion of fresh greenery grew thicker and darker and lower, becoming tunnel-like in its intensity. Sudden clouds of midges or gnats or whatever they were would envelop her then just as quickly vanish after she had inhaled several thousand.

Spitting and snorting, she should have reached the mulch site by now but she certainly couldn't see it and now she couldn't see the creek either.

After so many sparkling crisp clear glorious spring days, it had become gloomy and overcast. No telling where the sun was; not that she was sure how that would help anyway – certainly no pioneer woman here who could navigate by the heavens. If only she could find the creek. It had been right here a minute ago.

By now bent double under the low-hanging vines that could have supported a hefty and overly athletic Tarzan, Melody McCullough started to ponder the possible ignominy of her fate. She could see the headlines now: "Area Scoured For Missing Policewoman," "Body of Partially Clad Policewoman Found In Woods," "Foul Play Suspected In Death of Partially Clad Policewoman Found In Woods."

The press could never be relied on to get things right. What did they mean, "Partially Clad?" Good God, what had happened to her? They'd have the wrong age and weight. (Weight! No one ever reported weight, did they?) Watch, this would be the one time some overly detail oriented obsessive-compulsive journalist out to make a name for himself would go on about her weight and what were the police thinking hiring someone so out of shape and there'd be all those doughnut emergency jokes, although those were usually about firemen. And her car! That really gave Melody McCullough the horrors. They'd talk about the Froot Loops and dirty laundry; oh it just wasn't fair!

All she wanted to do was solve the murder of Eunice Kingston – no – Kingblade. Blade, how could you forget a name like that? Born to be killed although of course that was her married name. Born to be a killer? Her husband? Hadn't used a blade however. One always did look at the spouse first despite protestations of devotion. Not that he'd made them in this case, it had to be admitted; and he did not have an alibi. She'd learned that from Olney's notes. But it was the lack of an alibi that made him believable. On the other hand, that Dash Lethaby was just too good looking to be guilty.

So it had to be somebody else. If she ever got out of this damned jungle she would find out who!

The day had become oppressive and humid and a low rumble of thunder added to the summerlike atmosphere. "Sodden Body of Missing Policewoman Found In Mulch Site." Mulch site! There it was. She could smell it: the tannic spores with oblique fungal accents. She had stumbled into it. "Another Body In Mulch Pile." What will this do to soil acidity or alkalinity or phosphorous or nitrates? No, that was bacon. All those bad things that made stuff taste good. Ooh – she still had some cookies from Mrs. St. Cyr's in her pocket.

Munching hungrily on the ginger snaps, Melody McCullough could now walk in a normal upright position of Homo sapiens through a small tree nursery on the border of the mulch site. Then she skirted the black ooze of the retention basin and made it into the huge open area of the mulch site. At first seeing no one, she surveyed the scene. Wait a minute! What were those old bats doing here?

41.   GRACE AND IVY INVESTIGATE

Grace stumbled over yet another dried rut in the path. This was absolutely ridiculous. Dried mud clods were so hard to walk on. Deer Creek was just riddled with miles of bridle trails. The horses churned up the muddy ground, then it hardened into cement-like ridges that tripped you up and bruised your arches and threatened to sprain your ankles. The path on the opposite bank was much more level and open but then they would have to ford the creek to get to the mulch site.

Wellington boots are not the best things to wear when you need to move stealthily. But then Grace was not sure that Ivy could do anything without making noise. They marched along the bridle trail single file, Ivy exclaiming over spring flowers then clamping her hand over her mouth. There was no one around but Grace supposed that trying to be quiet was Ivy's way of adding to the suspense.

Ivy clumped along, cautiously mouthing "dog tooth violet" and gesturing dramatically toward "Phlox divaricata."

For heaven's sake, I know perfectly well what they are grumped Grace to herself, but then Ivy was just pointing them out in her enthusiasm – not implying that Grace did not know what they were. "Look: creek poppies!" Excitement had gotten the better of Ivy and her voice boomed forth. "They're taking over the entire bank. We'll have to organize a digging party to get rid of them. You can bring Parsley."

"But they are so pretty," was Grace's defense of the pariah plant.

Despite these observations and asides, Ivy was striding ahead. Well she has bigger feet, judged Grace a bit petulantly, and she should probably put mufflers on them. Maybe Ivy was right and there could be policemen or worse, journalists about. They had driven by the mulch site entrance to "case the joint" to make sure that it was deserted. Nevertheless, for added secrecy they had parked at Ivy's house and walked to the mulch site.

Grace and Ivy crossed the drainage ditch that went under the highway then climbed up along the abandoned railroad right-of-way. They could hear the rushing noise of cars but at least the spring leaves hid the highway from view.

Just pretend it is the noise of a lovely mountain stream as it falls over rugged cliffs, frothing its way to the boundless sea, Grace told herself. Maybe she should write a book. No, what she really needed to do was to go through Olivier's notebooks and get them ready for publication. His agent had been bugging her to let a professional editor do it, but Grace wanted to do it herself. It was the closest link to him that she still had.

"All right, we're getting there," huffed Ivy as the path got narrower and steeper. She stopped at the top of the rise and waited for Grace to catch up. They were approaching the small tree nursery that was at the edge of the mulch site. From there they could see the retention basin with some black water in it and the ring around the collar effect of crusty slime.

"Now THAT is a good place to hide a body. No one would look in there. It's too disgusting."

Grace examined it dubiously. "I don't think there's enough water in there to cover a body. That little bit is probably left over from the winter or even last fall."

The scene of the crime was on the far side of the open acres. Since they didn't see anyone, they cut across the enormous expanse, rather than skirt all the way around.

"I do want to go back by way of the perimeter though," said Ivy. "We need to search this place where Reavis was living."

"Good heavens, was he actually living there? I thought it was more of a daytime hideout."

"Well it isn't clear but regardless, we should take a look at it."

They were now at the pile of mulch where Eunice's body had been found. Some of the yellow "Do Not Cross" police tape was on the ground and some more was attached to Police No Parking signs, the kind usually used for when people were having parties. The only other times that Ivy had seen police tape was when the Deer Creek Garden Club members made it into garlands for the Police Department Christmas tree. It had been so much fun: looping yards of the tape around the tree along with star shaped toy sheriff badges, handcuff chains and flashing red and blue lights.

"Not very encouraging." Ivy's confidence at finding any clues was faltering. "It seems as if the police were very thorough after all."

"What did you think could possibly be here?"

"Well, I don't know, I just thought that it would be obvious."

Forlornly, Ivy turned around in a circle, regarding the vast space while Grace recited, "'Look on my works ye mighty and despair. Nothing beside remains. Something, something. Boundless and bare the lone and level sands stretched far away.' Well, they're not sands of course but they are lone and level."

Ivy smothered a sigh. Grace could be a bit odd at

times. She needed to be encouraged to action, not poetry. "I know Grace, let's reenact the murder. We'll work backwards. You be Eunice and I'll be the killer. Stand here."

Grace obeyed and Ivy continued with her version of the crime.

"So – the killer puts her in the mulch pile and covers her up with mulch." Ivy started to fling mulch toward Grace, who backed off. "I don't think we have to be that exact."

"Yes we do. See: now my hands are all dirty. So he must have used something to shovel the – ha that's it! He used a shovel! Reavis's pirate shovel!"

"Or he could have been carrying hand wipes."

Ivy stared at her friend. "Grace, you are the only person I know who could have possibly said that. A murderer carrying hand wipes around in case he has to kill somebody."

"I always carry hand wipes around," said Grace. "But not because I plan to kill anyone," she added quickly.

"Yes, everyone knows that you always carry hand wipes. In fact may I have one now please? But we are getting off topic here. Let's move on."

Grace did not think that it was off topic. One heard of fastidious killers, or at least careful ones. A glimpse of a tabloid headline whilst in the checkout line could tell you that. But how on earth could "everyone" know about her hand wipes? Although there had been that woman in the airport who had approached her to ask if she had any antiseptic hand wipes. Grace had immediately produced two different types: organic lavender scent, and industrial-strength-kill-every-germ-in-sight-guaranteed-to-wipe-out-entire-populations scent.

Accepting some, the grateful woman had added, "You just look like the kind of person who would have hand wipes." Grace still didn't know how to take that remark but apparently her proclivity was obvious to the general public, a general public that in Grace's opinion would certainly benefit from the use of more cleaning products.

Ivy scrubbed at her hands and stuffed the grubby hand wipe into her pocket.

"Okay, now the killer used a shovel to cover her up. So he probably used it to kill her too. But I don't remember seeing a shovel lying around when we got here that morning. Do you?"

"No, and remember that's why Gardenia was there: to get the Garden Club of St. James's shovel!"

"Yes, and she couldn't find it! Okay, okay, this is fantastic! Now we just have to find the shovel."

Grace and Ivy scanned the lone and level non-sands, rotating slowly in silence only to see the bulk of Melody McCullough hove into sight.

After staggering through that bug infested jungle, wondering if she'd be found lost and dead and partially clad, Melody McCullough was not in a particularly welcoming mood. Then what does she see but two women scrabbling around in the mulch. Pulling on her jacket and cramming the last cookie into her mouth, Melody hurried toward them quelling the deep desire to draw her weapon. They had garden club written all over them.

"This is a crime scene. You have to leave immediately."

"Oh is it still considered a crime scene, officer? It is clearly unguarded and the police tape is just fluttering around." Realizing too late that she should have been

GRACE AND IVY INVESTIGATE   163

prepared for something like this, Ivy's persona wavered between insulted royalty and "silly little ol' me."

"I could arrest you for tampering with evidence." That was a ridiculous threat, but Melody hoped that it would scare them off.

"Ha!" Ivy chose the haughty approach. "I would hope that the Deer Creek police are competent enough to have already collected all the evidence. SUCH as it is." Her intonation and dismissively flickering fingers indicated withering disdain.

Melody did not want to deny competence but she did not like having evidence insulted. Could these two actually have found something? Were they concealing it? Did they have additional information about the murder? Her eyes and mind narrowed as she considered bringing them in for questioning.

Grace had to boldly intervene before Ivy got them arrested. This earnest and beefy young gal projected serious intent. Although the cookie crumbs down the front of her jacket suggested otherwise.

"We just needed to check on the flowers, Officer," she peered at the name tag, "McCullough." At the same time, she identified the cookie crumbs as ginger snap. Officer McCullough must have been at Gardenia's. Grace gestured toward the office trailer that had two freshly planted window boxes and walked toward them. "We planted them just the other day and due to the, umm, all the activity, we have not been able to care for them properly. Would you like to see them? Lovely pansies for right now. We'll switch them out for begonias later in the season. We'll just give them a good watering and then be on our way. Are you interested in gardening? Maybe your job doesn't give you time to garden. What a shame. Now where is that hose? It was here a couple of days ago. Ivy, do you know where the hose might be? It's one of those terrible kink free hoses that leak all over the place. If you ever take up gardening Officer McCullough, do not buy a kink free hose."

Ivy marveled at how easily the usually reticent Grace chatted away in her gentle, friendly voice, effortlessly trailing the now docile policewoman behind her.

This is the kind of woman that I do not know how to talk to, Melody panicked. She's similar to that Parsnip Woman, but not goofy somehow. She is so soothing and reasonable that there is nothing to contradict or object to or find fault with. As she listened to Grace's lilting tones of advice, Melody found herself nodding and imagined gardening on her little patio with flowerpots overflowing with blossoms outside her apartment door.

"Oh, you can do so much in flowerpots," Grace continued. "And you know, the garden club does all the planting at the village hall and the fire house and the Police Department. The firemen grow their own vegetables and herbs. We put the herb garden in for them and Ivy gave them a cooking lesson on how to grill with herbs. Firemen are great grillers, apparently. So reassuring in a way."

By now they had tramped around to the back of the office trailer, where the spigot was. To-ing and fro-ing, trying to skirt the mud, they searched high and low, well just low really, but the hose remained elusive.

"You see what I mean by those kink free hoses leaking. That's why it's all muddy back here. But why on earth would someone take the hose? Unless Mungo put it away in a shed somewhere."

Seizing the opportunity that this presented, Ivy said, "Ha! We better search the sheds."

Melody had to get these two snoops out of here now. She would come back later to search the sheds by herself. Pulling herself back from the brink of succumbing to a bright gardening future, she said, "No, I am sorry but you will have to leave. Any search must be done with proper protocol by the police to protect the chain of evidence."

"Oh for heaven's sake," broke in Ivy. "We are only looking for a hose, not evidence and didn't you say that the police had collected all the evidence?"

Melody McCullough recovered her professional bearing and spoke sternly to Ivy.

"You might contaminate something."

"Nonsense. We have hand wipes," Ivy announced, just as sternly back.

Melody stared and nearly said out loud, "Not to mention mental problems."

"I will escort you to your vehicles," she said in carefully measured monotones, not wanting to set off the disturbed housewives. Not seeing any vehicles, her detective instincts kicked in. "Where are your vehicles?" Maybe she could bring them in on concealed vehicle violations.

"We came on foot and we will leave on foot thank you very much," said Ivy huffily.

"You walked here!" Melody couldn't help but express her astonishment. There was that one crazy woman who walked all over the place, people were always seeing her, but surely most people in Deer Creek, even these two, drove cars. This was looking more suspicious every minute.

"Thank you Officer McCullough for all your help. Do let us know if you find the hose," said Grace, turning away from the city-bred policewoman and throwing Ivy a warning squint.

Melody had no intention of falling for that ploy: those society women think that they can turn this into a missing hose case. Something of no consequence, so I'll leave them here alone. Chief Hequembourg would probably jump at a missing hose case, but not Melody McCullough.

"I'll drive you home."

Grace and Ivy did not want to leave the grumpy cop here on her own to tear the place apart. Goodness knows what she might do to the window boxes. So they turned as one to accept her somewhat grudging offer. Plus maybe we can worm some information out of her about any progress or lack thereof in the case, schemed Ivy.

Silence fell as they walked out of the mulch site with Ivy trying to formulate the right tactic to pursue. Taking the road back to the Racquet Club was much shorter and easier than going through the woods on the bridle trail. Grace started to worry about their muddy shoes and tracking up a police vehicle. Why do police always say "vehicle" instead of "car"? Except there was no police vehicle or car. It appeared to be the officer's own vehicle or car.

"Oh dear, I'm afraid that our shoes are quite muddy Officer McCullough."

Melody studied Grace guardedly with total incomprehension as she opened a back seat door. The resulting cascade of empty cups and candy wrappers and dingy underwear explained her bafflement. Grace was about to refuse to get in, but Ivy had already bustled around to the other side and was pushing the debris aside so she could sit down. Grace held her breath and gingerly lighted on the edge of the seat. Well, she no longer had to feel bad about her muddy feet. In fact, the mud mopped up the stale Froot Loops. Melody grabbed the fallen articles off the ground and stuffed them in through the open front window of the passenger side. Grace got all the hand wipes out of her bag and started swabbing away at the seat and door handle.

As they pulled away from the Racquet Club, Melody McCullough was starting to think that maybe she would bring them in for questioning after all. They must know something. She wasn't going to fall for that flower watering excuse. They'd been looking for something in the mulch pile. Should she take the tough, grim-eyed (Bad Cop) approach or use the menacing, brutal (Even Worse Cop) method?

Ivy was still mulling over whether to continue her high-handed manner with the officer or to throw her off balance with a surprise attack of sycophantic praise. Certainly there was nothing in the car that could remotely warrant a compliment and a comment on her appearance did not even bear thinking about. Those ginger snap cookie crumbs were very unprofessional. She must have been at Gardenia's. Ivy was coming up blank when Grace, having used up all the hand wipes, asked innocently, "How was Gardenia St. Cyr this morning? She was quite upset by all this especially as Dash is her cousin."

"AND, we all know that he didn't do it," added Ivy staring accusingly at the back of Melody McCullough's neck.

What! Were these women psychic? How could they know that she had been at Parsnip Woman's house? How did they "know" that he didn't do it? No question about it: these garden club ladies were in cahoots. Officer Melody McCullough sped off to the police station with her two (2!) suspects in custody.

42.   CUPPY AND THE OBITUARY

It wasn't until the third phone call that it dawned on Cuppy that he had sent in the wrong obituary: the brandy fuelled one. The first call had been from the pastor asking if he was all right. Cuppy had taken it for general solicitude or part of the guy's job.

Some of the pastor's remarks had puzzled him, though. What had he meant by saying that the unhinging effects of grief and a possible psychosis of emotion could manifest themselves in the polar opposite of true feeling? That hadn't sounded particularly comforting or even kind. It had been more like an Old Testament warning, chapter and verse from the Book of Freud. Cuppy put it down to disproportionate dedication to duty or the man's clinically lugubrious nature, which was certainly a detriment to his chosen profession.

Then that busybody Beatrice Plumpting from next door had just "popped" in with a casserole. She had entered his house after just the faintest of taps on the kitchen door. He guessed that Beatrice would claim that her status as a neighbor granted her entitlement. It was all Cuppy could do not to throw the casserole and her out the window, although she would require a bay window and that would have meant hauling her into the living room. One of his first promises to himself after Eunice's death was that he would never eat another casserole. Beatrice compounded the offense by saying that it was one of Eunice's favorite recipes.

Lulu started screaming, "HAVVACUPPATEA HAVVA CUPPATEA!"

Beatrice kept harping on and on about the ill effects of bitterness, the lack of dignity in spiteful invention and making mountains out of mulch piles. That last cryptic comment was so insensitive it was off the Eunice Scale. The phone rang to save him from more of her perplexing lecture but it also left her free to rummage through his refrigerator and cupboards on the pretext of seeing what he needed.

"Hey pal." It was McKnight checking in. "How about I come over with a bottle of scotch: one of the finest, a Bowmore 25 year old." Since it was 9:12 AM, this was early even by McKnight's standards. Although tempted, thinking that it might counteract the aftershocks of yesterday's bourbon and brandy spree, Cuppy really just wanted to be left alone.

He thanked McKnight in mournful tones, hung up and nearly shoved Beatrice out the door. He was just getting a breather when his lawyer called. Isaac "Icy" Sencindiver spoke in his usual doom and gloom of frigid legal admonitions: do not speak to the press, do not call attention to yourself, do not say anything else in the least negative about Eunice. This superfluous advice compounded the pounding in Cuppy's head. Icy's parting shot was to recommend a retraction.

The resulting mental alarm bell nearly caused brain damage. Cuppy grabbed the newspaper that Beatrice had brought in. Feverishly ripping the pages, he found the Death Notices.

He moaned as he beheld the words that he had written in drunken idiocy – "combative and unpleasant" – an exercise meant to provide cathartic relief – "monsoon in Bangladesh" – from his anger and genuine distress but would now – "repel magnets" – be viewed as further evidence – "not tax deductible" – of his possible guilt. He considered calling McKnight back, but instead just collapsed into the hard metal chair at the rigid kitchen table.

"HAVVACUPPATEAHAVVACUPPATEA!"

He was going to kill that damn parrot. Leaping toward the cage, he grabbed it and shook the shrieking bird around in it. Now there were seeds and water all over the kitchen floor and a dazed and ruffled Lulu huddled under her perch. At least she was finally quiet. Cuppy flung the cover over the cage and figured he'd clean up the mess later.

Then the doorbell rang. This was just too much. He would kill himself and the parrot in a murder suicide right after he killed whoever was at the door. Cuppy stomped to the front door and flung it open to find Father Wedgewood.

Although Father Wedgewood was a Catholic, he was the kindest person Cuppy had ever met. Neither Eunice nor Cuppy were members of his congregation, Eunice keeping the Episcopalians from lapsing, prone as they were to doing so, and Cuppy seeking refuge from her as a Marginal Presbyterian. Yet here Father Wedgewood was in person.

Most everybody in Deer Creek considered Father Wedgewood a friend. A magnificent skater, he coached the local Young Hockey Players League. Swirling around the rink in his long black robe, he cut a distinctive figure and had developed several championship teams. Although the Bishop took a dim view of hockey, he did value (although not acknowledge) Father Wedgewood's positive influence in Deer Creek.

"Hello, Cuppy. I was just reading the newspaper and thought that I would stop by to see how you were doing."

"Oh Father Wedgewood, I really appreciate that. Would you like to come in?"

"Well just for a minute perhaps. I don't want to intrude."

"No, no. You're not intruding. I'm glad of the company," which was true Cuppy recognized happily. "I was starting to feel that people think I killed Eunice."

"Oh surely not!"

Cuppy had turned and was walking toward the kitchen. "C'mon back. I'll make some coffee."

Father Wedgewood followed him into the kitchen, which had apparently been designed in the culinary brutalism style. Thinking vaguely of Mussolini and the Bishop, Father Wedgewood warily surveyed the scene. Something was all over the floor, so he stood still while Cuppy crunched up to the stove to put the kettle on.

"Have a seat."

Father Wedgewood cautiously snapped, crackled and popped his way over to the table and sat down, having identified birdseed as the cause of the kitchen floor's gritty condition. The hard metal chair was hideously uncomfortable, even worse than Lutheran pews.

"Do you, umm, like birds, Cuppy?"

"I like to hunt birds."

Father Wedgewood shifted uneasily around in his seat and hoped that hunting did not take place in the kitchen. Maybe Cuppy was a dangerous lunatic after all.

"Oh, oh you mean why is there birdseed all over the floor. Eunice's parrot had a little accident." He gestured toward the covered cage.

The thing must be the size of an ostrich to cause this much mess. Father Wedgewood could feel the seeds working their way into his sandals and between his toes. The Bishop would tell him that this is what comes from calling on Presbyterians.

There was also a peculiar smell in the kitchen: hauntingly familiar yet elusive, with more than a hint of potential indigestion. When Cuppy shoved a bunch of stuff farther along on the kitchen counter to make room for the coffee cups, Father Wedgewood recognized one of Beatrice Plumpting's casseroles.

In a rare flight of levity, the Bishop had christened this particular incarnation a Last Supper Casserole because it was the last time he was going to eat supper at Father Wedgewood's church St. Melchior of the River. Yes. That was the odor all right: a Last Supper Casserole. Cuppy was in bigger trouble than being suspected of murder.

How could he help this poor soul? Greater love hath no

man than this…. "I see that Beatrice Plumpting brought you a casserole."

After Father Wedgewood left with Beatrice's casserole, Cuppy had some time to rest. But as soon as he sacked out on his beloved La-Z-Boy (the only piece of furniture unsanctioned by Eunice), there went the doorbell again. It was exhausting being bereaved with everybody calling and dropping in and bringing you food. Why were people so thoughtless? He pretended not to be there but the person started knocking then banging on the door.

"Cuppy! It's me! Kimberley!"

Oh my God! Cuppy raced to the door, wrenched it open, pushed out the storm door and grabbed her by the arm. He shoved her inside, did a quick 180 look then darted back in and slammed the door. Breathing heavily he said, "What are you doing here? Are you crazy?"

"Well you said not to call so I thought that I'd come over."

"Jesus Christ that's worse than calling! What if some one sees you?"

"I'm in Personnel! This is office business. I have to counsel you and go over things and stuff. I had to bring some important papers or something. Jeez Cuppy, you're not very appreciative. I had a hard time getting away. The place is going nuts. Wally in Mechanical started a Guilty Or Not pool."

That had to be payback, Cuppy figured, for the time he poured glue into the vent in his office to try to stop the excessive billows of heat pouring out. The system cooked you to death in the winter and froze you to death in the summer. He was convinced that Wally did it on purpose in order to prolong his employment, always pretending to be "fixing" it while blaming the architects and HVAC engineers. Right: job security for Wally. He should have seen that the glue helped with that.

Kimberley was walking slowly around the living room, taking it all in, eyeing the dark brown rugs and the even darker brown venetian blinds, the colorless paintings and the sort of bland, even cheap looking furniture. Huh, kind of a boring-modern blah house. It was just so, so ugly. It was downright ugly! It should be a lot fancier and bigger. But nope: with all the venetian blinds closed, it was plain and pale and dim, and Cuppy was too, now that she studied him more closely and objectively.

Viewing Kimberley with somber clarity in this setting, Cuppy registered with a slap of perception her appalling youth. He impassively acknowledged that he was a tired, middle-aged fool, one in a line of millions who had gone before him and the untold millions who would undoubtedly come after him. Cave/Fort/Castle/Office/Space Station affair with much younger woman. Everybody must know about it. Wally was probably running a pool for that too: Executives Who Cheat. At the moment he just didn't care about anything. He slumped onto the unyielding sofa and closed his eyes.

Kimberley had a rare flash of insight. What a fool she had been. What a cliché: office bimbo has affair with older married corporate bigwig. Was everybody laughing at her? Were all the guys exchanging rude remarks in the men's room? Or even beyond the somewhat limited confines of the men's room? Wally was probably running a pool: Office Sluts.

Kimberley gazed dispassionately at Cuppy, who was either asleep or comatose. You know, she'd been getting tired of him anyway. They never did anything any more; not like at first with dinners and trips and shopping. He was too worried that Eunice would find out. Oh no, Eunice this, Eunice that. He had said himself he was so tired of his wife. "Why don't you do something then?" Kimberley had demanded.

Agh, maybe he had! What if he HAD killed her?

"Ya know what, I think I better go back to the office." Cuppy didn't open his eyes. "Okay."

After the front door closed, Cuppy said, "Eunice, I'm sorry."

43.   MEMORIAL CONTRIBUTIONS

Ivy sighed. Only Eunice would have a memorial charity that was not tax deductible. Amateur Herbal Tea Brewers Association indeed! Never heard of it. Really, the woman reached out from the grave to cause difficulty. Now what do I do? The Deer Creek Garden Club tribute fund was the only answer. Not that she would contribute to a cause solely for the sake of a tax deduction. Ivy's irritation betrayed a shameful meanness of spirit, which she hastily suppressed by writing out a check of guilt-induced magnanimity. But surely, some aggravation might be warranted. Ivy huffily sighed again and slapped the checkbook closed.

"Now see here Gardy ol' gal." Gardenia did not like

it when Herbert called her that. It meant that he was being jovial and there was no reason whatsoever for him to be jovial over Eunice. "How about a contribution to a home for defective kink free hoses? Use it to start The Tournament of Hoses! Heh heh,heh. An endowment for a Federally protected bush honeysuckle preserve? A Parrots For Pirates adoption program? The prospects are endless. Think of the good she would at last achieve the world over. Heh heh heh."

Herbert returned to one of his several Monopoly boards. They were all in different stages of progress because he was practicing for the upcoming tournament. Trying to acquire St. James Place, he had become mired in a tricky deal with "Brutus." Herbert always named his fictitious opponents – made the game much more challenging. His own moniker was "Omnivore."

Gardenia did not find Herbert funny or helpful, and he was making that annoying whistling noise when he breathed.

"Oh do stop breathing like that!"

"What? Stop breathing? What do you mean stop breathing? You stop issuing death threats – telling me to stop breathing." Herbert could be seriously frivolous at times. Times like this, for example, when she needed advice.

Perhaps the only thing to do would be a contribution to the garden club tribute fund, although should it be the Deer Creek Garden Club, of which Eunice had been a longtime member and President at the time of her death, or the Garden Club of St. James, of which Gardenia was the current President? They were both ex officio honorary members of each other's club so it was all to the same purpose really, agonized Gardenia as she poured beseeching looks at Omnivore, who was still chortling (and breathing) over the Monopoly board. Really, men were so childish. Why couldn't he decide for her? She would call Dash; that's what she would do.

The irony of consulting a murder suspect about a charitable donation in memory of his alleged victim completely escaped Gardenia. Dash marveled anew at his cousin's obliviousness. She didn't even seem to realize that she possibly came under the heading of "person of interest." He rather liked Herbert's suggestions, especially the pirate one.

Gardenia's phone call made him realize that he should make a contribution as well. Might be a point in his favor with the judge and jury so Dash recommended donations to both garden clubs. Gardenia hung up in grateful relief. Omnivore bought a hotel for St. Charles Place.

Grace and her mother sat at the kitchen table and stared at each other. Then both turned their gaze toward Parsley, who stared back at them. There was an awful lot of staring being bandied about in this kitchen; too much so from Parsley's point of view. What had he done now? Oh no, he could feel it in his bones. There was a ruckus coming on. BURGLARS! Bounding and barking, Parsley surged toward the front door, scattering the rain rugs and almost banging his nose. Jolted out of her chair by the eruption of noise, Grace flurried after him to let the ferocious guard dog out to patrol the premises for lurking garbage men or invading squirrels.

"Perhaps a contribution to the Red Cross might be

best," said her mother calmly. "Think how relieved they must be."

"I think that a lot of people are relieved. How sad."

Far from feeling relieved, but certainly sad, Reavis sat morosely in the Deer Creek jail cell with the ferrets. He didn't kill the Mean Lady. The ghost did. Worried sick about him and Reavis not having alibis, Mungo kept busy inspecting potholes and putting up stop signs. The ferrets slept with the depth of innocence.

44. FATHER WEDGEWOOD AND THE CASSEROLE

"Who will rid me of this troublesome casserole?" declaimed Father Wedgewood melodramatically as he drove away from the Kingblade Manse. It would probably end up more well traveled than a fruitcake, although it certainly did not have the shelf life of one. Beatrice Plumpting's Last Supper Casseroles were studded with unidentifiable ingredients that were even more mysterious than the ways of God.

Known for her reckless use of mushrooms and pineapple, the admirable woman generously supplied every church event and the downtown soup kitchen with endless peculiar variations. The director of the soup kitchen happily reported that the number of homeless showing up for food was down, the good man attributing it to improved circumstances in the community. Father Wedgewood privately suspected that it might be Beatrice's casseroles. How could he use this in a homily?

The other thing that he had to get rid of was the birdseed that he had tracked into his car. Were other rooms in Cuppy's house encrusted with birdseed? Most unsanitary, but would it be a motive for murder? It was more likely to be a motive for going to the car wash. He would certainly have to go there before he drove the Bishop anywhere.

Souls in torment: did he know of any? Brightening, Father Wedgewood figured that Police Chief Hequembourg had never met a casserole he didn't like. Perhaps he would just swing by the Deer Creek Police Department before going to the Hose and Elbow, the unauthorized car wash that Mungo ran behind the Department of Public Works buildings in back of the village hall. McKnight had coined the name of the car wash after Mungo had assured him that all car washing took was a hose and elbow grease. Of course officially, Mayor McKnight Freemantle was not aware of an unauthorized car wash being run out of the Department of Public Works buildings behind the village hall.

Olney Cowperne was manning the desk when Father Wedgewood strolled into the Deer Creek Police Department and nonchalantly placed the casserole on the counter. He hoped that it would go undetected until he managed to make his getaway to the car wash.

45.   *DANNY BOY PLUMBING*

The guy from Danny Boy Plumbing was hanging around the village hall. His name was either Frank or Matt (people could never keep them straight). He was hoping to catch sight of that new policewoman. The Police Department was right next to the village hall and Frank or Matt had to go there to apply for construction permits. Since seeing Melody McCullough for the first time though, Frank or Matt found that he needed a lot more permits. Plumbing was not a good business for meeting girls.

At the moment, neither was police work. This society murder must have all the cops busier than beavers on an anthill. Fifteen phony and two legitimate permits later and Frank or Matt hadn't seen her for what seemed like days. With molasses-like tread he eased slowly out of the village hall and loitered with intent across the parking lot. He had parked as far away as possible in order to eke out the time that he could spend there on stakeout.

Finally! Melody McCullough's car pulled up in front of the Police Department. Frank or Matt reversed direction but halted when a woman got out of the back seat. Melody swung around to the other side of the car and opened the back door and another woman got out. All of a sudden the place was clogged with women. Frank or Matt recognized them: American Standard and Crane.

Grace had her hands full of the used hand wipes when the now confident seeming young officer marched around the car to open the door for her. The three of them followed a puzzling trail of birdseed into the Deer Creek Police Department. Had a bird feeder thief been apprehended? It was really quite an exciting prospect until they came upon Father Wedgewood, whose sandals were clearly the source. Had he been on some mysterious St. Francis sort of pilgrimage? Was it a penance of some ornithological order?

Despite these worrying theological questions, Ivy beamed with satisfaction. Ha! Once again, they had infiltrated the fastness of the Deer Creek Police Department. Sure as shooting, they would discover something this time.

46.   THE POLICE STATION

"Wasn't that Frank or Matt from Danny Boy Plumbing out there?" asked Ivy (American Standard).

"Yes, but I can never remember which one is which," said Grace (Crane), with a note of contrition.

"No, nor can I. I don't think anyone can. Oh well… I wonder how long this is going to take." Ivy wandered around the room for a while looking at the dingy certificates on the faded walls, but she soon lost patience.

"This is getting awfully tiresome," Ivy announced to Grace and Father Wedgewood who were sitting patiently at a grubby faux Formica-topped table in the Deer Creek Police Department Snack/Interrogation Room One. Officer Melody McCullough had deposited them there and then had vanished, allegedly to get some coffee. Ivy was marching back and forth. "Are they going to arrest half the town and still not get the right person?"

"Now Ivy, we haven't been arrested; and I guess the policewoman may have had reasonable suspicion, seeing us rummaging around in the mulch."

Father Wedgewood wanted to lighten the mood a bit. "I think that I'm being held on one count of casserole possession. Although they haven't formally charged me." Grace smiled gratefully at his gentle humor. "Then they would have to arrest Beatrice as an accomplice," he added.

The sight of a police officer accompanying Grace Mere into the police station had shocked Father Wedgewood to his core. Grace was one of his favorite parishioners so he wanted to do everything that he could for her in this her Time of Need. Although what the Need was for this Time mystified him. It was most confusing. He was also intimidated by the rather strident Ivy, whom he did not know well. She was probably an L.E. (Lapsed Episcopalian). As she regarded him suspiciously, he quickly continued, "Were you really rummaging around in the mulch? Whatever for?"

Sensing an ally, although in her opinion priests were kind of fishy, Ivy scraped out a chair and plunked herself down. "The police don't know what they're doing. And now they're not doing anything. We know that Dash did not kill Eunice. We were looking for clues. Why haven't they arrested Cuppy? He is a much more likely suspect. And so are a bunch of other people. There are loads of possibilities. Dash is just a slam dunk, that's why they are going with him. They're too lazy to see beyond the obvious."

Father Wedgewood had gotten to know Dash through

Madeleine. The dear girl was a delightful addition to his little flock at St. Melchior of the River. Although her husband did not take religion seriously, surely he did not merit the description of "damn skunk." And he had been most gracious when Father Wedgewood had called on him after his arrest.

"Well, I just came from visiting Cuppy. After reading that peculiar obituary, I thought that he might need a steadying influence."

"Yes, that was odd. My mother and I were quite puzzled over what sort of donation to make. How did he seem?" asked Grace.

"He seemed fine actually. The kitchen was a mess though; birdseed all over the place." Father Wedgewood contemplated his crunchy feet. "He said that Eunice's parrot had had an accident." He lifted his feet off the floor and banged them together a couple of times. The birdseed was gradually falling away. He would just have to go back to wearing socks. Unusual situations cropped up occasionally (although this time was far beyond the norm) and footgear could be so unreliable. Father Wedgewood was going to add something about the "toothsome" female in the red car who had pulled into Cuppy's drive just as Father Wedgewood was leaving, but managed to refrain. Was gossip a sin? He certainly was not going to seek the Bishop's opinion on that thorny topic.

"Ha! There you are then. How could he be fine if his wife has just been bludgeoned to death with a garden club shovel?"

"Kind of appropriate in a macabre sort of way," said Grace. "That it was a garden club shovel I mean."

This somber observation brought a sad quietness to Snack/Interrogation Room One. Melody McCullough's volcanic return shattered that silence.

47.   IN THE LOOP

After leaving Snack/Interrogation Room One to search for coffee, Melody had discovered a meeting going on with the Major Case Squad officer, Chief Hequembourg and Mayor Freemantle. *They can't keep me out now!* She avalanched toward the table, shoving it into the mayor's bumper-like middle and landing in a chair more or less accurately, right next to Chief Hequembourg.

Looking extremely annoyed, the Major Case Squad officer grudgingly pushed a copy of the final police report toward her, concluded briefing the mayor on the successful apprehension of the murderer Dashiell Hammett Lethaby and announced that they could now release all the details to the public. "Our PR Liaison Officer will handle that," he said as he got up to leave. "See you at the trial."

"I still don't believe it," said McKnight. He also couldn't believe how boring a police report could be. It really surprised him at how monotonous were the endless petty details about blood and fingerprints, the lists of dozens of names of people talked to and all their stupid observations. The police report in his book wouldn't be boring. He would see to that right away. McKnight struggled to get out of the ugly metallic chair, which was nearly impossible to push back, certainly didn't swivel and had no lumbar support whatsoever. He would have to look into getting better chairs for the police, but maybe uncomfortable chairs encouraged them to go out and catch criminals. Shelve it. McKnight took his copy of the final report and returned to his office and a surprise visit from Pinckney.

Melody McCullough sat alone at the table with a copy of the final report. As soon as I am in the loop, the case gets solved. They had the perpetrator, although he was out on bail, which bugged her – these rich people – and the murder weapon, which was in the Broom Closet/Evidence Room. Case closed. Everybody can take their gun and go home. Why hadn't anyone told her? She fumed her way slowly back toward Snack/Interrogation Room One. But maybe there was still something. Both those women and the mayor really think that he didn't do it. Could there be something in this? Was it local knowledge or just local loyalty?

Mulling over the report, Melody McCullough made her way back to Snack/Interrogation Room One. She got there just in time to hear Ivy's and Grace's comments on the shovel.

"How do you know that?" she thundered at them. "That detail was not released to the public!" Looking like a hungry bulldog with malocclusion, she slammed her hands down on the table and jutted out her chin.

Father Wedgewood jumped. Grace sat back, sharply stunned while Ivy stared in disbelief at the exploding policewoman.

"Know what?" Ivy recovered first.

"Why don't I say a nice calmness prayer? Oh, Lord grant us…"

"I don't want prayers!" Melody cut him off. "I want answers! Or I'll arrest all of you!"

"See," said Ivy, "I told you that they would resort to arresting the whole town."

"…grant us calmness of spirit and…"

"The only way you could know about the shovel is if you had something to do with it!" The bulldog's decibel level vaulted into the red zone.

"…and let there be an end to quarrels…"

"Ha! It's just common sense that it was a shovel!"

"…an end to strife…."

"And we knew that it was a garden club shovel because Gardenia told us that she had left it there."

"In our midst be charity…"

"So she's in on it too!"

"Who? Charity?" By now, Ivy was having fun.

"No! That Parsnip Woman St. Cyr."

"…charity and love…."

"Parsnips! What do parsnips have to do with anything?" Ivy was in her element. Gosh, you couldn't make this stuff up. A frozen parsnip that you had first sharpened before putting it in the freezing compartment would make an excellent weapon. Then you could eat the evidence. I could write one of those silly garden club murder mysteries, she told herself exultantly.

"Please sit down Officer McCullough so we can hear your theories on this case." Grace had had enough and her clear, cultured and bell-like tones soothed the savage beast.

Ivy couldn't help herself. "Maybe she was digging up

parsnips with the shovel."

"We beseech Thee and cry out to Thee to bring us peace."

Melody subsided into a chair at the grubby faux Formica-topped table and everyone stared at everybody else.

"Through Jesus Christ our Lord, Amen."

"Amen," Grace said automatically.

"Thank God," said Ivy.

After they had all breathed carefully for a while, Ivy finally sighed.

"Listen, we've all known Dash for years. Aren't there any other possibilities? Someone trying to frame him maybe or someone who wanted to get rid of both Eunice and Dash?"

Grace got caught up in the speculating. "What about somebody else who wants the mulch site? Some ruthless out-of-town conglomerate or evil consortium of foreign developers?"

Father Wedgewood jumped in, "A conspiracy of Godless infidels."

"The Mafia!"

"The government!"

"Would Godless infidels be redundant or an oxymoron?" mused Father Wedgewood. He would have to take it up with the Bishop.

It was a three person tennis match and neither Melody McCullough's neck nor her mind could keep up. She hauled herself up and backed away from the table realizing that she did not have the stature to loom over them, so she would have to intimidate by volume. "That's enough.

Quiet all of you!"

Frank or Matt from Danny Boy Plumbing had followed the trail of birdseed and muddy Froot Loops into the police station. When those clues petered out he followed the noise of the ruckus. Mesmerized, he crept closer and closer (although with that racket no one would hear him) to the half open door of Snack/Interrogation Room One.

The thrilling fierce authority of Melody McCullough's voice paralyzed his caution and propelled him ever onward toward the source of his billowing passion. He could hear Wonder Woman giving those dangerous criminals what for! He had forgotten all about Crane and American Standard. Was the bold Officer McCullough holding violent gang members at gunpoint? He had to see. He worshipped the linoleum she walked on.

Dazed with love, Frank or Matt tripped on the worshipped linoleum and fell into the empty trophy cabinet. Hearing the crash and rattle, Melody McCullough ripped open the door just in time for Frank or Matt to rebound off the cabinet and into her impressive chest. Her arms and the aroma of cookies enveloped him. He was a man whose dreams had come true.

"Hey! I could arrest you for assaulting a police officer."

Handcuffs. Frank or Matt smiled. This was getting better and better.

Once it was established that he was a plumber, Melody hauled him off to the so-called Ladies' Room, where there was no hot water and you always had to jiggle the handle of the toilet to get it to stop running and that was after it had taken forever to fill. He turned out to be awfully nice despite his damp handshake, but that could be forgiven in a plumber.

The grappling out in the hall ceased, leaving it quiet and empty. Ivy grabbed the police report that Melody McCullough had left on the grubby faux Formica-topped table and gestured forcefully at Grace to shut the door. "Wait, Father Wedgewood, would you stand outside and keep watch. If anybody comes along, cough or something. Start blessing them or whatever." She was sure that a Catholic priest could come up with something devious.

Ivy started to leaf through the police report quickly, Grace looking with her to glean something, anything to go on. "Blah blah blah, yeah, yeah yeah, aha Fingerprint Report: three sets on shovel; Dashiell Hammett Lethaby, Gardenia Cadwallader St. Cyr and Sigismonday Rache Vellacotton. Grace and Ivy stared at the last name then at each other. "Who on earth is that?"

"Well it must say, someplace." Grace took over the report and scanned it hurriedly. "Here it is: Assistant to the Mayor."

"The mayor? You mean our mayor? McKnight?"

"Yes. Although I didn't even know he had an assistant."

"Assistant? Ha! Assist with what? Getting rid of empty scotch bottles?"

Grace was looking very puzzled. "Do you think it's a man or a woman?" Grace was running through her mind all possible people she may have seen at one time or another at the village hall and she just couldn't imagine who it could be.

"I don't know, but a name like that would be enough to turn anyone to a life of crime. Let's take this with us."

"Oh, Ivy, I don't think that's a good idea."

After perusing it fairly thoroughly, Ivy reluctantly placed the report back on the table and motioned with her head to get out of there. She opened the door slowly and leaned out into the entrance hall to see if the coast was clear. Father Wedgewood was at his post, but Melody McCullough and Frank or Matt were nowhere in sight.

"I need to go to the car wash," Father Wedgewood whispered. "Where are you ladies off to?"

"Officer McCullough was going to drive us home but now I guess we will have to walk," Ivy replied in an equally low tone.

"I'd be happy to drive you," offered Father Wedgewood, "but I really do need to get the birdseed out of my car first."

"Okay, thanks. We'll just pop into the garden club closet for a minute, then meet you over there at the car wash. We call it the Hose and Elbow. Elbow for elbow grease. Be a great name for a pub. Maybe Mungo should sell drinks too."

That proved to Father Wedgewood that Ivy was an L.E. Although perhaps not so L. after all. Those Anglicans were always thinking about pubs. He smiled. "My, that does sound like a pub. I'd never thought of that before."

Grace and Ivy strolled out of the Police Department, crossed the parking lot and went in the front door of the village hall.

"I assume that we are doing this so we can reconnoiter the area."

"Yup – the closet is just an excuse to let us wander around the building. So walk slowly, Grace."

The two sleuths proceeded casually down the hall toward the open office space that had a couple of desks. The only person there was Eloise Lutjens, the receptionist, who was on the phone. She waved friendlily at the garden club ladies. She often helped them set up their meetings that were held in the council chamber. Ivy and Grace continued to walk toward the garden club closet, which was off to the right at the far end of the hall.

"Let's just peek into the closet to pretend to look for something then walk back. At least we don't have to worry about running into anybody. No one ever goes in there if they can help it."

48. REALLY MCKNIGHT

McKnight was starting to get the feeling that Pinckney was checking up on him these days. She had rarely visited the village hall in the past and if she did so it was for garden club reasons, not to see him. But lately she had been ominously present, cropping up at miscellaneous times, often carrying large packages. One day she was lugging a chair in – what was going on?

McKnight really didn't want to know. She had to be manufacturing reasons to spy on him. She was not only checking up on him but giving him advice. This called for evasive action, but he did not know what form that might take. He began to leaf through the bunch of brightly colored brochures that she had dumped on his custom milled antique mahogany desk. They were samples of political ads and information.

"Oh, really McKnight, haven't you ever noticed? You're the only person Siggy ever talks to. She's weird. She's creepy. Her eyes are upside down. I don't care how efficient she is. You need someone not just professional, but outgoing, friendly, good looking. I mean – there is something wrong with her. And all she wears is white: her clothes are white, her car is white; and shoes: white shoes – after Labor Day! She looks like a ghost. I mean, really McKnight!"

McKnight sighed and idly kicked the wastepaper basket in an experimental sort of way. "Oh I know. She creeps me out sometimes too. But I feel kind of sorry for her and she does a good job. I can't just fire her out of the blue." He knocked over the wastepaper basket and started kicking the wadded up pieces of legal pad paper that fell out. The novel wasn't going too well just then.

"You don't have to fire her, although I don't know why not. Just hire somebody new for the campaign. Ask Cuppy for ideas – there are lots of gung ho marketing types over at Tirano. She can keep doing the mayor stuff and when you leave here, you leave her too. Make it clear that she is not doing any work on the campaign. For heaven's sake, stop kicking those things around. Really McKnight."

Behind the partly closed door, Siggy's hands were shaking. She clenched and unclenched them, watching the tendons turn white until they formed a dinosaur's spine. Her hands had always acted on their own while she observed them with total detachment. She hated with cold, indifferent malevolence. If left to their own devices, her hands would go around that woman's neck and squeeze all the pinkness out of Pinckney.

Siggy had already done a lot of work on the campaign, just to be prepared for when McKnight needed her. She had written up press releases, speeches (which were especially good), position papers, summaries of the issues, lists of words, phrases, sayings and humorous anecdotes to use or to avoid. She was going on that campaign. Oh yes she was. McKnight would see that he had no need to feel sorry for her. Pinckney must have put that idea into his mind.

Hearing the snap snap snap of Pinckney's little shoes on the parquet wood floor gave Siggy time to ease into the shadow of a closet door. Pretending to look for something, she kept her back turned as Pinckney went by.

Pinckney quickened her pace as she passed Siggy, acting as if she did not see her. Ugh. Although it might be funny to shut her in the closet. Pinckney giggled away down the hall to complete her mission.

She had come over to the village hall to see the newly redecorated Garden Club of St. James's closet. Really, we should stop calling them closets. Gardenia had called her to say that the last pillow was in place. She peeked into the room and gasped. It was so fabulous! That precious cast-off Duchess of Windsor style: so rarely imitated, so rarely attempted, so rarely achieved. Yet here it stood before her. Oh the chicness of pale blue silk; the romance of brocade and toile; the delicacy of all those Louis 18 or 19 chairs. (She could never keep those roman numbers straight or understand why people used them anyway. They should use American numbers.) All that was missing was the gilding around the mirror.

Pinckney imagined herself in the South of France,

sipping champagne with mysterious, well-dressed yachts-
men and clean but brilliant artists. Hearing approaching
footsteps, she turned to see Ivy Wilcoxen and Grace Mere.

49. THE DUCHESS OF WINDSOR SUITE

Grace and Ivy turned the corner to see Pinckney
Freemantle in the doorway of the Garden Club of St.
James's closet. Pinckney turned toward them in surprise
but with a big smile. "Isn't this beautiful? Have you seen it
yet? It is so amazing! I just can't believe it! This room was
such a shabby old dump for years and now – oh – so, so
Duchess of Windsor – don't you think?"

Ivy had never had much time for Pinckney. What?
The Duchess of Windsor? The woman was an idiot. How
could they get rid of her? She said rather tartly, "I rather
liked the shabby old dump, myself."

Ivy's comment caused Pinckney's face to fall a bit so
Grace hastily came up with, "It certainly is quite a trans-
formation. Do you know who was responsible?"

"Um well, um well." Pinckney glanced left and right for
possible spies then whispered, "It's a secret until Gardenia
and I ooh — I mean, I think this is lovely.... And VERY
chic," she added stoutly.

Ivy had been looking around more thoroughly. "It had
to be a committee. No individual could come up with
this. No wonder you want to keep it a secret."

"Oh really, Ivy! It's clearly the creation of sophisticated and cultured interior designers." Pinckney thanked her lucky stars that she was not a member of the Deer Creek Garden Club, with crabby frumps like Ivy Wilcoxen and a moldy, messy closet. At least Grace Mere was nice and had beautiful, unique clothes that were always right for the occasion. At the moment she was looking kind of tweedy, as if out for a walk in the English countryside. She smiled at Grace and said as much.

Grace thanked her and explained, "Oh, well we were over at the mulch site, so these seemed appropriate."

Aghast at such a prospect, Pinckney actually took a step backward, hand to her heart. "The mulch site! You were at the mulch site?"

Ivy hadn't paid any attention to what Grace was wearing and the conversation with Pinckney was starting to grate. "Yes, and now Grace and I need to discuss a report on the science of mulch production. It's in our closet." She gestured across the hall and started moving toward it figuring that would send Pinckney off, but it just revved her up.

"Mulch production! They should close that mulch site after what happened to Eunice. Build nice townhouses like Dash wants. Somebody's trying to frame him just to keep it a mulch pile. I don't believe for a New York minute that he killed her. It has to be some drug dealer. I mean really! YOU don't think he killed her, do you?"

"Well, no, but I seriously doubt that any drug dealer would be hanging around in a mulch site," said Ivy, trying to be patient and wondering if a New York minute would be long enough to throttle Pinckney.

"But didn't you hear? Mungo and Reavis were growing marijuana over there. It could have been a drug deal gone bad and Eunice just happened to get caught up in it."

Grace ventured, "Have you brought this to the attention of the police? Maybe you should go over there now and talk to Officer McCullough about it." Ivy gave her a thumbs up behind Pinckney's back. Grace was so diplomatic.

"Oh, Pinckney, wait." (Not that she showed any signs of moving.) Grace went on, "I just had a thought. Do you think that McKnight's assistant, sort of an odd name, might know who redecorated your garden club closet?"

Pinckney tossed her perfect little hairdo. "Siggy? That nobody weirdo? Absolutely not! She's too busy looking after McKnight. Gotta run. Nice to see you, Grace." Pinckney threw a sweet smile at Ivy. "You must feel right at home in your moldy old closet. Enjoy!" she called and clacked away in her perfect little shoes.

Grace and Ivy waited until they could no longer hear the pitter-patter of Pinckney's beautifully pedicured little feet before entering the Deer Creek Garden Club's closet. The reassuring musty smell told them that all was as usual.

"Siggy – good work Grace," admired Ivy.

"Well, at least we know it's a she."

Something was different after all. It was either something extra or something missing. But what? Then the awful truth struck them simultaneously: the wine bottles and the flowerpots were gone and in their place was a collection of empty scotch bottles.

Ivy picked one up. "What on earth is going on in here? I was kidding when I made that remark about scotch bottles. It has to be that Siggy person, but why would she take the wine bottles and put scotch bottles in here?"

"And that's why there were so many wine bottles in the other club's closet. They fit in well with the décor however."

"The Duchess of Windsor Suite? I suppose so. Although didn't they all drink gin back then?"

"Well, that's the least of our worries now. Let's go over to the car wash to see if Father Wedgewood's car is ready."

"Tell me about Father Wedgewood," said Ivy. "It's hard to believe he never thought about the Hose and Elbow as a pub's name. Ha! Those Catholic priests are always thinking about pubs." Ivy's remark nettled Grace but she ignored it for the time being, despite wanting to defend Father Wedgewood. She would have to save that for a more suitable occasion.

They walked back along the front hall, past Eloise still on the phone. Beyond her was McKnight's closed office door. They turned left into the short corridor with the restrooms, made another left to go past the coffee room, then right to get to the back door: nobody in sight and quiet as the tomb. Ivy shrugged at Grace.

"I guess she could be in with McKnight. Why don't we go tell Father W. that we have work to do here? Then come back and tackle McKnight."

They walked more quickly now, through the parking lot and past the Department of Public Works buildings. Right in front of the big beehive-looking structure, they found Mungo and Father Wedgewood drying the clerical black Volkswagen. Another car was parked there, seemingly waiting its turn. It was white, which really showed up all the mud on it.

Ivy elbowed Grace. "Gosh, look at all the mud on that car. I wonder where it could have been?" They turned to look at each other with wide eyes. The mulch site: all that mud behind the office trailer. Where Reavis said that a car started up sometime after the ghost drifted past.

"Hey Mungo, whose car is that?" called Ivy.

"That's Siggy's. She works for the mayor. Always bringing her car over here and never tipping. Just counting out the exact amount. Humpty Dumpty! Everybody else leaves a bit extra. Mayor Freemantle, he's real generous; even pretends he doesn't know about the car wash – so I don't have to pay taxes or fees or get a business license." Mungo's honesty about legal business particulars added to his appeal and in no way diminished his income.

Mungo was going on. "Even when she brings the mayor's car here, she never tips. But maybe that's because she knows that the mayor will give me something later. Sometimes he'll give me a big tip and say get something special for the Ladybugs – that's what he calls my little girls."

Father Wedgewood's car was ready but Grace thanked him for his kind offer of a lift and said that they had to go back to the village hall instead. So he putted off with a birdseed and casserole-free car.

50. FATHER WEDGEWOOD

Father Wedgewood made a mental note of the conversation and resolved to up his tipping from then on.

The Bishop, who was somewhat frugal in the tipping department, would be none the wiser as Father Wedgewood used his own funds for discretionary spending. Perhaps the diocese could have its own illicit car wash behind the cathedral. Cathedral Car Wash had a nice ring to it and he could feel a homily coming on about washing away sin while raising money. The Bishop would certainly approve of the latter.

Father Wedgewood was feeling a bit tired as he turned into the rectory driveway and pulled around to the back. Maybe a little nap was in order and then he would look for the Biblical Allusion Dictionary. Perhaps the Lutherans had borrowed it, although he couldn't imagine the Bishop allowing that.

"Oh Father, thank goodness I've caught you!"

Father Wedgewood marveled at the accuracy of Mrs. Tumbledry's vocabulary. Of course her name wasn't really Tumbledry, but that was how Father Wedgewood referred to her. She was always rolling around through parish life with warmth and an admirable lack of static cling. She served as the softener of the congregation, a benign influence bringing concord, cooperation and casseroles.

"Yes, Father it's true. I'm afraid that it is all absolutely true."

Casting aside the immediate idea that she was referring to the possibility that she had poisoned several parishioners, Father Wedgewood composed himself to hear the fatal truth.

"They're all gone! Every single one! I've looked everywhere and called everyone. I've prayed to St. Balistica and St. Decahedron to no avail. One must be careful of those post Vatican II saints, they so often let one down."

Father Wedgewood started to remonstrate with her, trying to summon words in support of post Vatican II saints and to point out that Sts. Balistica and Decahedron weren't post Vatican II anyway. In fact they weren't even saints. The Bishop had advised against correcting her because Mrs. Tumbledry's financial support of the diocese was as generous as her imagination. It was the only instance that Father Wedgewood could think of when the Bishop had taken a lenient view of anything, let alone something liturgical. There was no stopping her, however, and Mrs. Tumbledry's oration continued to steamroll right over him.

"That time my bunion was acting up I prayed to St. Podia and wouldn't you know it, the next thing I knew I was buying lots of new shoes. Some lovely ballet flats and some navy pumps and some moccasins. Even cocktail shoes!"

Father Wedgewood could not even remotely imagine Mrs. Tumbledry in moccasins. And what precisely were cocktail shoes? Did they have to be red and steep?

"And some orthopedic Mary Janes that didn't look orthopedic at all, quite the opposite really, as if they would glorify your feet while praying."

As that sounded even more incomprehensible than cocktail shoes, Father Wedgewood smiled at her understandingly.

"Have you ever noticed Father – oh perhaps you wouldn't, not ever being in the right location – but you see the bottoms of people's shoes when they're praying and you are sitting behind them and sometimes they are so dirty and worn and have gum stuck on them. And did you realize that kneeling scuffs the toes of your shoes?"

Father Wedgewood squinched his toes around in his sandals. He had sprayed his feet off at the car wash and now a homily was coming on: were their souls as dirty and worn as their soles? Could chewing gum be equated with sin? What about working in birdseed as it had worked its way into his sandals?

Mrs. Tumbledry stared at him as if he were about to reveal the whereabouts of the missing.... He still did not even know what was missing. But did he want to? Perhaps God was protecting him from Too Much Mrs. Tumbledry. How grateful that made him, as did the realization that one could not scuff the toes of sandals. But what about one's own toes?

Somehow Mrs. Tumbledry had wandered off, in search of the Bishop hoped Father Wedgewood a bit maliciously. But now, alone at last.

Father Wedgewood nervously glanced around the deserted hallway leading to the refectory. Finding the coast clear of bishops and parishioners he muttered, "Forgive me Father for what I am about to do." He then hastily blessed the roll of Tums that he was clutching with the fervor of a convert and thrust them into the pocket of his cassock. It was then that the lightning bolt struck. Or was it a message from God? The only thing to do about those Lutherans was to inflict one of Beatrice Plumpting's casseroles on them.

Father Wedgewood would ask her to make one of her famous Last Supper Casseroles to bring to the Lutherans the next time they invited him over to "see" their Biblical

Garden. "See" in Lutheran meant "help us weed." So far they'd gotten him twice but now he had a secret weapon.

Father Wedgewood did not usually plot against Lutherans, nor indeed against any denomination or crackpot spin-off thereof. We are all God's children he reflected piously; but then added a bit more petulantly, some are just more childish than others.

Have to write the ol' homily though, so he bustled off to the library munching on his holy Tums. The green ones were the best. He'd once offered them around as After Dinner Mints following a particularly idolatrous meal of burnt offerings, courtesy of the First Communion class parents. Indigestion was an occupational hazard as far as Father Wedgewood's inner workings were concerned; but with the Tums, hope springs internal.

Maybe he could somehow bring food into the homily. But what if that approach inspired Beatrice Plumpting to new heights of inedibility? Scrap that idea. The Solace of Tums? If only he could choose the topic, his words would speed onto the page like a winged chariot or some such biblical allusion. Note to self: look for Biblical Allusion Dictionary when you take the Last Supper Casserole over to the Lutherans.

Vowing to make the best of things, even Apocalyptic Casseroles, Father Wedgewood noted the Readings and Gospel for the coming week and settled down to work.

51.   MCKNIGHT BESEIGED

As soon as Pinckney had left, McKnight had gotten out his secret manuscript: *Bet Noir – A Casino Mystery*, even though he had been getting a bit discouraged lately. McKnight readily acknowledged that he was no Raymond Chandler and never would be, but then Raymond Chandler had never been a mayor had he? He probably hadn't belonged to a garden club either. With his confidence reasserted, McKnight set to work.

He had somehow wandered off on a tangent based on a garden club meeting. Last month, the program had featured an excruciatingly well-organized and in-depth speaker on daffodils (dear God every known variety on the planet, although some of them sounded made up to him).

Why not have someone smothered with daffodil bulbs or tulip bulbs or beaten with a sack of mixed bulbs or poisoned! Were daffodil bulbs poisonous? He wished that he had asked that question. It would have been a lot more interesting than those self-aggrandizing anecdotes, "Recently when I was in Borneo/Tanzania/the South Pole camped on the banks of the Amazon having just shot a crocodile, I espied some daffodils." Yeah right, bub. Daffodils In Borneo. That was it! He had his title. It was worthwhile going to those garden club programs after all.

DAFFODILS IN BORNEO

"So there I was see, wandering

> lonely as a cloud in a clear blue
> tropical sky. The dame evoked
> familiarity, but maybe that was
> only because I wasn't wearing
> my glasses. She had on a bright
> yellow dress with sleeves flaring
> like trumpets and a frill around
> the hem. I guess somebody's old
> couch lost a slipcover. Reminded
> me of something … that was it - a
> daffodil. That dame was a floozy
> daffodil."

McKnight read through the paragraph, hoping that people would pick up on his literary allusion and see that he had certainly improved upon the original.

His office door was now open so Grace and Ivy marched right in. Surprised, McKnight pushed the legal pads aside and sighed as if things were very hectic and he was in great demand.

Well, he had been in great demand actually. Thinking back to that scoffing urban mayor: we now have crime too buddy, with good ol' Eunice packing it in at the mulch site. The media coverage had been spectacular – just the thing to launch his run for higher office – and he had bought several new ties to keep up with the interview demand and to give the illusion of even more numerous appearances.

Strengthened by the good lumbar support of his Revolver, but wishing that it had a pusher-upper feature – an eject button perhaps – he unfolded gallantly from a sitting position to shake hands with Grace and Ivy and wave them gently into distressed leather club chairs.

"So, what can I do for my two favorite constituents?"

Since McKnight ran perpetually unopposed, he could certainly assume that they supported him. "Would you like a drink?" He sure needed one: first Pinckney and now them.

"Oh, no thank you McKnight. Actually…" Grace got up and shut his office door. That move struck him as ominous so he opened his desk drawer to reach for the reassuring bottle of scotch. "But you go right ahead. We want to talk to you about Dash Lethaby. Ivy and I do not believe that he killed Eunice. So we are investigating and we would like your advice." An appeal to his vanity always helped with McKnight.

McKnight slapped his desk authoritatively. "I was just saying the same thing to Chief Hequembourg and the Major Case Squad guy. That I couldn't believe that Dash had done it I mean. But they consider the case closed."

He could have kicked himself for not investigating on his own. Why did he just feebly accept what the police report said? Dash was a friend. Grace and Ivy had more sense and caring than he did. He put the bottle back in the drawer and settled into his chair.

"What have you found out so far and how can I help?"

"Not much, unfortunately – what can you tell us about your assistant?"

"Monday?"

"No," Grace sounded a bit puzzled. "Now."

"Right, right, I know now, but her name is Monday."

"Oh," sounding more uncertain. "We thought that it was something like Siggy."

"Well her name is Sigismonday – God knows why – so most people call her Siggy, but I call her Monday – you know – my girl Monday instead of Friday."

"Okay, now that we've got that cleared up," said Ivy, "What can you tell us about her?"

"Why on earth would you want to know anything about HER?"

"Wait Ivy," said Grace. "Let's start in general, McKnight. Please tell us about the meeting on the night that Eunice was killed."

"Well, I assume that you know the basics: Dash wants to show prospective investors how much better it would be to build houses rather than have the mulch site. Eunice crashes the party; still don't know how she found out about it. Causes a scene. Monday bundles me out of there tout suite. That's it as far as I know."

"So Monday left with you?"

"Well, she came in her own car. We didn't come together. In fact, she wasn't going to attend because this was more social really, so I was kind of surprised when she showed up, but umm…" McKnight stopped to think. He wasn't about to explain that Monday had suspected that Eunice might be there and had come as a buffer so to speak. Minder might be more appropriate, he ruefully admitted to himself. He also didn't want to bring up the fact that Monday and Eunice had had a bit of a contretemps at the village hall that afternoon. Eloise Lutjens had filled him in on all that hose business, but he was thinking about the Kimberley business.

"Did she say why she decided to come?" Grace was relieved that Ivy was keeping quiet and letting her ask the questions.

"Well, not really, I mean we didn't have a chance to talk. There were lots of people milling around – should have had drinks there – and then Dash started the presentation and his dog was snorting around and digging."

"So did she leave when you did?" Grace cocked her head at Ivy. Were they getting somewhere with this?

"Sure – she was right behind me."

"So you saw her in her car and she left right after you did?"

"Well, yeah. Yes. She must have."

"McKnight, would you swear in a court of law that you saw her leave the mulch site when you did?"

McKnight was feeling confused. What did this have to do with anything?

He squinted slightly at Grace and shook his head. "What difference does it make?"

Ivy had been quiet long enough. "Tell us about her: how long has she worked for you, what is she like, did she know Eunice?"

The light bulb finally went on. "Wait, this sounds like you suspect Monday."

Grace and Ivy just sat there, waiting.

"Noooo, no, no, no, no. She's this timid little nothing; hardly says a word to anybody and she told me that she left right away and oh, now I remember, she told the police that too. That's right – yeah – I saw it in the report."

"McKnight," Ivy said heavily, "Her fingerprints were on the shovel."

"Oh, that. She told the police that she tidies the closets from time to time and she had recently handled the shovel. That's why." McKnight sighed with relief. Fortunately, Monday had not told the police about rearranging the garden clubs' belongings in order to foment discord.

McKnight's hope of a garden club free village hall was beginning to dim.

"Believe me, she's a nobody. People don't even remember her. She just does her job and fades into the woodwork. She has a talent for drudgery." McKnight had read that phrase somewhere and it had been percolating in the back of his brain. He had to get it down in his book right away or he would forget – totally forget these brainstorms that came to him out of the blue. He also wanted to get Grace and Ivy out of there before he somehow let it slip that he had encouraged Monday to get the garden clubs moved out of the village hall.

After his police interview, Monday had told him of her elimination method of moving the contents of the closets around in order to stir up animosity, figuring that it would lead to a mass exodus of garden clubs. In theory, it sounded brilliant, but she did not know garden club ladies – a tenacious breed when they dug themselves in – ha-ha – garden club humor. Maybe he could use that in his *Daffodils In Borneo* book. McKnight jumped up with newfound agility.

"Well, listen, ahh, Grace and Ivy, thank you for coming to see me. This has been really interesting and I will see what else I can come up with. After all, Dash is our friend and we've got to stand by him. I'll be in touch. And seriously, with Monday, you are digging up the wrong tree. Ha-ha, garden club humor – just a little joke. Barking I mean, barking up the wrong tree. You two need to wake up and smell the roses."

52. GIN AND TONIC WEATHER

"My word, that was rather sudden." Grace raised her eyebrows at Ivy.

"It sure was. The attempt at humor was somewhat dubious too. I wonder if he is up to something."

"Like what?"

"Oh, I don't know. But we now know the explanation for her fingerprints on the shovel. Here I thought we were really on to something. Hmm... I wonder if Siggy/Monday is here now. We should still talk to her."

"Oh Ivy, I think we need to talk this whole thing through a bit more before we tackle her."

After such an eventful morning, and it was early afternoon by now, Grace and Ivy were really hungry, so they walked up the road to Shady Grove. They could ask Lenny to drive them home after lunch. It was a nice walk up from the village hall and the day was lovely but with a promise of spring rain. Ivy was trying to decide whether she was going to get a hamburger with extra onion rings or a fried egg and bacon sandwich with extra onion rings. "Oohh, I wonder if they're serving outside."

"You know Ivy, I wonder if Lenny could shed any light on this whole mess. He might have seen something, but doesn't realize it could mean something."

"Great idea. We'll grill him on the way home. Speaking of grills, I think I'll have the hamburger. Do you think it's gin and tonic weather yet?"

The day was becoming oppressive with vague rumblings in the clouding over skies. The screened log huts

were open, however, and Grace and Ivy sat down gratefully onto the uncomfortable metal folding chairs. Having
determined that it was definitely gin and tonic weather,
Ivy ordered a whiskey sour and Grace a glass of Chablis.
They didn't need to look at the menu. No one did. You
just ordered.

"Okay Ivy, let's make a very clear plan of attack here
because this is starting to get nerve wracking."

"Nerve wracking? Really? I find it rather exciting."
This was worrisome. What if Grace pulled out? "Would
you rather not be involved?"

"Of course I would rather not be involved, but that
is not the point. A friend is wrongly accused. We have to
do something. So first, we need to talk to the main people
before we tackle this assistant Siggy person. Sigismonday
Vellacotton – good grief. For clarity, what do we want to
call her?"

"Ha! I know! We have to come up with a code
name! Velvet cotton sounds like a rabbit. Or terra cotta.
Operation Terra Cotta! Operation Flower Potta!"

Grace hoped that Ivy was not going to order another
drink. "Let's just stick with Siggy. McKnight said that is
what most people call her." Fortunately their food arrived
and Ivy tucked in.

With her finger, Grace traced the drops that were bead-
ing on the outside of her rather large wine glass. "We've
already talked to Reavis, Pinckney and McKnight. So that
leaves Dash, Cuppy and Gardenia."

"I talked to Gardenia at the mulch site."

"Yes, but that was before Dash was arrested. We have
to ask all three of them if they saw Siggy leave. The point

that seems so odd to me is that she claims to tidy the garden club closets. I've never heard of that before and it might explain all the odd things missing and moved around. But why?"

"If she's this bland little nobody, then probably no one will have noticed when she left. Or have ever realized that she was messing about in the closets. You're right – that really is strange."

"Pinckney and McKnight think she's a nobody, but then Pinckney thinks that most people are nobodies."

"You know, Grace," Ivy leaned back speculatively in her chair, "that is the first even remotely unkind thing that I have ever heard you say. I mean about Pinckney being that way. Which she certainly is! I'm not disputing that."

"Oh." Grace blushed a bit and took a sip of wine. "Well, McKnight thinks that Siggy left right after he did because she told him that she did. He never definitively said that he saw her leave."

"Okay, fine, but what possible motive would some mousy little secretary have to kill Eunice? Did she even know Eunice?"

"That's another good question for McKnight. Plus she can't be too mousy if she can make somebody believe something by just telling them so."

"But Grace, McKnight trusts her, so of course he believes her. He has no reason not too. I don't think that it's a question of mind control or something."

"Maybe, but remember, we're talking about McKnight who is probably pretty easily led. Let's figure out how we are going to approach her."

"Good plan. How about another drink?"

53. DEATH BY TYPEWRITER

```
    The dame was called Tuesday
and she had a face that looked
like someone had gone at it with
a typewriter; which someone had
because the dame was dead and the
typewriter wasn't looking too good
either. Blood soaked, the black
typewriter ribbons snaked around
the dame's neck. They were an
improvement over the cheap jewelry
she usually wore. The typewriter
had typed its last letter; had the
final word so to speak.
    I expanded with relief into my
swivel chair with the good lumbar
support.
```

McKnight discerned a subtle evolution of his writing style. He reread the last paragraph and then checked his watch. It was way past lunchtime. Well, he'd been assaulted all morning by prying women.

"Tuesday! I mean Monday!" Where was the blasted woman?

Monday spread in like lukewarm Elmer's glue.

"Oh, there you are. Would you call Shady Grove and tell them I'll be right over and tell George not to put me next to a table of cackling women."

George answered her call so she just had to say, "The mayor is on his way."

"Got it. No cackling women, yeah, yeah."

Monday hung up and began organizing the jumbled legal pads on McKnight's desk. He had started another chapter in his book and he had been unusually prolific that morning. In general, he was pretty good at first paragraphs of first chapters and the last sentence of the last paragraph. It was the in-between stuff that proved elusive. So sometimes Monday filled it in for him. What would this one need?

MORE THAN LUNCH

The dame was a nobody named
Tuesday but she looked like a bad
Saturday night and was harder to
get rid of than a Sunday morning
hangover. At first I didn't care,
see, as long as she did her job and
kept quiet about it. Her job was to
file papers and to keep my desk
tidy and hang up my coat and make
lunch reservations for me and
the Clientele. The Clientele being
mostly and very female.
    I felt sorry for Tuesday but she
had a talent for drudgery and I let
her keep the job out of pity. She had
no family, no boyfriend and about
as much hope in that department
as a lemming in Kansas. I soon
realized that I had to get rid of
her once the Clientele started
pointing out that she was weird
and creepy and dressed in white all
the time and wore white shoes even

after Labor Day.
  The Clientele that day was a
dame dressed in a snappy little
black number and looked like she
expected a lot more than lunch.
Getting rid of Tuesday would have
to wait until Wednesday."

Siggy read the two chapters with a cold burn in her
chest. It is just a story. You know how he is: melodramatic
without meaning. Yes, she would have to add to this one.

TUESDAY'S STORY

  Working for the detective had
given Tuesday a whole new look on
life. She wanted one. Not day after
day of dreary typing and filing
and making phone calls and lunch
reservations. Didn't he realize that
her little suggestions, questions
and remarks were what prompted
his ideas and brought about his
ultimate success? Maybe she should
just clam up and watch him flounder
his way through unsolved cases; let
him follow red herrings, let him
lose clients, let him find it hard
to pay the rent, let him scrape the
bottom of the scales of justice. Then
he would realize the truth and see
her as his savior. But right now she
had bigger fish to fry.
  The Dame had had it. In fact
the Dame was fed up. This two-bit
detective would never discover

where her two-timing rat of a husband had stashed the gold bullion. Two times two meant four times the trouble with both those guys. Do the math, buster.

Time for Tuesday to step in. Her white dress clashed with the black one of the Clientele's but she didn't care. They could not afford to lose this job. Her boss had stepped down the hall so here was her chance. Teaching him a lesson would have to wait. The Clientele eyed her with suspicion and disdain as she flicked open her gold cigarette case. Not bothering to offer Tuesday one, this cool cat slowly lit the cigarette and gave it a cynical drag. She perched on the edge of the boss's desk and exhaled like a Nascar tail pipe.

"So tell me. Is your boss going to get my money or my husband back? Which is it? I only want the money."

54. KIMBERLEY DRIVES CAREFULLY

Kimberley drove slowly away from Cuppy's house, a lot more slowly than usual. She already had two speeding tickets. Both from this fat woman cop with a bad complexion. She was a slob too. Something all down the front of her shirt. Yuck. Now if it had been a handsome young policeMAN, she wouldn't have minded so much about the messy shirt. There didn't seem to be too many around. Handsome young men that is. Certainly not at Tirano. That must have been why she took up with Cuppy. The speeding tickets were bad enough because they were more expensive than she could have imagined, but now after this Cuppy mistake, she would have to get a new job.

She had planned to take the rest of the day off to be with Cuppy, but now that was out. Maybe she could go over to the village hall. Her mother had told her that the mayor was an old family friend and he had got her the job at Tirano. Maybe he could pull strings at some other company. She guessed that she should have thanked him, but her mother had said that he did not want anyone to know that he had helped her because then he would have to help everyone. Well, no one has to know anything. She certainly wouldn't tell. OOH, maybe he could do something about the speeding tickets too! But first, maybe a little shopping would cheer her up.

McKnight had just gotten back from lunch and was working on his book. He had told Monday not to interrupt him so he flung his head up irritably when his office door opened. That feeling changed however when one knockout dame waltzed in. Now where had he seen her before? The question tantalized him for a second. Realization slammed into him just as she introduced herself. He had to remember to breathe. Blood pressure soared into the stratosphere. It was pounding in his ears. Chest pains! He was going to die! Things were going black. Didn't he get a dying wish? What was his dying wish? His dying wish was that he wouldn't die. Was that a priest? "Pinckney," he managed to gasp.

Oh my God, he was almost passing out and was all pale like Cuppy had been. What was it with these old coots?

Kimberley grabbed his arm and eased him back into his swivel chair with the good lumbar support. He needed a hell of a lot more support than lumbar right now. "Do you want me to get you some water?"

McKnight scrabbled at the lower left-hand side drawer of his custom built antique mahogany desk. Kimberley jerked it open, rattling the medicinal scotch bottle. McKnight grabbed for it but Kimberley got there first and handed it to him. Despite being in extremis, he couldn't quite bring himself to just chug the scotch (it was an exclusive triple malt) right out of the bottle. He swiveled expertly around to reach for one of the beautiful heavy crystal glasses with his initials and a duck etched on them. The glasses were arrayed on a lovely silver tray that Pinckney had given him when he had been elected mayor.

The force of his takeoff and expertise at swiveling caused him to whack one of the glasses to the hardwood parquet floor where it shattered like his dreams of higher political office. This was a disaster. His chair kept spinning until Kimberley slowed it down and brought it to a stop. They stared at each other face to face. A face that was familiar somehow. Of course it was.

When Kimberley's mother had called McKnight out of the blue after so many years (25 or something like that; or maybe longer?) he had been horrified. In fact, he could only vaguely picture her. She had been a waitress at Shady Grove: this healthy young country lass who probably drank gallons of milk every day. They'd had a bit of fun and then she had gone back to the depths of farm country never to arise again. Until now. NOW! Why now of all times? Not that any time would be good for this kind of news. She had called to ask him to help their daughter (THEIR DAUGHTER! AGHHHH!) get a job.

"How do I know she's mine?"

"I think that you should remember me enough (he did by now) to believe me (he did) and she looks just like you. I'll send you a photo." Even if she hadn't been an absolute replica of him, McKnight would have had to do something for her just to keep it secret.

After a partial recovery from the Kimberley Heart Attack, induced by her unexpected visit, McKnight went home to take a nap. Thank God Pinckney was out. The day was sort of gloomy and oppressive. He found that he couldn't rest after all, so he wandered around the house at loose ends pondering Life. Now that Eunice was dead, and the prospect of running into her was just as dead, perhaps she hadn't been THAT bad after all. Quirky one might say. One might, but not him.

McKnight moped around some more and ate some stale potato chips, peered into the refrigerator then stared out the kitchen window. The dogs had been interested in the potato chips but had now gone back to sleep. He didn't even feel like drinking. That was scary.

The first thing that he had to do was fix Kimberley's speeding tickets. That was easy: just make another contribution to the Olney Cowperne Retirement Fund. With all that McKnight had paid in over the years, what with the kids' speeding tickets and Pinckney's DWIs, the guy should be in Branson by now.

The second thing was harder: get her another job. Kimberley had told him that she wanted to leave Tirano for a career in fashion or modeling. For some reason, a bio-engineering firm did not offer these opportunities. Not that she wasn't grateful for the job. She really appreciated his help and she really liked the job and Mr. Kingblade was a really great boss, but it was time to move on.

At least that was a relief – knowing that Cuppy hadn't put the moves on her. But fashion? Modeling? He was stumped on that and it certainly was not Monday's forte. Pinckney would know about that kind of stuff. She'd be the ideal resource, but did he dare?

55. AFTER LUNCH PLANS

After reviving drinks and fortifying food (Ivy did get the hamburger with extra onion rings and Grace got the Special Salad), Ivy outlined their first step. "We have to talk to Dash. Let's just go over there. He has to be at home if he's under house arrest. Lenny can take us."

"Well, wait. After all that rambling along the bridle trail and searching the mulch site and riding in that policewoman's dirty car, I just feel so grubby and icky. I would like to go home first to shower and change. Then we can call on Dash in time for tea or early drinks." In Ivy's opinion, Grace remained as immaculate as ever but the prospect of a rest certainly appealed to her.

"Good idea. I'll take a nap."

Grace and Ivy were among the last of the lunch crowd. Lenny moved the two remaining cars so they were right by the side entrance, then pulled up his car to drive them home. On the way, Ivy quizzed him about the night of the murder.

"What time did Dash get there? Who else was there? When did they arrive and leave?"

"Police asked me that too. I don't keep track. Lots of people, very busy. I do remember Dash because he was already loaded, but I can't pinpoint the time."

"Ballpark?"

"Seven? Eight?"

Grace found it impossible to believe that Lenny did not know that type of information to the minute. He had made a career out of being discreet and protective, however, and he was going to stick to it. She wasn't sure what the information could add anyway. Although there was one thing that she definitely wanted to find out.

"What was Cole doing all this time?"

"Oh, he helps me park cars then stays overnight at my house. Dash picked him up on his way home the next morning."

"So Cole stayed overnight at your house? But where was Dash?"

"At Shady Grove. He sometimes kind of falls asleep on that old sofa in the Pine Room. So he picks up Cole on his way home the next day." Ivy lifted her eyebrows at Grace. This kind of behavior certainly did not help his case.

❦

56.   THE MINISTERING ANGEL

Although Cuppy had enjoyed a respite after Kimberley left, he was still emotionally drained and another doorbell ring nearly finished him off. Why can't they make silent doorbells? Sell 'em to bereaved people. Make a fortune.

Donning his sorrowing widower's face, he opened the door with tired sadness. His expression blossomed into a smile when he beheld the delectable Madeleine Lethaby on his doorstep.

"Hi Cuppy. I'm not sure you remember me."

"Oh, of course, of course, I remember you," he managed to get out, but then stood there like an idiot mentally salivating over this vision of loveliness.

Madeleine returned a wistful look to convey tremulous tenderness. When he just kept standing there though, a slight tremor of alarm, a far-off warning bell rang in her consciousness. Was it possible that his vacant stare indicated homicidal guilt or only incipient drooling?

She broke the silent standoff with, "Ah, I've brought you a casserole. Would you like me to take it to the kitchen?" Madeleine wasn't about to just hand it over. She was bound and determined to get inside that house and question him.

Sensing that speech and possibly even movement were called for, Cuppy found himself able to utter the words, "Oh, yes, please come in, so kind umm," as he ushered her into the front hall. Madeleine stepped into a space that had all the artistry of a manila envelope. Was that a bouquet of sticks?

Rotating robotically, Cuppy clipped the edge of the hall table, knocking over the vase full of dead twigs as he led the way into the kitchen. God she was gorgeous! She smelled like spicy peaches and, with that dab of a French accent, he would happily forgive her anything – even a casserole. But how could anyone French make a casserole? Surely they would be tumbrelled off to the guillotine for cooking such an American abomination. Or maybe they just called them something else over there and they were fabulous. Bouillabaisse he guessed wildly or cassoulet. Cassoulet, casserole – must have the same origin. Then he remembered that Madeleine was French Canadian – so that explained it.

Madeleine regarded the kitchen floor with horror. This was even worse than Dash's kitchen. Why were men such slobs when left on their own? She smiled in what she hoped was a sympathetic way and tiptoed through the minefield of disgusting grit to put the CorningWare dish of "Tropical Spring Medley" on the counter. She hoped that he would be able to follow the directions that she had printed clearly in her precise small handwriting on a 3 x 5 index card. "Preheat oven to 350 degrees. Remove lid, put casserole dish in oven and bake for 30 minutes."

"Would you like a drink?"

Although Madeleine usually did not drink in the afternoon, she had come there to get information and what better way than to let him think that he was plying her with liquor?

"A glass of wine would be lovely, thanks." Oh dear! What if he meant iced tea? People here drank gallons of the stuff – day or night. She couldn't get used to it.

Cuppy had been thinking along the lines of bourbon or scotch mais bien sur (see, his French was coming back to him) how French (Canadian): wine in the afternoon! Now that was civilization for you. Christ he hoped he had something decent. Yes! Somebody had brought him a bottle of wine the other day and he had just shoved it into the refrigerator. It turned out to be a California chardonnay with an acceptable looking label. He grabbed the bottle and two wine glasses and gestured for her to go ahead toward the sun porch, which was by far the least gloomy room in the house. Eunice had never wanted to let the sun in. Sun in a sun porch? It might fade the upholstery – gasp – horrors! How could beige get any less beige? Well it was curtains for her, but not for him. Ho ho ho. Things were looking up.

Madeleine sat down on a small sofa that turned out to be surprisingly rock-like. Cuppy set the bottle and glasses on the table then had to go back for the corkscrew, which he had forgotten. Madeleine immediately examined the glasses. Thank goodness, they were clean.

She furtively scraped her feet on the slate floor, trying to get rid of the clinging crunchy stuff. What WAS it? Cuppy returned and she smiled sweetly at him. He botched cutting the foil and nicked his finger in the process, but managed to uncork the bottle with ease if not flair.

"Well, cheers," he said somewhat inappropriately, but she didn't seem to notice as she responded with raised glass and took a sip. Ick – not very good, but as an undaunted investigator, she continued to smile.

"So," started Madeleine, realizing that she should have

prepared better for this interview. She had assumed that the conversation would just flow. It was unlike her not to have compiled a list of gambits and questions cleverly designed to elicit information. Time had been of the essence however and the stupid casserole had taken much longer to make than the book said it would. Wasn't the whole point that they did not take a lot of effort to make? She tried to think of what Father Wedgewood would say to prompt the confession of sins.

"How have you been?" she asked wincing inwardly at the lame opening, although really what else could one say?

"Well, okay I guess. One day at a time you know."

Cuppy continued to gaze at her in an unsettling and loony way. Her heart suddenly thumped. Was she in danger? She hadn't told anyone where she was going. Madeleine took a hefty gulp of the wretched wine, which went down the wrong pipe. Coughing and choking, with eyes tearing, she fumbled in her purse for a tissue. Cuppy sprang up to pound her on the back or render mouth-to-mouth resuscitation if necessary (or even if not necessary), but she warded him off with an upraised hand and managed to gasp, "I'll be okay, thanks. Oh gosh, sorry."

It somehow broke the awkwardness though and he said with a bit of a smile, "Is the wine that bad? I don't drink much wine myself. Someone dropped it off the other day. It was probably given to them too – one of those bottles people take to a party when they know that they aren't going to reciprocate. Would you like something else?"

"No, no I'm fine really. Thanks. I just wanted to see how you are. Dash and I wanted to see how you are," she amended.

Cuppy's eyebrows went up and his hopes went down. Were they back together?

"I was out of town when Eunice – when it happened. Dash's sister Christie called me to tell me that Dash had been arrested, so I came back. I know he didn't do it." Madeleine waited, hoping that Cuppy would say something incriminating.

He turned his head away from her. Dash had killed Eunice for all the obvious reasons and then with the police finding the shovel in his car, that was that. Dash wasn't stupid and mean, but he could sure drink himself stupid and mean. And that was what had happened. He was just drunk and he did it. So drunk he didn't remember, but he did it all right. What about those hitting motions with the shovel that Dash had made behind Eunice that night? They'd been so mesmerizing, hypnotic, a trance of death. He could have done it himself, had done it himself... had done it himself... had done it himself.

57.   THE VIOLET HOUR

Grace picked Ivy up late that afternoon, planning to arrive at Dash's around 5:30-ish or so – that nebulous time that could work for tea or cocktails. Although some people, usually nautical folk, declared that the violet hour (otherwise known as cocktail time) started at 5:03 PM. This calculation held fast regardless of where the sun was in relation to the yardarm and regardless of Mr. DeVoto's declaration of 6:00 PM as the appropriate starting time. Despite this difference of opinion as to timing, the Lethaby clan had embraced *The Hour: A Cocktail Manifesto*, as a family creed. Cross-stitched by Dash's mother then framed and hung in the pantry, it read:

> *"This is the violet hour, the hour of hush and wonder, when the affections glow and valor is reborn, when the shadows deepen along the edge of the forest and we believe that, if we watch carefully, at any moment we may see the unicorn."*

Dash opened the door looking worried and clearly adhering to the 5:03 tradition with a glass of scotch in his hand. Being arrested for murder was liable to put a damper on anyone's week and drive one to drink. Not that Dash needed any transportation in that direction. But it turned out to be something much more important.

"Have you seen Madeleine? I thought that she'd be back way before now and it's getting kind of late. Cole's been back for ages."

"Oh she's probably just out shopping or something. Oh wait, do you mean that they were out together?" Ivy bustled into the front hall past Dash who continued to look outside.

"No, not together. Cole was with the UPS guy. He gives him rides in the truck but they left at the same time."

Cole came skittering toward them, thumping Ivy with his tail and snorting in great big waves of her delicious doggy Newfoundland smell. Ivy good-naturedly thumped him back then turned to Dash. "That dog needs a bath. Does he really ride around with the UPS guy? What fun! But first, we do not believe that you killed Eunice so we are doing our own investigation. Now, is there somewhere we can sit down and talk?"

Oh Christ this was all he needed. If they went bumbling all over investigating he'd get life for sure. How the hell could he stop that bulldozer Ivy? Maybe that zealot of a prosecutor could get him a restraining order.

"Um, sure, let's go into the living room. Would you like something to drink?" He needed time to think of a strategy and drinking always helped any situation.

Cole had been greeting Grace, who gave off a faintly terrier-ish air. Gosh, he really did need a bath. Maybe she could have Parsley send him a present of Doggy Bath. It had such a nice fresh scent, not perfumey at all. Parsley hated Doggy Bath and would be happy to send all of it to Cole, perhaps by UPS.

Dash was explaining. "One day the UPS truck was just parked there while the guy took a package up to the Toynbee's house. Apparently Cole just got in. The guy takes off then realizes he has Cole with him. So he just drove around the block and dropped him off. Now he picks him up whenever Cole is out there and drives him around the block."

Grace did not think that she would let Parsley ride around in a UPS truck. He might fall out.

Ivy chimed in. "Didn't Cole used to ride around in golf carts too? I think I remember hearing something about that."

"Oh yeah. That was a disaster. He ended up driving one into the pond on 17. Do you know how much those things cost?"

"Good heavens. How on earth did that happen?" Grace found Dash's attitude toward his dog rather casual.

"He'd just go over there…"

Meaning that he had to cross the road by himself, Grace frowned.

"…and wait for someone to stop. Most folks know him and they'd give him a ride for a hole or two. Then one time, these guys were searching for a ball and they had just left the cart there for a while so Cole got in and we guess that his foot hit the pedal that released the brake. It was on that downward slope right above where the cart path turns, but instead of turning it went straight into the pond. So, one golf cart was added to the bill that month and Cole was banned from the club."

Grace did not think that she would let Parsley ride around in a golf cart either, especially if Cole were driving. She definitely needed a cup of tea.

"By any chance do you have any tea?"

"There may be some tea bags somewhere…" Dash trailed off doubtfully.

"Oh well, never mind – that's all right."

"No, no, I'll go out to the kitchen and look."

"Let's just talk in the kitchen," said Ivy and led the way. "Quite different than in your parents' day, Dash."

"Yes, I'm afraid that Mad got a little carried away."

"Ha! Mad went mad, so to speak."

"Yeah, that about captures it all right."

They walked past the closed double doors to the dining

room. Grace restrained herself from opening one to peek in.

"Do you still have the dining room furniture?" Compared with the simplicity of the rest of the furnishings in the house, the dining room was an anomaly. The table and chairs were massive, of a brooding dark wood with extraordinary medieval carvings on the legs. Carved animals climbed up the backs of the chairs – a different animal on each chair. Great had been the fights in the Lethaby household to claim ownership of a particular chair.

"Oh yes, she didn't get rid of anything; just redecorated and added – added a lot. Here we are: Vi-o-la – tea bags."

"Vi-o-la?" questioned Ivy.

"A family catch phrase – instead of voila. Can't remember how it started."

The kitchen had been partially restored and they sat down at the old library table. It was long and beat up and practical. At each end there was a Captain's chair with a raggedy cushion tied to the spindles. The other chairs had come with the table. Dash managed to locate some cups and saucers and even found an unopened tin of Danish Butter cookies. "Here we go. These things last forever."

Ivy dug into the cookies. "Okay, first thing. Have you ever heard of a person named Sigismonday Velvetcotton?"

"Vellacotton," corrected Grace. "Or the nickname Siggy or Monday?"

"I have absolutely no clue what you are talking about. Who the hell is that?"

Grace did not like Dash's language but she forgave

him due to the extreme circumstances. "She's McKnight's assistant."

"Oh, well I knew that he had an assistant because he told me that she was typing his book for him but I never knew her name. Good God."

"McKnight's writing a book?" Ivy was flabbergasted. "About what?"

"Some hardboiled mystery apparently. But he asked me not to tell anyone. He only told me because he wanted some advice about publishers and he knows that Adele, my stepmother, has published some novels. So I put him in touch with her, but I haven't heard anything more about it, from him that is. Adele told me that he sent her part of his book to read, which she did. So she sent him a book called – oh – it was something like *Thirty Seven Fiction Writing Blunders and How to Avoid Them.*"

"Bet he loved that," said Ivy drily. "But how exciting that your stepmother writes novels. I've always wanted to write one. Maybe about garden clubs. What does she write about?"

"Oh some torrid romance things about Indians. She's written the Gitcheegoome series and the Daughter of the Moon series. Deer skin bodice rippers I guess you'd call them. Christie's read some. Says they're terrible and wildly inaccurate historically, but they sell like hot cakes."

"Ivy, let's tell Dash what we've found out so far and go from there. There's a third set of fingerprints on the shovel."

Dash sat up and stared at Grace. "The police never told me that."

"They belong to McKnight's assistant. According to

McKnight, she says they are on there because she straightens out the garden club closets from time to time, which was news to us, and she claims that she had moved the shovel that very day, before Gardenia came over to get it. Do you remember seeing her at the presentation?"

"No but there were lots of folks there and, since I don't know her, I probably wouldn't have noticed. Plus I was really busy and then focused on dealing with Eunice."

"So you wouldn't have seen her leave?"

"Obviously not. Let me tell you what I remember." Dash poured an encouraging slug of bourbon into his cup of tea. "I went over this about a million times with the police, so here is the basic version. Eunice shouting. Everybody leaving. Hit Eunice with car. Drove around. Went back to mulch site. Nobody and No Body. Capital N. Capital B. Saw Gardenia's shovel. Put in car. Big Mistake. Capital B. Capital M. Went to Shady Grove. That's it." Dash got up and went to look out the window. "Where the hell is Mad?"

Grace and Ivy flicked glances at each other. Had Madeleine moved back in? Grapevine hadn't reported that.

Grace tried another tack. "What if the killer wore gloves? Oh but wouldn't that have smudged the other prints? I wish that we had taken that police report with us."

"Ha! I told you we should take it!"

"I know Ivy, I know. Misplaced propriety."

"You need to be more devious, Grace."

"But one shouldn't have to NEED to be devious. Besides, I don't WANT to be devious."

A devious Grace Mere. Dash didn't think so but at

least this was getting more promising. They had discovered that there had been a third set of prints. Why hadn't the police told him? Why couldn't the killer be this velvet woman? Who straightens out garden club closets anyway? That was suspicious right there. Had she been looking for something? Hiding something? Planting something? They just had to find a motive.

"How did you get a copy of the police report?" Maybe Grace and Ivy were more effective than he had given them credit for.

The kitchen door opened and Madeleine stumbled in over the sill. It never ceased to amaze Dash how clumsy a ballet dancer could be in regular daily life. She had explained to him that dancers were like that. They needed music to guide their movements. If she could live to music then she wouldn't go around bumping into things and stubbing toes and what not. Dash tried to conjure up what kind of music would enable her to enter a kitchen without falling into the table.

Cole scrambled up to greet her, rooing and thwacking her legs with his tail. She'd been gone for months and months!

"Where have you been? I've been so worried about you." Dash enfolded her gently in his wonderful, welcoming arms. Sometimes she just wanted comforting and affection.

"Oh, hello Grace, Ivy," shaking their hands and hugging Cole. "Well, I probably did something stupid. I went to see Cuppy. I took him a casserole."

Grace and Ivy grimaced at each other, knowing how Cuppy hated casseroles. Madeleine may have narrowly averted death.

"He was perfectly nice but when I was there I had this sudden thought, what if he is the murderer and kills me? And I hadn't told you where I was going, oh Dash." She leaned against him.

"What did he say?" Ivy grabbed the opportunity for more information as she tried to formulate a more substantial reason for calling on Cuppy than just condolences. They needed something that would take a while and give them a chance to search the house or at least look around, something beyond a casserole. Beyond A Casserole – sounded like a culinary romance novel. Maybe Dash could suggest it to his stepmother.

"What casserole did you make?" Grace took a dim view of casseroles but was curious nonetheless. And a casserole was still a casserole, no matter how well intentioned.

Dash did not see how casseroles were relevant. "Mad, Grace and Ivy are here because they are trying to figure out who killed Eunice, but I don't think..."

Madeleine cut him off, "Well I am too! Why do you think I went over there? Making casseroles is not easy. I made something called Tropical Spring Medley. It took forever and it had way too many ingredients."

Oh God, now there were three of them. He was as good as convicted. His case would go down in legal history as the failed Casserole Defense. Where did Mad find ingredients? She was even more resourceful than Grace and Ivy. Maybe things were looking up after all, but they had to step away from the casserole.

"Jesus, can we move beyond casseroles?" This was getting annoying not to mention possibly incriminating and

Dash wanted another drink, which was not tea. "What did you say to him?"

"We just sort of chatted." Madeleine was disgruntled. "He didn't say anything about her at all and when I said that you didn't kill her, he didn't answer. He just looked at me kind of weirdly." Madeleine was tired and discouraged and vaguely weepy and wished that Grace and Ivy would go home. They were firmly ensconced at the kitchen table, however, so she put more water in the kettle to make a fresh pot of tea.

Grace could tell that Madeleine wanted them to leave and under normal circumstances she would have taken the hint. Instead, she said sympathetically, "It's tiring being a detective, but I have an idea about going to see Cuppy. Maybe Ivy and I could get more out of him since we've known him so much longer."

Dash sat down with a refreshed drink. "What do you mean?"

"The kink free hoses. They're still in his garage aren't they? He probably wants to get rid of them, so one of us can call him and offer to come over and take them away."

"Brilliant!" Ivy beamed at her. "Let's do it tomorrow. We can search for gloves. But right now, Dash – let's go over the whole evening in detail – start with who was at the presentation."

"Oh man, I don't want to go through the whole thing again. Besides, it seems to me that the person to investigate is the assistant. Cuppy's fingerprints aren't on the shovel are they? Okay, he could have worn gloves. He probably has work gloves in his truck. In the meantime, why don't I call Gardenia and see if she knows about McKnight's assistant moving stuff around in the closets. I also want to know if the police told her about the other fingerprints."

58. *LONELY SPLENDOR AT THE ST. CYR'S*

Gardenia would be dining in Lonely Splendor that night. Lonely Splendor was what she called the dining room when she was all by herself. She liked to pretend that she was keeping up standards in one of the last outposts of the Empire. Dinner would consist of a small, ladylike portion of the Cocktail Buffet Dish that she had made just that afternoon. It was intended for her bridge group luncheon the next day.

Herbert was out at a Monopoly tournament. She used to accompany him to the tournaments but it became awfully boring standing around watching other people play Monopoly; especially as they were all so dreadfully serious about it and never appreciated her advice. Her favorite properties were the yellow ones and the green ones. They were such pretty colors.

Her darling baby Worcester was away at Princeton where for some inexplicable reason his friends at the eating club called him "Sauce." Herbert's two children by his ill-advised first marriage were safely married and living elsewhere. One was in California and the other in a reassuringly remote section of Oregon. Doing something earthy apparently, the Oregon one that is, and quite successfully so according to Herbert. Oregon was the place for earthy doings. How one measured success in earthy terms Gardenia did not know. The California one was successful just for living in California.

That had been her less than riotous prospect for the evening until Dash called. Gardenia leapt upon the phone as if it were a life vest and she a drowning shepherdess although why would a shepherdess be drowning? Shepherdesses were usually found on hillsides or in meadows or sitting on tuffets, not falling off cruise ships.

It was such a relief to hear Dash's voice. "Oh Dash dear, come over for dinner. I've been so worried about you."

"I'd love to Gardy but I'm under house arrest. I can't go anywhere."

"Well, just tell the police that you will be at MY house instead. It's a perfectly suitable house."

"I don't think that they think like that. Listen, Gard, I called you because..." Gardenia cut him off. "I know: I'll bring dinner over to your house and we'll have a lovely evening there and the police will never know."

"Ah... well, sure that'd be great. Mad's here too, oh and Grace and Ivy. But really I just need to ask you about...."

"My word – quite a party." Gardenia slashed in sharply. She was hurt at being the last to be invited, but she had the Cocktail Buffet Dish already made. That would be perfect. She could figure out something else for the bridge group. And she always had salad fixings. On the way over, she would stop at the club to pick up some of those butter top rolls and a bunch of half-dipped chocolate macaroons for dessert. That darn policewoman had eaten all the ginger snaps.

Gardenia cheered up mightily. "An impromptu dinner party – what fun! I have a Cocktail Buffet Dish and salad. I'll bring everything. Don't you worry. I'll be over there shortly. You do have wine dear, don't you?"

She hung up abruptly and Dash sighed. "Well, she's on her way over."

Madeleine let out a small moan.

"But she's bringing dinner for all of us."

"As long as it isn't a casserole," Madeleine muttered.

Ivy rolled her eyes. "Oh Gardenia doesn't make casseroles. She makes Cocktail Buffet Dishes."

"What's the difference?" Madeleine wanted to understand these curious Deer Creek rituals and vocabulary.

Ivy snorted, sounding remarkably like a Newfoundland. Looking surprised, Cole got up and leaned against her legs then started licking her knees. Hmmm... earthy tones, traces of floral accents with a hint of grass and a nice oaky finish.

"There is no difference. That's the point. They're both a one-dish meal. Gardenia always has to make things more important than they really are and different from everyone else. It's often funny, sometimes endearing and usually ridiculous." Ivy flapped Cole's ears. "Look! He's trying to fly! He's trying to fly!"

"You have to admit though," said Dash as he opened a bottle of wine, "Gardenia's Cocktail Buffet Dishes are really good." With this positive prospect in mind and glasses in hand, everyone started to relax. The murder could wait until Gardenia and the Cocktail Buffet Dish arrived.

Feeling faintly sordid and crusty from the birdseed, Madeleine longed to get cleaned up and changed. "Do I have enough time to take a shower?"

"Oh sure. It'll take her a while to get here because she doesn't turn left."

"She doesn't turn left? What do you mean?"

"My dear cousin Gardenia," said Dash in quite a mocking lofty tone, "does not make left turns while driving. She considers it dangerous."

"Oh good grief." Although she had to admit to a grudging respect for someone who made her own rules. There were plenty of left turns that Madeleine did not like to make either. Dash, on the other hand, zooming around as he did at breakneck speed, made just getting out of the garage a death defying exercise. Madeleine went off to see what she could dig up to wear and Grace, Ivy and Dash moved into the living room.

It too had returned to some of its former, if not glory, then original state. The fresh paint and clean upholstery did lighten up the old place, Dash had to admit. Once he had pulled down the horrible curtains and gotten rid of the pillow infestation and those stupid mirrors, it wasn't too bad really.

The rainstorm that had been brewing finally broke and the air turned sharply colder. Thunder and wind smashed and clashed around the old chimney, which channeled in the wuthering noises. Dash got some dry logs that had been sheltered on the back porch and started a fire. Madeleine had just returned wearing one of Dash's shirts over some old ballet warm-up pants when the lights went out.

Ivy called home to let Merit know that she was safe at Dash's house. It had taken him a while to answer the phone and she could hear all sorts of racket in the background, almost drowning out the storm. He sounded a bit out of breath.

"The boys and I are just practicing lacrosse shots."

Ivy closed her eyes. Oh well, the house couldn't possibly be in much more of a mess than it already was. A massive crash jarred her eyes open.

"What was that?"

The unmistakable sound of a receiver clattering onto the floor came over the line.

"Merit? Merit? Helloooo…"

"Hi Mom. How are you? Dad's um busy right now. He's um letting in some fresh air. But we're fine."

Merit called out something indistinct and annoyed.

"Dad says don't worry about us. Have a nice time. We'll send out for pizza. Bye!"

Ivy studied the silent phone and then the ceiling, which was also silent. The immense silence convinced her that Dash's wine selection needed immediate attention. She also had the feeling that he was not thrilled at the prospect of them investigating so this might take more careful handling, not a quality that she was known for, but tough toenails, this was a life or death situation.

59.   GARDENIA ARRIVES WITH THE COCKTAIL BUFFET DISH

"Tidying? Tidying? My foot! She was causing mischief that's what she was doing. Oh this explains so many things. Things missing and rearranged and in different places and gone and back again. Why Eunice accused me of taking their tacky vases! And all along it was this, this evil assistant Miss Sigman person moving things around and stealing no doubt. Flowerpots! The flowerpots are all gone! And I saw her, that very day too. I wonder if McKnight knows about these goings on. And more to the point: what about the police? This sounds like criminal behavior to me, stealing flowerpots. Murder would be just a step away."

Gardenia bustled around, artfully arranging the dishes and serving pieces. Madeleine had already set the table and Dash was filling the wine glasses with a nice white Burgundy. Eyeing the table critically and deciding that it passed "mustard" (as her darling little Worcester used to say), Gardenia graciously invited the others to sit down. She then gracefully placed the perfect amount of the Cocktail Buffet Dish on each plate and passed it along. The salad bowl made its own way around the table as did the warm rolls.

Gardenia continued her diatribe. "Those policemen obviously have no idea what they're doing – really – arresting you, Dash dear. Heck would never have arrested you. They should arrest that Miss Sigman person. Anyone who would tamper with garden club property would certainly be capable of murder. It's those out-of-town policemen. They never told me about her fingerprints on the shovel. They should let the locals handle it – the case that is, not the shovel. Although that policewoman didn't seem very effective and she ate all my ginger snaps and left before I could tell her everything!"

Grace tried to get a word in edgewise for the purpose of stemming the flow of Gardenia's observations, but Ivy got in first with the unfortunately encouraging, "What did you have to tell her?"

Grace could see Dash clenching his teeth, so she counterattacked with, "Oh Gardenia, this dish is just marvelous! Doesn't everyone think so?" which elicited enthusiastic and agreeing ums and oh yes – fabulouses and oh I want seconds, which for a while held off the onslaught.

The pretext had not been needed however because Gardenia's mind was roiling, positively roiling. Had it ever roiled before? Once or twice perhaps. She told herself to remain calm and look vague, something she excelled at; a master, one might say.

Everybody else had tucked in right away to the Cocktail Buffet Dish of creamy tender chicken with petit pois and baby carrots and the most beautifully formed little broccoli florets all swooning in some kind of heavenly brandy mushroom sauce with perfect ephemeral herbs and spices on a bed of wild rice. The butter rich rolls soaked up every last drop of the luscious gravy and equally complemented the tangy fresh salad of spring greens that were dressed with the lightest of French vinaigrettes.

The lights had come back on and Madeleine had turned on the classical radio station. Dash hoped that now maybe she wouldn't drop anything, although Philip Glass might be a problem. The gentle chatting, banter, laughter and reminiscences continued and Dash was quite enjoying himself. Perhaps because Gardenia had been oddly quiet for a while, which had allowed the coherent and interesting conversations to flourish.

Gardenia gazed at her cousin, his wife and their friends with confident gratification. People always praised and appreciated her cooking. She hadn't really eaten that much herself. She'd been thinking about what she had been going to tell the hefty policewoman. If only she'd known about the fingerprints! Then she would have told the officer about the argument between Eunice and that assistant person.

Noticing that Gardenia showed signs of getting cranked up again, Grace lifted her eyes at Ivy and tilted her head in the direction of the kitchen. They cleared the table, going back and forth, catching bits and pieces of Gardenia's monologue to Dash, while carrying everything out to the kitchen where Madeleine loaded the dishwasher with industrial efficiency.

"As I was saying, I never got a chance to tell that policewoman everything and she was asking me about the shovel and I was going to tell her how I cleaned it all up for you Dash dear, do you remember and Eloise Lutjens – you know the village hall receptionist – told me that she had heard Eunice yelling at that Miss Sigman person that very afternoon. And then the meeting started and she must have been there, that Miss Sigman person I mean. Did you see her Dash? The more I think about it, I think that I saw her there and then you know with Eunice shouting it was so terrible and I zipped out and drove so fast to get home but I had to go all the way around. That's another thing that's wrong with the mulch site: to get back home I have to turn left. Maybe you can fix that when you build those nice houses. Where was I? Oh, and Herbert was there and he didn't say a word about the flowerpots so

I went right to bed." Gardenia finally fizzled out when she saw Dash's head nodding toward his chest.

Heartened by the first really good food that he'd had in a long time, and mellowed by quite a lot of wine, Dash had been feeling much more optimistic about his chances of acquittal so he let Gardenia's puffy meanderings float over him. First thing in the morning, he'd call Heck and ask him about McKnight's assistant. What was Gardenia going on about? He was pretty sure that she had the name wrong. Gardenia so often got hold of the wrong end of the stick. Eunice yelling at Miss Sigman; now he was doing it. It wasn't Sigman it was Siggy Velveteen. No, that was some rabbit in a children's book. Dash yawned a real jawbreaker. First time he'd relaxed since he'd been arrested.

There wasn't much washing up really, since Gardenia had brought everything – just the cocktail buffet dish that had certainly been scraped nearly clean, the salad bowl and the wine glasses. Ivy washed and Grace dried while Madeleine drifted around humming and carefully swirling and pirouetting, but pausing every now and then to put the glasses away. The three of them plotted to go over to Cuppy's house in the morning. Ivy said that she would call him first to make sure that he was there.

Gardenia drove home in a deeply pensive mood. She would go over to the police station first thing in the morning and talk to Heck about that Miss Sigman person, but it would take careful planning. She would have to get her account of events absolutely right. Did she tell that policewoman who was recording it all that Herbert wasn't at home when she got there? Oh dear. Gardenia resolved to practice what she was going to say. Sometimes people did not take her seriously because she did blither so, but this was too important. She had to make sure that Dash was freed and that horrible Sigman woman was arrested. Once the police had Gardenia's testimony, they would understand the significance of those fingerprints. That would straighten things out!

60.   IVY GOES HOME TO THE BROKEN WINDOW

Merit was peeved. Merit was frequently peeved. Why the hell wasn't Ivy home to deal with the broken window? She was pretending to be a detective that's why. La-dee-dahing over there at Dash Lethaby's house. Having a nice dinner that Gardenia had made. I bet there was dessert too. The pizza had been okay, but pizza was becoming his only form of food these days. If Ivy didn't give up this investigating he might never eat a real meal again. What if she took it up professionally? There could not possibly be enough crime in Deer Creek to support such an enterprise. She was a really good cook when she took the time and he wanted her to take the time.

Lingo and Wooly started barking and ran to meet Ivy at the door. She'd been gone for months and months! They herded her into the kitchen and checked her into the boards of the cabinets. After patting them reassuringly for a while, Ivy flapped her hand in the direction of the window and said, "I'll call the hardware store first thing in the morning. They can fix anything. For right now, let's put one of those extra shelves in front of it."

Ivy soon had it propped up and fairly snug – certainly a decent solution. She was good at creative patching, using unorthodox methods to tape, glue, wire and shore up all manner of broken objects. They started out as temporary solutions but frequently just faded into long-term makeshift relics: the sofa with the brick under one leg, the fishing wire on the shower curtain, the heavy duty electrical tape around the sink pipe in the downstairs half bath. Merit would give the shelf over the window two weeks, then call the hardware store himself.

61. THE TROUBLE WITH FRENCH CANADIAN CASSEROLES

Cuppy carefully read Madeleine's beautiful handwriting – just as beautiful as she was. He loved good handwriting. Eunice had written in a rather crabbed backhand, tilting so far to the left that it was nearly horizontal.

Pre-heat oven to 350 degrees. Ho, ho, ho – he could do that. Remove lid – bingo. I'll just add a splash or two of brandy on top. Can't go wrong with brandy. Cuppy smugly put the casserole in the oven. Cooking holds no mysteries for me. He couldn't find the timer, but it was just now seven o'clock so he would remember when the 30 minutes were up. Cuppy poured himself a refreshing scotch and went off to take a shower.

Instead of taking a shower right away, Cuppy lay down on the bed for just a few minutes first. It had been a trying day and now it was a nightmare. Eunice was calling him, "CUPPYCOMEHERECUPPYCOMEHERE!" Cuppy sucked in some croaky slobber and pushed himself up. He shook his head groggily and peered around with half open eyes.

"CUPPYCOMEHERE!" This time it ended in a screech that made him leap off the bed. He could smell smoke and it was wafting into the room. Sort of a pine-appley scent, vaguely tropical, and that sounded like a parrot. He was in a smoky jungle. "CUPPYYYYYYY!!!" His foot was asleep, so he had half collapsed when he hit the floor. He clumped down the hall. The kitchen was on fire! He had to save Eunice! Pineappley? It was that #!%!***!@#$ French Canadian casserole! And that was Lulu, not Eunice! Eunice's parrot was in there calling him for help!

He could now hear fire sirens approaching, but he had to save Lulu. Before he had fallen asleep, he had been feeling bad about having shaken her around in her cage. Parrots were very sensitive and human-like. Smarter and nicer than a lot of humans too. Nicer than I am, he thought miserably. He had to save her!

Choking and clawing, Cuppy stumbled into the dense gray cloud in the kitchen, grabbed the cage and turned toward the kitchen door. Thick, enveloping smoke and flames billowed and swirled around him. A huge batch of papers (DWI reports that Eunice had pilfered from the village hall attic to mine for ammunition) puffed and whooped into jets of fire. The spilled birdseed was exploding like popcorn. Raging flames were blocking the kitchen door. Staggering with the covered cage, he reeled around, banged into the wall, rebounded into the hall and ran for all he was worth to the front door. He ripped it open and fell out onto the front porch. Hacking and snorting, he ran out into the weedy lawn with the still covered and now silent cage. Oh please don't let her be dead.

Fire engines stormed up the drive and everyone was swooping around with hoses. Hoses? He had a garage full of hoses! He could have put it out himself. Well, maybe not. How did the fire engines get here? Beatrice was running toward him clutching a watering can, water slopping over the sides. She must have called the fire department and was coming to save him with a watering can. Only a garden club member would think of that. He moaned at the idea of repaying those favors. If only she had let him burn to a crisp.

"Are you hurt?" asked Beatrice anxiously. The poor man must be in terrible pain.

The brave firemen swirled and shouted and flung hoses about in a water ballet of synchronized action. It was over quite soon really. The kitchen was partially burned but because it was mostly metal and stone the basic structure remained intact. It was the first time Cuppy was glad that he didn't have comfortable flammable chairs and curtains. One of the firemen pointed out that curtains are the worst culprits in terms of fire propellants. You couldn't get venetian blinds to burn if you wanted them to. And Cuppy did want them to, or he had.

Cuppy had left the covered birdcage where it was in the middle of the lawn. Now that the worst was over he approached it cautiously and slowly lifted the cover. A huge sad eye met his, but then the bird suddenly perked up in either happiness or relief at seeing him. "Are you okay Lulu?"

"CUPPYCUPPYCUPPY!"

Thank goodness! He sank down into the damp, scratchy weeds. First thing tomorrow, he'd call the parrot club and find somebody he could give Lulu to. Taking care of a large tropical bird was just too much of a burden. And Lulu had really loved Eunice. Probably the only one who ever had. She needed to live with people who understood her. Or maybe she could live at the zoo with lots of other parrots and they could sing parrot songs together or whatever it was parrots did.

Tropical bird almost became part of Tropical Spring Medley! Cuppy started to laugh, then hoot, then positively turn into a hyena. He fell back onto the sodden but prickly brown lawn and roared with laughter. But the heaving quickly turned to shaking sobs. A couple of the medical team guys ran over to calm him down. It was a completely normal reaction for someone who had just undergone such life wrenching catastrophes. "He must really love that parrot," commented one of the firemen.

Beatrice came over to Cuppy with a cup of tea.

"HAVVACUPPATEAHAVVACUPPATEA," screeched Lulu. Things were getting back to normal. The firemen were there quite a bit longer: rolling up hoses and stowing equipment, making sure all the embers were out. Two of them accompanied Cuppy back inside so he could get some essentials because he would have to move out for a while. The smoke smell was overpowering and particularly pungent, probably from the burning of Eunice's herbal teas. Cuppy offered the firemen the kink free hoses in his garage, but the well-known saga of their defective nature caused the firemen to diplomatically decline.

"Looks like the oven was set at 450 and the casserole must have been too full so it spilled over. Had a whole lot of liquor in it too."

"It was a French Canadian casserole," Cuppy explained. The Fire Chief gave him an odd look then told him, "That parrot probably saved your life."

In a wave of euphoria at being alive, Cuppy promised Lulu that he would keep her forever. How could he not? Maybe even get another parrot to keep her company. The garage was detached, hence smoke free. He would get rid of the kink free hoses and turn the whole garage into an aviary. If only he'd had the foresight to store the hoses in the kitchen.

Cuppy smiled at Lulu, who waggled trustingly back and forth on her perch at him.

"Lulu, I think this could be the beginning of a beautiful friendship."

62. *CUPPY AND LULU STAY WITH THE FREEMANTLES*

Pinckney was being so pleasant and welcoming. What the hell was the matter with her? McKnight had been the one to issue the invitation to Cuppy. He'd zoomed over there as soon as he was notified about the fire. The second after he had said that they'd be happy to have Cuppy as long as necessary, and the parrot too of course, he had a mental crisis about how Pinckney would react.

Au contraire: she was sweet and sympathetic and did not even quail at the sight of the parrot. She stroked the smoky parrot, even making parrot sort of noises at it. Why on earth do people do that? Lulu was looking around with great interest.

"Let's put her out in the Florida Room. She'll love it out there and ooh – look how well she goes with the tropical colors: that green is just transcendent!" Parrot as decorating accent. McKnight shook his brain. Did she mean the green of the room or the green of the parrot? Or maybe she meant iridescent? Translucent? As a novelist, McKnight harbored a fleet of words.

Having gotten the parrot settled with fresh water and a big dish of seeds, Pinckney led the way to the "Guest Wing." It was the original maid's room with attached bath and they had offered it to Valentine when she had first come to work for them but she had declined. Valentine shrewdly suspected that she would end up on call at all hours of the night and day if she lived in.

So Pinckney had declared it the "Guest Wing" and had decorated it to the eyeballs. The cascading result would have overwhelmed Marie Antoinette. Now she was fluttering around, asking Cuppy what he would like to drink, showing him where the towels were and how the byzantine apparatus of the foreign shower worked. She plumped up the pillows and got out an extra blanket. God, next thing she'd be tucking him in!

McKnight went off to get the drinks and as he neared the kitchen a high-pitched voice called out, "HEREBOYHEREBOYHEREBOY!" Ford and Field trotted past him into the Florida Room. He followed to see them standing expectantly in front of the parrot's cage, gazing up at it. Splat! Splat!

Both dogs recoiled, scraping and pawing at their muzzles. That goddamn parrot had spat seeds on them. He was going to kill it. "Ford! Field! C'mon." They sprang after him and he let them out the back door. Field started sneezing and sneezing, slamming his snoot onto the back steps and then into the lawn. Ford surged away happily into the darkness, malevolent parrot forgotten.

McKnight tromped back into the Florida Room to stare at the unrepentant bird. It would be feathers in the Florida Room if that parrot didn't watch out. Feathers In the Florida Room – what a great title. First book in The Parrot Murders series. Everyone who owned a parrot was being killed. Maybe that's why Eunice had been killed. Had the police considered that angle? Maybe he should call Heck.

Obviously, Cuppy loved the parrot. Perhaps he and Eunice had been vying for the parrot's affection. That might be motive. Although that parrot didn't look very affectionate to him. McKnight covered it up for the night, let the dogs in and poured himself another scotch.

63.   THE BATHOS OF FIRE

The first thing on the news the next morning was about the fire at Cuppy's house. That melodramatic young TV reporter Roman Messina was broadcasting live from the long since extinguished scene, decrying the pathos (or was it bathos?) of the terrible tragedy that had struck once again in the heart of this posh community, usually immune to the slings and arrows of outrageous fortune, but not immune to inheriting an outrageous fortune. Mr. Kingblade and his heroic parrot Lucy, who had saved his life, were said to be recuperating from smoke inhalation at an undisclosed (but soon to be ferreted out) private residence within the bucolic burg.

Grace was pretty sure that the parrot's name was Lulu not Lucy; but regardless, this obviously changed their plans about going over to Cuppy's house. She was wondering if 6:45 AM was too early to call Ivy when the phone rang.

"Grace – I knew you'd be up – are you watching the news?"

"Yes! Bucolic burg! But I just turned it on – have they said anything about what caused it?"

"Not that I've heard. Do you think that he might have been trying to kill himself?"

"Good heavens, that hadn't occurred to me. It seems like a very unreliable method. They said that the parrot saved his life."

"I heard that, but I thought the parrot's name was Lulu. Not that that has anything to do with saving him."

"No, true, but I thought it was Lulu too." There was a

bit of silence, then Grace said, "Well this certainly changes our plans for going over there, so I think that we ought to concentrate on McKnight's assistant. Why don't I call him at the village hall around nine?"

"Ha – do you think he gets in that early? Or up that early for that matter. I'd call him at home around eight. This is murder after all; and possibly arson!"

"Arson? Do you think that someone wants to kill both the Kingblades? Cuppy's fairly innocuous really. I can't imagine anyone having a motive to murder him; especially McKnight's assistant – would she even know him?"

"You know what Grace, I'm starting to get feeble echoes of last night. Now admittedly I wasn't listening to Gardenia because she is so terminally goofy and also admittedly I'd had a good bit of wine but she was saying something about Eunice yelling at that Miss Sigman person as she calls her and then something about the shovel. Do you remember any of that?"

"Oh dear, I wasn't paying attention either. I'll call her right after I try to reach McKnight."

"Rather you than me. Just let me know."

64. *PINCKNEY MAKES BREAKFAST*

Pinckney was up early and bustling around in the kitchen, mixing pancake batter then carefully folding blueberries into it, all while opening a package of sausages. McKnight aggrievedly appraised her enthusiastic energy.

She hadn't made blueberry pancakes and sausage for him in a really long time. Fresh coffee was brewing in the resurrected Mr. Coffee. The juicer was out and the big serrated knife was lying next to a heap of oranges. Where had all this stuff come from?

Pinckney turned toward him with a big smile. "Oh McKnight, good. Would you do the oranges please? I thought that Cuppy would need an extra good breakfast after his ordeal, so I got up early – you were sound asleep – and went to the market."

McKnight violently slashed open the oranges and begrudgingly squished them down on the reamer, which made perilous cracking noises.

"Be careful!"

A morose McKnight did not acknowledge Pinckney's warning. What about his own ordeal? Ordeal By Kimberley. What the hell was he going to do?

"Oh McKnight, you know what you can do?" Pinckney stopped to plop a blueberry into her mouth. Fibrillations threatened until calmed by her continuing with, "Take Cuppy a cup of coffee. Take Cuppy a cup! Oh how funny!"

"Hilarious," McKnight mumbled mentally. He clomped over to the "Guest Wing" taking care to slop some coffee into the saucer. He had put five sugar lumps and an unhealthy dollop of cream into it then stirred it with his finger. McKnight started considering what substances might disrupt a parrot's digestive system.

Cuppy woke up to pounding on the door: where was he? Oh yeah: the Freemantles. Boy this was a comfortable bed.

Although McKnight rather aggressively thrust the cup

of coffee at him, Cuppy accepted it gladly until he tasted it. McKnight stomped away so Cuppy stuck out his tongue – bleck – and put the cup down on the Louis the So-and-So bedside table.

Cuppy stretched, feeling surprisingly good and full of energy. He had another wonderful shower under the enormous rosette shower head, thinking of the thin spindly stream at home. This was like being under a waterfall. Not that he'd ever been under a waterfall. He'd had a shower last night to get rid of the smoky smell and had just reveled in the cascade. Those clothes were headed for the trash.

He got dressed in the stuff that he had grabbed out of his drawers and closet last night. Fortunately it had only a faint whiff of smoke, so he was able to follow the scent of coffee into the cheery bright kitchen.

"Oh Cuppy, how are you doing? Did you get a good night's sleep? Sit down right here and I'll get you some blueberry pancakes and sausages. First let me get you some fresh squeezed orange juice. And there you go, here's the syrup. Oh, what about coffee? Didn't McKnight bring you a cup?"

"Yes, yes he did. Thank you. Wow, this looks great, Pinckney! Thanks!"

"McKnight had to leave – to go to the office."

"Kind of early for him, isn't it? Oh, man, this orange juice is really good."

It had seeped into Pinckney's consciousness what might be making McKnight grumpy, which gave another little lift to her spirits. It was nonetheless a relief that he had left. Now she could have a nice little chat with Cuppy and find out more details about the murder and the fire.

Pinckney fixed herself a plate with a dime-sized pancake and half an inch of sausage. Sensing rightly that condolences might be awkward, she proceeded directly to her mission. "So Cuppy, are you going to sell the house?"

"You bet I am. As soon as possible. I'll move a few things out then sell the place as is."

Pinckney shuddered internally, thinking about that horrible beige house. Eunice hadn't had any decorating sense or ability at all. Her color palette had been brown and brownier. In fact, Eunice had never had anything going for her, really. Except the parrot of course. At least Lulu was decorative.

"Oh but you'll get a lot more for it if you redecorate it first. I can help you with that and Misty Tallois just got her real estate license and a divorce so she can list it for you."

"What, a divorce is a prerequisite for a career in real estate these days?"

"Oh Cuppy – you're so funny!"

So Misty Tallois was divorced. That was food for thought – rather tasty food at that. Maybe start off with a few little hors d'oeuvres? "Pinckney, I just want to get rid of the place. Maybe Misty could find me a small house to rent until I find what I want."

"What do you want?"

"I definitely do not want a big house. Just, you know, a small, traditional place. Eunice liked bare contemporary stuff. I want a nice old normal looking house with big, soft sofas that you can sink into with lots of needlepoint dog pillows and old leather chairs and warm heavy curtains in burgundy and hunter green and patterns with ducks on them and wallpaper with historic scenes."

That sure sounded like decorating to Pinckney. As to the house, Misty would bring him around. Small, old house indeed. Misty would skillfully demolish that notion, making it his own idea to buy the brand new four bedroom with a pool. And as for his ideas of decorating.... Pinckney smiled and poured him some more coffee. Oh there was so much to look forward to!

Cuppy leaned back in the comfy kitchen chair and sighed contentedly. He would leave Lulu with Pinckney who appreciated the parrot's artistic enhancement of the Florida Room. Then he would get a dog, a big furry one. "Here boys." Ford and Field trotted over to him and he patted them happily. Maybe he could sneak one of them into his room tonight and let him sleep on the bed! Oh there was so much to look forward to!

65.   *PHONE CALLS*

When Grace called the Freemantle's, she was surprised to learn that McKnight had already left for the office. Pinckney was even perkier and chattier than ever, told Grace all about the fire and that Cuppy was staying with them and the parrot matched the Florida Room and that she had made blueberry pancakes for breakfast. Grace was torn as to whether or not to say anything to Pinckney about the suspicion regarding Siggy/Monday. It might unduly alarm her and cause goodness knows what hysterics.

So she listened patiently a bit longer and was finally able to hang up.

An uncharacteristically grumpy McKnight answered his office phone. Pinckney's fussing over Cuppy had irritated him and now he'd had to answer the phone all by himself, Monday having evaporated off somewhere. "Either she's not here when you need her or she just suddenly beams up and scares you to death," crabbed McKnight.

"Well, actually it is good that she isn't there at the moment, because Ivy and I want to come over to talk to you about her some more."

That was the last thing that McKnight wanted to do, so he let out an exaggeratedly aggrieved sigh. "I'm afraid I'm all tied up this morning and I'll be out this afternoon. What more is there to say anyway? Monday's too much of a nothing to be anything."

Grace let him go and called Gardenia.

That morning, Gardenia had risen earlier than usual, so she was all showered and dressed before Herbert left for the office. She wanted plenty of time to rehearse what she was going to say to the police, but without Herbert there. He so often pooh-poohed her ideas or compared them to some situation in Monopoly and she just didn't feel like putting up with that this morning.

First things first, however, so Gardenia fortified herself with a comforting breakfast of a four minute soft boiled egg with toast soldiers. She could cleanly decapitate a soft boiled egg with a single blow of a sterling silver butter knife. Her outfit was commanding yet feminine: a grey pleated wool skirt, a ruffled white blouse and a smart looking navy blue jacket.

After reciting her lines and practicing her moves and expressions one more time, Gardenia regarded herself as ready for legal action. Onward to the police station! She would have Dash released from house arrest in time for a celebratory lunch at Shady Grove. She would just have to put the bridge group off. Then the stupid phone rang. Despite the seriousness of her mission, she was too conditioned to answering to just let it go.

"Good morning, Gardenia, this is Grace Mere calling. How are you?"

"Oh, fine thank you Grace. How are you?" No mission could stop the social niceties.

"Fine thanks. I just wanted to call to thank you for the lovely dinner that you provided last night."

"Oh my goodness, you're quite welcome. Wasn't it a fun evening? But really I am literally flying out the door to go see Chief Hequembourg about that Miss Sigman person's fingerprints because, you know, I told you last night, I cleaned the shovel right before I took it over there so she has to be the killer and not Dash who we all knew wasn't the killer anyway, except those out-of-town police. But now they can arrest her instead. So I'm afraid that I really must go Grace. Thank you so much for calling."

The click terminated what had to be the shortest phone conversation anyone had ever had with Gardenia. Grace excitedly called Ivy with this startling development and they arranged to meet at the police station.

🍂

66.   MERIT TAKES CHARGE

"Lethaby? Wilcoxen here. Merit Wilcoxen."

"Oh, hello Merit." Dash was a bit surprised at the phone call because he did not know Merit very well, Merit not having grown up in Deer Creek. Not sure where Ivy had found him. Up East probably – one of those tweedy New Englanders who ate clam chowder every day, and beans, lots of beans. No wonder he was such a windbag.

"Do you know what the girls are up to?"

Now this was a loaded question and lately Dash had become more and more careful with his mental processes and corresponding answers. He was certainly interested in knowing what particular girls were up to but he couldn't imagine what girls Merit Wilcoxen was talking about.

"Ah, what girls might those be?"

"Ivy and Grace, and now your Madeleine apparently." Merit sounded impatient. "Playing detective – damn foolhardy I call it. Can't have women running around looking for murderers. Too dangerous."

"For them or the murderers?" That had come out inadvertently.

"Now see here Lethaby."

You might feel differently if you were the one who'd been arrested bub. Dash managed to keep his mouth clamped shut this time. Last night he hadn't wanted Grace and Ivy prying into things because he figured that they would make it worse for him. He hadn't considered the danger aspect of it and a faint and temporary flush of shame bubbled up. Not that he was going to admit that to this self-righteous blowhard Wilcoxen who sounded as if he were auditioning for the role of Colonel of the Regiment.

"What do you suggest we do?" Dash threw back at him. If this guy couldn't control his wife, Dash certainly wasn't going to try. Ivy was a formidable gal and Wilcoxen shouldn't have married her if he couldn't keep her in check. Serve him right as a matter of fact.

"I told Ivy nothing doing. If we men stick together and all do that, then we can nip this in the bud."

Yeah right, pal. As of last night, it's already in full bloom. Dash stifled a snort and said, "What about Grace?"

"What do you mean?"

"Her husband's dead." Poor guy. At least he had been married to Grace for a couple of years. That would have been worthwhile. Olivier Mere had been a WWI poster incarnate, a poet or flying ace: boyish, impossibly handsome and doomed.

"Oh, right, right... hmmm," Wilcoxen humphed. Just like a woman to lose her husband. "Well, I'm sure she'll follow Ivy and Madeleine's lead."

"Good plan old boy. I'll tie Madeleine to the bed and that will free up the police to do their job by golly. Much obliged – got to go find some rope. Tally Ho."

Christ, what an idiot! Tally Ho – that'd be a good name for a dog. Tally, here Tally. Dash clumped the phone down, but brightened at the prospect of tying Mad to the bed. No need to mention Wilcoxen's phone call. Rope. Now where could he find some rope? There was the rope that they used to tie the Christmas tree onto the roof of the car but it was kind of rough and grubby. Hmm – ah ha! Those tie back things on the horrible curtains that Mad had put in the dining room. Thick, soft twisted gold twine with tassels. Perfecto! Now where the hell had he thrown them?

Cole helped him rummage around for a while, but to no avail. Feeling hungry, they went out into the kitchen, which was the cleanest they had seen it in months. Well, no wonder, with Ivy and Grace and Mad all thrashing around in it last night with soap and water and dish towels. Last night was coming back to him in more detail, as the alcohol leached out of his system and the early morning haze lifted.

Gardenia had said something about cleaning. She said that she'd cleaned the shovel before she brought it over to the mulch site. So, Dear God in Heaven! That woman had done it. She'd killed Eunice! Her prints got on there AFTER she had allegedly moved the shovel at the village hall and AFTER Gardenia had cleaned it.

Crazed with excitement, mind churning ferociously, looking for any fault in this theory he shouted, "Mad! Mad!!" Cole was excited too, so barking and bounding they thundered up the stairs to find Madeleine.

They burst into the bedroom only to find that the bed was made. In Dash's experience, a made bed was never a good sign. So they ran to the window, Cole putting his paws up on the scratched sill, just in time to see Madeleine pull out of the driveway in her Peugeot.

"Damn! Cole, we have to get over to the village hall. I'm going to get that woman myself. C'mon!"

They hurtled down the stairs, rampaged through the kitchen and out to the detached garage. He immediately realized he no longer had the jeep; it was still in the police impound. Fortunately, the police had missed another means of escape.

"Cole! The golf cart!"

Golf cart? Music to Cole's ears! Dash wanted him to get into a golf cart! Yippee! They chugged down the drive and out into the street. Barreling along! Speed! Freedom! Out into the main road, leaning forward to get the cart to go up the hill, whooshing down the hill, hurtling across the country club grounds, tearing right through foursomes, bumping out the other side; now just a bit more downhill to the village hall. They were in the home stretch to justice!

67. MERIT DOES SOMETHING CONSTRUCTIVE

Merit regarded the phone with a bit of amusement. Must say the fellow was taking his arrest in good spirit. Oh wait, maybe Lethaby WANTED the girls to investigate. He'd grasp at any straws or girls to prove his innocence. Although grasping at girls was not conducive to innocence. What a muddle life was!

Merit tried to think of something constructive to do. His eyes narrowed as he contemplated the lawn. The hoses! He'd take those goddamn kink free hoses to the dump. That would make it up to Ivy for telling her not to investigate the crime. He might even ask her to tie him to the bed. She could investigate something else.

The dump was in the old quarry. For a very reasonable annual fee, a Deer Creek resident could throw just about anything in there. Although one did not literally throw it in. One left whatever it was there, on view, so to speak – giving others the chance to scavenge or rescue – depending on your point of view.

After the item in question had sat there for a strikingly arbitrary length of time, Mungo and Reavis would either use it or sell it or give it the Old Heave Ho. The last was Reavis's favorite option, but it actually did not happen too often. As a result, there was still a lot of space left in the quarry, which guaranteed years of profitable non-use.

It was too difficult to coil up the hoses, so Merit dragged the roiling feet and feet and feet – good God how long were these stupid hoses? They were all dirty too. Man, he'd forgotten how bad these things were. Merit threw them down in disgust – disgust in the dust – that was a good phrase. He smacked his hands together up and down then wiped them on the sides of his trousers. Ivy would have to deal with the hoses and do something about these stains too.

Why on earth do people in general, and Ivy in particular, need to garden, he asked himself with superior irritation, when there were so many more pressing matters, like laundry and dinner? Maybe he would write a letter to the editor about it. Too bad he hadn't come up with that disgust in the dust line for his letter about the hoses. Maybe he could use it for one about the dump. The dump! Why hadn't that occurred to him? It was a perfect topic for a letter to the editor. Possibly more than one! Oh there was so much to look forward to!

68.   THE NEW SHOVEL

Clutching the brand new shovel, Gardenia surged into the police station only to find that Heck wasn't there. That hefty policewoman who had eaten all the ginger snaps was manning the phone and dispatch.

"Chief Hequembourg is out sick today."

"Oh dear, well, what about Olney?"

"He's out sick too. Yesterday an as yet unidentified assailant dropped off an anonymous casserole. The alleged casserole gave them food poisoning."

"Well this is a sorry state of affairs, I must say. How trying! Perhaps the police should not eat so much."

Gardenia marched out in a huff, thumping the handle of the shovel on the grubby linoleum. Maybe McKnight was in. She could tell him, as a rehearsal, and he could take immediate executive action to arrest the guilty party. Why that Miss Sigman person was probably the one who dropped off the poisoned casserole in order to hamper the police effort! Gardenia certainly wasn't going to trust that overweight young officer with this crucial information and insight.

Gardenia charged into the village hall and made a beeline for McKnight's office. Oh, but what if she ran into that Miss Sigman person? That would be horrifying. Gardenia swiveled her head around as far as it would go each way: no one in sight. Holding her breath and the shovel, she ducked in front of the counter in the reception area. Then using it as cover, she scuttled down the hall and peered around the corner. In a burst of speed Gardenia sprinted down the fifteen feet to McKnight's office, plunged in and slammed the door behind her.

Had his chair with the good lumbar support not been so deep, McKnight would probably have fallen out of it. As it was, Gardenia's unexpected and dramatic entrance pinned him into the dimpled leather with the g-force of an F-15 takeoff. He stared at her open-mouthed then managed, "What is going on?"

"McKnight, thank goodness I found you. You might be in danger. I might be in danger. All of us might be in danger. Oh, oh."

As if fearing for their lives, she locked the door behind her. "There! We should be safe enough although Chief Hequembourg has been poisoned just when I need him and a murderer is walking around free dropping off deadly casseroles while poor dear Dash languishes in prison."

McKnight was too stunned to point out that far from languishing in prison, Dash was at home under house arrest with Madeleine; a situation that undoubtedly did not include languishing. The other stuff was just too crackpot to take in.

"McKnight, I know that this will come as a shock but your assistant, that Miss Sigman person, she – she's the one who killed Eunice! I can prove it! And now she's trying to kill the police!"

With dropped jaw and stuck open eyes, McKnight goggled from a ringside seat as Gardenia's bravura performance went off without a hitch. Indeed, further inspiration came to her as she projected her lines to the person

in the back row. She was the lawyer for the defense in oratorical summation, dramatically brandishing the shovel.

"So, ladies and gentlemen of the jury, this incontro-
vertible evidence proves that my client, Dashiell Hammett
Lethaby is innocent and so must you find him!"

She brought the shovel down with a mighty bang on
McKnight's desk causing him to jump ten feet, and then
stared right into his face, breathing a bit heavily.

McKnight had been feeling increasingly alarmed as he
regarded this new Gardenia. She had somehow cast off
her usual vagueness and was being suspiciously coherent, even about the nutty poisoned casserole angle. The
blow to his desk caused his heart to ricochet around in his
chest. Fortunately, the pile of legal pads had protected the
custom milled mahogany from shovel damage. He tried
to collect himself so he could calm her and the ol' ticker
down.

"Well, Gardenia, that's a good point. About her fingerprints. Umm, do you mind taking that shovel off my
desk please? That she must have handled the shovel after
you took it to the mulch site. But what if she got hold
of it during the meeting? Just to move it or something.
Or dig something up – potatoes, I don't know. Umm yes,
you make a good point, but it doesn't really prove that
Dash DIDN'T do it. I mean theoretically, any of the three
of you could have done it. Or somebody else. Not that I
think so of course."

Gardenia sank into a chair and stared at him in be-
wilderment. What was the matter with him? The truth
was absolutely clear. Had she overdone it? Had she gotten
carried away into a different persona in her determination

to be believed? Why hadn't he immediately pounced into executive action and used his emergency powers as mayor to expedite the arrest of that Miss Sigman person?

McKnight just sat there staring back at her. The old gal had clearly gone round the bend. She thinks this is some kind of play and she has the lead role. She wants to be a heroine and has come up with this scenario in order to garner praise and admiration; be the center of congratulatory attention instead of that silly Gardenia who gets confused over a game of tic-tac-toe and can't even turn left.

In McKnight's opinion, the murderer was without doubt some outsider who had worn gloves or had burned his fingerprints off with acid. He had read about that somewhere – the acid thing – and planned to use it in his book. Grapefruit juice was supposed to work too. Then you could drink the evidence! Now how was he going to get rid of Gardenia without setting her off again? He was trying to figure that out when she jumped up and announced that she had to take the new shovel to the garden club closet. Rattled but relieved, McKnight made some positive noises about justice, then closed his office door behind her. Sheesh, what a relief. Could be time for a little nip of the Ol' Scotcheroo.

McKnight put the scotch bottle back in the drawer and sighed. Now what was he going to do? He picked up the receiver to call Heck but, oh that's right, he was out sick. He did not want to deal with Gardenia anymore and he did not want to be involved in the case. McKnight was more determined than ever that he had to get both garden clubs out of the village hall. Now how could he turn this situation to his own advantage? Monday – maybe this could lead up to a way of letting her go? Good thinking: very mayoral and politically savvy.

"Oh, there you are. Monday, listen, just a heads up: Gardenia St. Cyr was just in here with a crackpot theory. She says she cleaned the shovel before she took it to the mulch site so your fingerprints on it mean that you killed Mrs. Kingblade. Now, she is convinced that she is right, but that gal has always been mixed up and silly. So I wouldn't worry about it, but I thought that for the time being, you could take a leave of absence. You know, you do not want to cause disruption to the office of the mayor of Deer Creek. So until this matter is settled, you are requesting a leave of absence or we could even say you had tendered your resignation in light of pending litigation. Something like that. You'll know what to say. You always do."

While talking, McKnight had been rustling around with various legal pads of his novels. All this had given him a great idea and he wanted to get it down before he forgot it entirely or became confused. Plus he didn't want to look Monday in the eye. Her silence forced him to glance at her.

"What?" he said to Monday who was just standing there.

Siggy observed him from afar. So this was how he was going to get rid of her. That St. Cyr witch was going to accuse her of killing Eunice Kingblade, and McKnight wasn't going to do a thing about it. He wasn't going to defend her. He wasn't going to help her. Instead, he was going to use this as an excuse to fire her. Resignation! Over her dead body.

No one would believe her. They'd all believe Mrs. St. Cyr. She must be lying about the fingerprints to protect her stupid cousin Dash Lethaby and frame me, Sigismonday Vellacotton, that poor drab nobody, the mayor's assistant. Who cares about her? What motive could they attribute to me though? Lethaby had plenty of reasons to kill her; so did her husband. Kingblade could have done it; sneaked back to the mulch site. By now she was sure that Cuppy did not know who Kimberley was. It would have come out if he had. So no one would be able to fix a single motive on Siggy. With McKnight's assistance, she would not only be in the clear, she would wield more power than ever.

She had hung around that evening at the mulch site, wanting to keep an eye on things. She'd seen Lethaby brush Mrs. Kingblade with his car, but the old hag got right back up. By then, the only other one there was the one who would die, alone in the empty mulch site. She had walked away into the dusk under Siggy's malevolent gaze.

Dash Lethaby, Cuppy Kingblade, Gardenia St. Cyr: all those rich people stuck together. They would not believe that poor Siggy, which is what they were probably pityingly calling her, in a million years. They'd probably manufacture a motive too. But what about McKnight? The end of his telephone conversation, that she was too much of a nothing to be anything, had been loud and clear. To him she was a minion fit only for secretarial duties, scarcely human. She was going to change his opinion now. Use this to her advantage. What could she get McKnight to do for her now? She would make him defend her. This would test all her power over him and then increase that power beyond her wildest dreams. Siggy locked her eyes on his and slowly stalked toward him until she stood against the front of his desk.

"You have no idea what I have done for you."

She was so quiet that he had to lean forward a bit to hear her. Siggy could smell the scotch on his breath.

"I have done everything and more that you have asked me to do. I helped you with Kimberley, your illegitimate daughter. I never told a soul. I helped you with the media and the police. I made your lunch reservations. I wrote your speeches and press releases. I took your car to the car wash. I endured your wife's hatred of me. I tried to get rid of the garden clubs by mixing things up in their closets. I typed your book. I wrote some of your book. I went on and on – enduring, sacrificing, slaving, believing in you. Knowing that you really needed me and that you would never let me down, just as I would never let you down."

Siggy's voice had been slowly but inexorably getting more and more quiet, but the words came more quickly. Now they spewed forth in a hissing whisper: "Do you know what I did for you? Will you ever understand what I did and continue to do for you? If I killed her, I killed her for you. For you." Siggy was slowing down now but continued with deadly intensity. "She was going to tell Pinckney and everyone about Kimberley. That would have ended your political career and your place in society. You would have been ruined. You would never eat lunch at Shady Grove again."

"You owe me. You owe me big time. You're mine now. If you don't support me, I'll tell everyone about Kimberley.

You have the power to help ME for a change. You have power, McKnight. You're an important man. And with my help you'll be even more important. With me at your side, you'll move into higher and higher political office. That's what you want, isn't it?"

Siggy's voice was drifting away but her hypnotic hand swayed near his face like a cobra about to strike.

"All you have to do is say that we came back here to work late that night. You know I'm right. Do you believe me? Do you believe me, McKnight?" and ever so gently caressed his cheek.

Instead of the respect, gratitude and awe that she had expected to see, followed by a pledge of loyalty forever that she had fervently relied on hearing, McKnight's face sank and contracted in sickened horror and revulsion. He shriveled back into his chair. Was she going to kill him? If he hadn't been shaking so much, his hand would have fumbled for the scotch bottle; maybe he could hit her with it; or stab her with his engraved sterling silver Georg Jensen letter opener. McKnight scrabbled desperately at his stack of legal pads and flung them at her. That gave him a chance to wrench open the right-hand drawer and grab his antique Smith and Wesson revolver with the rosewood grips and wave it tremblingly in her direction. He couldn't remember whether or not it was loaded.

Siggy had gambled all and lost all. She quietly let herself out, clutching his car keys to her heart. She had to find Gardenia St. Cyr right away. That stupid fat rabbit was probably in the garden club closet. Siggy streamed silently along the corridor toward her prey. She wasn't going to let her get away with this.

McKnight stared mesmerized at Monday's departing back. He could now reach the scotch, but it was an almost full bottle of some really expensive triple malt, which he hated to waste by hurling it at her. So he fired the Smith and Wesson, which just clicked a disappointing empty. Bullets! There was a handful of them mixed in with the paper clips. He spilled the dish of them out all over his desk and frenziedly loaded two of them – bullets he made sure, not paper clips – into the chamber.

McKnight fired the two shots into the carved acorns and grape leaves on his custom milled old forest oak office door. His hand was a bit calmer now so he quickly loaded three more bullets, then fired, taking out the antique sconce to the right of the door, the umbrella stand to the left of the door and the telephone on his desk. Now he was out of ammo and couldn't even call the police. He was also out of luck if it rained. At least he hadn't shot the scotch.

69.   MELODY MCCULLOUGH
IN CHARGE AT LAST

Across the parking lot at the Police Department, some popping noises that sounded vaguely like pistols penetrated Melody McCullough's consciousness. But the idea of possible gunshots was so absurd that she dismissed the notion. Probably just Mungo clanking around with ladders or chain saws, or his crummy old pickup truck backfiring.

After handily getting rid of Parsnip Woman, Melody

McCullough had sprawled back triumphantly in the chair and interlaced her fingers behind her head. Yes sirree Bob, she liked being in charge. This was where the action was. She would get first crack at anything that came in: bank robberies, shootings, maybe even another murder! No more lousy assignments or bum steers from Heck or Olney; no more hoity toity Major Case Squad guys.

All she had to do was wait for the phone to ring or dispatch to light up. In the meantime, she could think about what she was going to wear that night for her date with Jeremy from Danny Boy Plumbing. It turned out that his name wasn't Frank or Matt. When his father Roger bought the business from brothers Frank and Matt Piper, it had come with a huge inventory of shirts embroidered with the names Frank and Matt. Seeing no need to waste good office supplies, Roger, Jeremy and the other two employees had been wearing the shirts for years and there were still dozens left.

Jeremy had said that he would stop by that morning. Melody craned her neck to spy out the window, hoping to spot him, but instead, the Mayor's car zoomed out of the parking lot going about a hundred miles an hour! It must have been stolen! She hastily dialed his direct line but nothing happened. His phone must have been sabotaged. What if he'd been kidnapped or killed? Mayor Freemantle never drove that fast.

Melody McCullough sprang into action. She ran out the door of the police station and ploughed smack dab into Jeremy. It was true love indeed, as they dazedly fell into a golf cart that some nut had left parked there.

70. THAT MISS SIGMAN PERSON

Yes, Gardenia told herself, she had overdone it with McKnight. But that was all right. That is what rehearsals are for she told herself stoutly. Find out what works and what doesn't. Her presentation to Chief Hequembourg would be a return to her usual self. In the meantime, she was going to nip over to the garden club closet to figure out where to put the new shovel. The sooner the better, to get it all behind her so that both garden clubs could move on. The shovel wasn't engraved yet but she would take care of that later. She needed to come up with a suitable inscription, something more than just the name of the club. Dedicated in memory of Eunice? No, no, maybe not.

Oh the new shovel was just lovely. So much better than the old one. Ugh. She did not want to think about what had happened with the old one. Gardenia hummed the new song that they were practicing in bell choir. Everyone would enjoy it so much more without Eunice there to criticize every ding and dong and glang and glung.

Humming and even trilling, Gardenia surveyed the newly decorated Garden Club of St. James's closet, which was now referred to as the Duchess of Windsor Suite. She did not understand why Ivy Wilcoxen found that so hilarious. But where best to display the shovel? Did the décor really do it justice? What would the Duchess of Windsor have done? Had she even been a member of a garden club?

The old shovel had just been sort of tossed in a corner

or shoved under the sofa. Shoved – that was appropriate for a shovel. Maybe she could have a nice shovel holder made. Gardenia was sure that the hardware store could come up with something along the lines of a gun rack, perhaps. Dash could advise them on gun racks.

In the meantime however... on top of the desk? Or leaning against it? Gardenia continued to gaze around speculatively. She had only partially closed the door. Ooh – what about behind the door? That might work. She pushed the door all the way shut and leaned the shovel against the wall. It teetered in a fairly stable manner and would probably be fine until she could get the holder installed. That was settled then.

By now McKnight would have called Heck and they would have arrested that Miss Sigman person. Oh but that's right: Heck is sick. Maybe she just better leave right away. Were those some kind of bangs going off?

Gardenia pulled the door open to find that Miss Sigman person standing right in front of her. "Oh, there you are!" Somehow the woman just appeared out of the blue. "Uh, uh, I was going to um leave now. Just just wanted to drop off the shovel."

Through the low-lying nimbus cloud that surrounded the stupid fat rabbit, Siggy's sight locked onto her prey. The word "shovel" echoed and reverberated in the small room. It pulsed and contracted, in and out of this pale cloud, in and out just like breathing. Breathing. Keep breathing. What was she saying? The cloud's voice came from so far away. Shovel shovel shovel.... A woman in white, clenching and unclenching tiny fists, little bitty hands, can't span an octave, can't reach around....

"Miss Sigman, Miss Sigman, are you all right?" Gardenia questioned with alarm as she tried to interpret the creepy woman's body language. It whispered illness, catatonia and threat. What if, Gardenia choked with a labored intake of air, oh no, McKnight could have told that Miss Sigman person about Gardenia's fingerprint testimony. That's why the woman, an accused murderer was here. She was going to make Gardenia the next victim!

Siggy shook her head and the skies cleared. She continued to stare at the stupid fat rabbit, mesmerizing it with snakelike intensity. Gardenia came into focus and Siggy fixed her python eyes upon her.

"Well, hrr, hnnn." A few nervous murmurs came out of Gardenia's mouth. She gathered herself up. "What a coincidence! I was just thinking about you. I wondered if you might be able to help me with something." She had to keep talking, make the woman stay here until the police could arrest her. Maybe McKnight had called that hefty young woman officer.

Gardenia stopped again. The woman hadn't moved from the doorway and Gardenia was starting to feel kind of trapped. Her breathing picked up and she motioned for Siggy to come into the room. "You see I just bought a new shovel for the Garden Club of St. James." Gardenia pulled the door out a bit from the wall so she could reach in and grab the shovel. "The old one – well we know what happened to the old one and the police have it now and we would never want it back anyway, but the new one needs to hang somewhere or have a special place and I thought that you would know about those sorts of things – hardware and hooks and and things...."

Gardenia found it difficult to swallow because she was so terribly thirsty. Her mouth was so dry. She held the shovel out toward the blank faced woman to show her.

"It's the same kind as the old one but it doesn't have the inscription on it yet." It was so odd. The woman wasn't even looking at the shovel.

"And, and it is so nice and new. Although the old one looked just as nice after I polished it up for Dash's presentation. It was rather dirty and grubby so I took it home and hosed it off and then cleaned it thoroughly with Murphy's oil. Uh, were you there? I didn't see you."

So it was true. The stupid fat rabbit was claiming that she had cleaned the shovel after she left the village hall, meaning that the only way that Siggy's fingerprints could be on it were if she had used it at the mulch site. Siggy's eyes flickered and darkened, closed and opened. May as well put her fingerprints on this one as well. Her small hands reached for the shining scepter. The tunnel was getting darker and smaller and filled with echoes. So full of echoes there was barely any other room. The echoes flew like bats and tore at her hair. McKnight. She had done so much for him and she had told him so – you will never know what I have done for you. How ironic was that. She would kill them, she would kill them all starting with this stupid fat rabbit. But the rabbit was facing her with binocular eyes. The witch had been walking away. Her mother had been asleep.

In slow motion and through a cloud, Siggy closed the door and reached for the shovel. Gardenia clutched it ever tighter and higher with shaking arms. Summoning inner power, she could do anything if she had to. The door flew open and slammed her, shrieking, into the wall. Dash and Cole catapulted into the Duchess of Windsor Suite. The full horror of the decoration hit Dash right before the shovel did. It was a glancing blow to the ribs that knocked him into the sideboard covered with empty wine bottles. Some fell off and broke into jagged projectiles. Grabbing one in each hand, Dash swung around and launched the rockets simultaneously. They smashed against the frame of the open door. Gardenia was still screaming.

"Dash, Dash, are you all right? I was trying to hit her not you oh oh oh...." In a full faint, Gardenia slipped gracefully to the floor right on top of Cole.

Dash scrambled over to heave her off Cole just as Grace and Ivy raced in and banged him with the door.

Siggy was gone. She cut her ties with earth. She was striding down the echoing halls of Valhalla. Her heels grew wings of speed and purpose. Swiftly through the building and out the back door. She had McKnight's car keys in her hand. More fingerprints. It didn't matter. Nothing mattered now. McKnight did not love her, did not even respect her, after all she had done for him. Oh the smooth purring ride that went faster and faster toward the concrete walls of the highway overpass. She hadn't put on her seat belt. There was no need. Siggy had always been so good at knowing what to do.

71.   *JUST STAY HOME*

The sickening and ghastly wreck was only a few hundred yards from where Eunice had died. McKnight was absolutely grief stricken. "If she was going to take her own life, why couldn't she take her own car?" Blueberry Rampant: his beautiful, classic dark blue Jaguar with the deep maroon custom leather interior was totaled. Not even the Leaper hood ornament that he'd had to special order was salvageable.

McKnight may have sounded like a horrible person, but he was only talking to Pinckney and he figured (correctly) that she agreed with him. "At least now I won't have the unpleasantness of having to fire her," he told Pinckney. A tiny bit of conscience niggled at him for thinking of his assistant's death so coldly, but not for long. After all, Monday hadn't just murdered Eunice, she had wrecked his car. The Major Case Squad had investigated her past some more. Some years ago, she had been suspected of killing her mother by suffocating her with a pillow, but the evidence was inconclusive. Well, this time it wasn't!

McKnight had hoped to finish his book before he set off on the campaign trail. But it was not to be. Monday wasn't there to type it anymore. He had found the part that she had written, Tuesday's Story, which wasn't half bad so he could use it somewhere, be really poignant. He had also found these other parts that he did not even remember writing. They showed a true evolution of style and some were fairly lengthy. Maybe he could continue to work on several novels while they were riding around in that campaign bus. What else did one do in a bus? Maybe they could sing songs! "The answer my friend is blowing in the wind...." That would be fun. He might even work it into one of his books.

Roman Messina, the recently fired news reporter would be handling the publicity. His TV station had uncovered the fact that he had been somewhat lax in terms of investigative reporting, frequently fabricating his own information and injecting his own conclusions. What a piece of luck: that was exactly what you needed in a political campaign P.R. guy!

McKnight had come up with his campaign slogan all by himself: "Just Stay Home." If people would just stay home more often, there would be less crime because the few criminals who didn't stay home would have fewer opportunities to burgle because the homeowners were home. And the roads wouldn't wear out so fast and develop potholes. And people would save money and fix up their houses. What about jobs though? How would "Just Stay Home" create jobs? He'd sic Roman on that one. Roman was proving very resourceful and indeed he solved the jobs issue with the snappy rejoinder "Because."

Kimberley would be taking care of all the practical stuff and logistics. It wasn't fashion or modeling, but the extremely generous wardrobe budget more than made up for it. Oh – maybe she could type his book. Pinckney was in charge of refreshments and decorating the interior of the bus. He must say, Pinckney had really stepped up to the silver plate – a real trooper – and he was positive that she didn't suspect a thing about Kimberley. Oh there was so much to look forward to!

72.   *PINCKNEY DRINKS AND THINKS*

Pinckney hauled the bottle of champagne out of the freezer. She had just slammed it in there but she couldn't wait for it to chill properly. Her fingers shook as she crookedly tore off the foil and wrestled with that wire thingy. It was called a cage or hood or something, something French. There was always something French. An article in the New York Times a while back showed how to make these cute little chairs out of champagne wires and those metal caps that were on top of the cork. Pinckney had fashioned quite a few (sure beat garden club workshops), but she didn't care about that now.

She usually held a tea towel over it but this time the cork rocketed out of the bottle and champagne frothed all down the side. She just poured madly anyway and the champagne overflowed the classic Baccarat flute. Gulping mostly fizz down the wrong pipe, Pinckney hacked and coughed for a while. By then the bubbles had subsided and she could take a really good swig.

Clutching the wet and sticky bottle and glass, Pinckney forlornly slumped out into the Florida Room and onto the sofa with the botanically correct tropical vegetation upholstery. Numb and exhausted, she just wanted to go to sleep. Lulu sighed sympathetically while she shuffled back and forth from claw to claw on the yellow groove bamboo perch in her new Palladian Parrot Palace.

As soon as Pinckney had met Kimberley, the

resemblance to someone puzzled her. The girl projected some vague familiarity. Then a shaft of sunlight had hit their profiles – Kimberley's and McKnight's – at just the right angle when they were looking at some papers together. The truth hit Pinckney like a New Year's Day hangover. She was going to be sick. Not that that was unusual, but it was always the morning-after, which was every morning these days and now here it was the afternoon. She suffered from morning-, noon- and night-after.

McKnight's recent brush with death while holding a killer at gunpoint had shaken Pinckney to her bone marrow. It made her realize that she would have been devastated to lose him. He really was a dear man and so unexpectedly brave and he had put up with a lot of her moods lately. But how was she going to deal with the Kimberley situation? Surely other people would eventually notice the resemblance and then you know how the old gossip machine would start cranking away.

"REALLYMCKNIGHTREALLYMCKNIGHT REALLYMCKNIGHT"

Lulu's new phrase startled Pinckney. Did she really say that often enough for the parrot to learn it? Well, obviously! How sad. The only person to ever quote her would be a parrot. "Oh Lulu. What am I going to do?" Lulu ruffled some feathers in reply. "Maybe I could learn to medicate like those Buddha people humming in India." Pinckney's tears plopped into her empty champagne glass.

After a few more refills, she stopped crying and began to strategize. How could she let McKnight know that she had discovered his secret without exactly saying so? Teach Lulu to say something? No, that was a bad idea.

She listlessly ruffled the pile of curly edged legal pads that McKnight had left on the rattan woven wicker coffee table with bamboo edging in refined cinnamon veneer. All this stuff was more of his silly book that she'd been reading when he wasn't there. He had never found that out, but by golly he was going to find out about her knowing about Kimberley. Maybe she could achieve two stones with one bird. Looking at Lulu for inspiration, Pinckney picked up the gold Montblanc fountain pen.

PINKERTON THE
CHIC SENATOR'S WIFE

Looking into the Rococo Mirror, the Italian marble fireplace mantle flamed with flaming flames and they rose up the chimney when Pinkerton checked her lipstick in it. For a well dressed Senator's wife with all the right accessories including a Kelly bag this was worse than when he walked on the Louis XVVIIII (replica but a good one) parquet floor with golf shoes on it! Now everybody would know about the illegitimate Senator McKay's daughter Katherine when he was her husband at the same time too but earlier! Pinkerton looked at her parrot Pooh Bear. Pooh Bear the parrot looked at her. She looked at Pooh Bear and sighed. Pooh Bear sighed too. (No wonder people got bored with books.)

What could Pinkerton do? Mend all

those ripped bodices that were hanging in the closet? No! She had a maid for that! She had two maids for that! So why weren't those bodices fixed by now? Yes! This would do it! She would start her own interior decorating color line! Holding a glass of champagne, the paint chips were all stupid colors like "Ulcer" and "Detergent! "No! No! No!" said Pinkerton triumphantly the chic Senator's wife with expression in the South of France. She would have colors like "Yacht" and "Pilates!"

Pinckney slapped the pen down on the coffee table. "There Lulu! That'll show McKnight. He isn't the only writer in the family and my story has a subclinical message too. I just hope he gets it." Pinckney frowned. She thought she meant subclinical – isn't that when you don't know what you're reading but your mind does? McKnight wasn't too good at subtle. "What do you think Lulu?"

"REALLYMCKNIGHTREALLYMCKNIGHT REALLYMCKNIGHT"

Neither was Lulu.

73. *TIME TO HANG UP THE SHOVEL*

It was several days after that poor Miss Sigman person died in McKnight's car. So tragic. But he could buy another car. Maybe a black one this time for a change from dark blue. Gardenia purred as she carefully placed the new shovel on the burnished bronze antique rifle rack that Dash had donated to the garden club. Maybe Father Wedgewood could come and bless it; sort of like the blessing of the eggnog that Mr. Savage the Episcopal minister did at Christmas but more formal. Catholics were so ceremonial, so good at pageantry. Maybe they could even have incense!

Mungo had put the rifle rack up that morning on the wall right behind the desk in the Garden Club of St. James's closet. It went admirably with the décor in the Duchess of Windsor Suite and Gardenia contemplated it with satisfaction. So nice and clean. Just like the old shovel had been, right before she took it over to the presentation. Well, it had been clean, but when she came out of the village hall ladies' room who was holding it but that awful Miss Sigman person. Gardenia had needed to get to the mulch site right away and hadn't had time to wipe it off again.

Everything had turned out so well. All for the best as people say. With Eunice gone, the Deer Creek Garden Club would elect a new President: someone with whom Gardenia could work in a friendly and dignified fashion. Grace Mere would be ideal, but Gardenia doubted that she would accept the nomination. She was so reserved and distant, not to mention going to Europe. Ivy would be a disaster: acerbic and opinionated, but she didn't think that Ivy would want the job either because she would regard it as too much bother. Beatrice Plumpting would be malleable but not much help. Well, anyone would be better than Eunice.

Or, or what about this? Could she suggest merging the two clubs? Consolidating her benevolent sphere of influence? Oh the good she could do! The civic improvements she could achieve! Now THERE was a Worthy Cause. Eunice could never have envisioned such a brilliant scenario. Oh there was so much to look forward to!

74.   GARDENIA TURNS LEFT

The most astonishing thing that had come out of all of this to-doing about Eunice was that Gardenia could now turn left. She was so proud of her courage that night of Dash's presentation at the mulch site. Eunice's accusations and insults had made it so terrible and nightmarish that she was desperate to get home. She tore away to the left, barely keeping the car on the road, but she had done it! She had done it! Then right, but still wildly. By going this way she had two more left turns to make. On the verge of hyperventilating, trembling hands trying to hang on to the steering wheel, legs shaking so much that they were slamming together, she was barely in the correct lane. Another left opposite Shady Grove. Now only one more to go. Yes! Whirling round the bend came the easy right to Home and Safety! Although she did run into the flowerpots in the garage, she had made it nonetheless. She had done it. She had done it. Victory!

Flailing herself out of the car, Gardenia staggered

into the house that night to find a fortifying drink and found Herbert instead. He was supposed to be out at a Monopoly tournament and he started up in surprise as she collapsed in.

"What happened to you?" His stately, composed Gardenia was the worse for wear.

"I, oh, Herbert, I turned left. I turned left. Because of Eunice. It was horrible just horrible. I had to get home as fast as possible so I turned left. Eunice... Eunice... it was so awful."

"She was so awful you turned left? Staggering. For God's sake, Gardenia, I am sick of hearing about Eunice. Hey, but if you can turn left now, she did you a good turn, heh heh. Good turn, get it?"

Other than this newfound ability to turn left, Gardenia had always suffered from Eunice's thunderbolts of scorn. Gardenia's complaints about her over the years had worn a rut in Herbert's mind. Boo hoo, Eunice said my bell ringing was out of tune and I came in at the wrong time. Eunice stole the garden club funds and bought kink free hoses. Eunice invaded the park. Eunice threatened Dash with a lawsuit to stop his development. Gardenia's explanation of the most recent atrocity went billowing over his head and beyond.

"And she called me a traitor. And now the flowerpots in the garage are broken."

"What? What on earth does Eunice have to do with flowerpots in the garage? You blame her for everything." Gardenia's voice hovered in the air but he no longer listened to it. Here he had envisioned a quiet evening alone so he could concentrate on Monopoly strategy.

"Just ignore her. Blast: Community Chest!" Herbert stabbed the battleship into the board.

"You always say that!"

"Community Chest?"

"Oh you know what I mean."

"Well, what else are you going to do? Kill the stupid woman? Eunicethasia – heh heh. She's been obnoxious since birth. It's a congenital defect."

"I'm going up to take a bath," Gardenia sniffed more wildly than usual and reeled up the stairs.

Unusually for Herbert's powers of observation, he perceived that she needed one actually. There was brown junk on her dress. Leaves or something. Oh, mulch obviously but something else too.

Herbert passed Go for $200 and landed on Baltic. Blast!

Upstairs in her bedroom with en suite bathroom, Gardenia's shaking hands fumbled through the medicine cabinet. Where were those sedatives that she used when she had to get on an airplane? Oh thank goodness, here they were. In a frenzy she struggled with the stupid child (and adult) proof lid, finally almost ripping it off. She considered going back downstairs for a bottle of scotch but gulped down four pills with the emergency bottle of sherry that she kept in her bedside cabinet, then turned on the bathtub faucets.

Gardenia wildly poured Arabian Nights Attar of Roses bubble bath into the raging torrent then tore off her clothes and threw them onto the floor. Oh she just wanted to be clean and relaxed, clean and relaxed, clean and relaxed. The events of the evening kept swirling around her, like bath water going down the drain, until the darkness of sleep fell.

When Herbert came up some time later, Gardenia was already in bed and sound asleep. The bathroom floor had water and her mulch infested dirty clothes all over it. There was something else on them too, sort of like blood actually. He hoped that she hadn't cut herself on some garden implement that was simply teeming with tetanus. Mulch piles were filled with dangerous germs and diseases. Heaps of soggy towels surrounded the ruined and possibly verminous garments. Herbert was an indoor man himself and regarded the distressing scene with exasperation.

This was unprecedented for his Gardenia. Clearly Eunice had upset her more than usual. Regret stabbed Herbert momentarily for not being more sympathetic but that pang might be due to the lack of dinner. He had been waiting for Gardenia to come back down. Well, now he would help by getting one of those big, black, tough plastic bags, stuffing the whole mess into it and chucking it out. Heck of a lot easier than hauling it down to the laundry room, and he wasn't about to run the washing machine. Herbert and sympathy had their limits. He didn't know how it worked anyway.

The trash men were coming tomorrow and Gardenia had a million outfits and towels. She'd never miss these. Plus, with her asleep, he could order pizza and continue with his devious multipronged Monopoly strategy. Back at the gaming table at last, Herbert rolled double threes and landed the Scottie on Park Place, giving him the monopoly. Yippee! Just wait 'til the next tournament! Oh there was so much to look forward to!

75.   TROPICAL SPRING MADLEY

Madeleine crashed into the kitchen to make Dash "Tropical Spring Medley" for dinner even though the casserole had been the cause of Cuppy's house fire, as he'd gone around telling everyone. That ungrateful liar. The big dope had caused the fire himself by not knowing how to turn on an oven and soaking the whole kitchen with brandy like an arsonist with gasoline. Well, SHE would do it right. You just had to follow organizing principles, even in marriage she had learned.

Oh organized married life was so wonderful. That had been the problem before: Dash was naturally disorganized. That judge had certainly seen that right away. Why hadn't she? Did she lack depth or insight or wisdom? Well, she had them now to some extent at least, so she would not let emotion take over from organization. To organize also meant to simplify, to streamline, to cut down to the bare bones, although perhaps that was not a very good formula for something tempting to eat. Too bad.

This time she would leave out the onions and carrots and celery. It was just too time consuming to cut them into those itty bitty pieces. Or she could put them in whole. Hmm… that might work. No, she had to stick to organization and efficiency. She'd use just the chicken and the pineapple. The béchamel was too much trouble too. It was easy to throw in lots of thyme and oregano, which came in those handy little jars all ready to go. That didn't look like very much food though so she put several cups of rice around the chicken. That made it tidy and rice was supposed to suck up the juices so she'd just pour in a lot of wine. Dash would like that.

In a couple of weeks they were going to celebrate Dash's freedom with a fabulous dinner party for their friends Chez Lethaby. This attempt for Dash would be the trial run for the improved version of the casserole. She would organize that recipe, Dash and his office too. Dash would soon realize what fun it was to be organized. Oh there was so much to look forward to!

76.   *MUNGO AND REAVIS (NOT TO MENTION FORD AND FIELD)*

At first, the job of having to move the mulch that Eunice had been found in was just too repulsive to think about. Where could he possibly put it anyway? Nobody would want it in their garden. Why the police hadn't confiscated it as evidence was a mystery to him.

Mungo stood there for a while, staring at the mulch pile and hoping that inspiration would strike. It didn't but another realization did. There was a lot less mulch than there used to be. He had been so busy bringing the marijuana plants back from the Department of Public Works and then planting some of them in the village flowerpots, that the absence just hadn't registered.

"Hey Mungo!"

It was Reavis with a wheelbarrow and a pitchfork.

"I replanted the rest of the marijuana plants and now I'm mulching them."

"Reavis: you are a genius man; a real genius."

Reavis beamed at him like a tropical sun.

"No I'm not. I'm the Happy Man and His Wheelbarrow!"

Mungo laughed and clapped Reavis on the back then went to look for a shovel. It would be a bumper crop this year. Oh there was so much to look forward to!

Right before Mommy and Daddy left for months and months, Ford and Field had accompanied them to the door in the mud room that opened out into the garage. "Be good doggies! Guard the house!" After the door clicked shut, they listened carefully, ears cocked. That was the garage door rumbling open, that was the new car starting, that was the grinding and thump of the garage door closing.

With the coast clear, they trotted into the Florida Room to observe that seed-spitting, smugly un-retrievable parrot. Good Mommy had tied a helpful fluffy thing to the bottom of the bird cage. Field approached cautiously, grabbed the tassel and pulled the cage as far back as he could, gave it a good shake, then let it go."REALLYMCK NIGHTREALLYMCKNIGHTREALLYMCKNIGHT"

77.   COCKTAILS

Madeleine and Dash Lethaby gazed happily around the front hall, waiting for their friends to arrive for the dinner party. Madeleine had wanted to cook the dinner but after the "Tropical Spring Madley" (as Dash privately called it) fiasco, both flammable and digestive, Dash had diplomatically suggested caterers so she wouldn't have to work so hard and could really enjoy the evening. Cooking just was not one of her attributes. That was a shame, but at least she wasn't one of those maniacal real estate selling, interior decorating females needlepointing belts and pillows all over the place, leaving sharp objects in the sofa. What a relief!

The doorbell rang and friends swept through the front hall and into the living room. Full glasses clinked, were emptied and filled again. The laughter and chatter of ten people ebbed and swelled, a tide of happy conversation. Cole greeted everyone rapturously, huffing and puffing, and thumping his tail around.

"Three hotels on North Carolina – I couldn't lose! Heh, heh."

"It's so exciting. Dash and I are going to work together on rebuilding the company. And, I haven't told him this yet, but I signed up for a real estate course and an interior decorating certificate program."

"My most recent letter to the editor was about Deer Creek citizens who leave their trash cans out overnight."

"Now that I have a Professional Digger – hello Cole – I'll be able to plant so many more vegetables. I'm thinking about grape vines too because Merit likes wine."

Dash stopped himself from saying that it would do Merit good to get out there and do the digging himself. "What's a Professional Digger?"

"Grace's dog Parsley. He's going to stay with us while Grace is in Europe with her mother. He's a terrier and they dig all over the place, halfway to China. Quite impresses the Newfies. Hope they don't get any ideas. All right Cole, that's enough."

"Oh Dash dear what lovely champagne and Pinckney likes it so much. I'll just take the bottle over to her so we can have a little chat."

"Gardenia, you have saved my life! Here, I'll take the bottle. When are we going to tell everyone the truth about the Duchess of Windsor Suite?"

"Shhsh dear, I was thinking at dinner you could make a toast and announce it. Have you heard that Dash gave all the stuff that dear Madeleine so naively put up to the Deer Creek Garden Club so they can redecorate their closet, not that it will be on a par with ours, of course, but an improvement nonetheless. Those mortifying curtains, she called them drapes, can you imagine?"

"Ha! So that's where those curtains came from and those puffy chairs. How's it all going to fit? You can barely get in the door. Liked the old beat-up stuff myself. And what happened to all the flowerpots?"

"Oh really, Ivy! Excuse me, I need some more champagne."

"I've finally realized that it's time to send all of Olivier's travel notebooks to his agent."

"Agent? You mean book agent?"

"Yes, McKnight, why?"

"Because… I have to make sure she doesn't hear me… because I just found out that Pinckney is writing a book! It needs tweaking of course, but as a novelist, I can help her with that."

"Well, how exciting, but why don't you want her to hear you?"

"Because I think she's keeping it a secret until it's farther along – I just happened to come across part of it right before we came over here tonight. So Grace don't say anything, but do you think your agent could take a look at it?"

"So I told her, Misty, the only thing that I am going to do to the house before it goes on the market is get rid of the kink free hoses in the garage."

"Whoa, you mean Misty Tallois?"

"The one and lonely. Talk about great real estate. Well, I'm going to go hit the bar. Want another one, Merit?"

"And bell ringing practice starts next week with the new music director who will be lovely I'm sure and without poor Eunice we will ring in harmony you know how trying she could be Cole stop that."

"Of course we realize that it will be impossible to go ahead with the development of the mulch site. Nobody will want to live on top of where a murder took place. Looks like Eunice got her way after all. So Mad and I are going to restructure the business and look around for other properties. Right, Cole?"

"Why don't you buy my place and tear it down? The fire really made it not worth rehabbing and I'm pretty sure the lot's big enough for two houses. I know it's small potatoes compared to the mulch site but what the hey? Misty Tallois's got the listing."

"Talk about great real estate."

"Oh Merit, calm down. I only agreed to take the position of interim President of the garden club if the new President is in place before Christmas – so I don't have to buy a sweater. You're the one who told me to take the whole job – remember? Right before Eunice died?"

"Well, yes but at the time I had no idea what was involved – what a time consuming trap it could be – taking away from our home life."

"Oh nonsense. Yes, Cole, I see you. Dash what do you think? Do you think that Madeleine would like to join the garden club? After your generous donation of furnishings, I think that the least the club can do is to invite her."

"What I think Ivy is that you need another drink. You too, Merit. What'll you have?"

"Pinckney! How's Lulu doing? I really miss the old bird – even all that screeching."

"Do you think he's referring to Eunice? Heh heh."

"Be quiet Herbert you never know how he may be feeling the poor man so bereft and left with all those kink free hoses too."

"Lulu's doing just fine. I think. Well, actually, I'm a little worried about her. Maybe she doesn't like being left alone because several times now, when we get home, we find that she's thrown seeds and water all over the Mexican quarry tile floor in the Florida Room. And I mean like all over! Really, Cuppy! Did she used to do that?"

"Well, Olivier's agent does only nonfiction, mostly travel. What is Pinckney's book about?"

"Well, it was just a short section and kind of confusing and I read it fast but it seemed to be about a politician's wife who finds out that he has an illegitimate daughter.... Uh, uh, oooh juff blig."

"Good heavens, McKnight are you all right? Here, sit down. I'll go get you some water. Where's Pinckney?"

"No, no, don't get Pinckney urg ohhh."

"Dash – McKnight needs some water!"

"Looks like he needs more than water. Here ol' buddy, take my scotch."

"I'll go find Pinckney."

"No, Grace, I don't want to worry her. I'm fine, just fine, please."

"Oh Dashley, guess what? Grace is going to teach me how to needlepoint when she gets back from Europe, aren't you Grace? Hey, what's the matter with McKnight?"

"Have you noticed that Mungo is giving such extra special care to the village flowerpots this year I'm sure it's because I encourage him and Eunice was so critical you know."

"No, I can't really say that I have noticed it Gardenia, but I'd be happy to write a letter to the editor about it. Our devoted village employees deserve our thanks and recognition on occasion."

"My Gardy is turning left all the time now, turning left, left and right so to speak heh heh. Probably passes herself coming and going. All started the night Eunice died apparently."

"I'm so glad, Herbert. Well, dinner is served everyone. Please come into the dining room and find your places. Herbert, you're next to me."

"Pinks, I'm fine really – just need a little something in my stomach. Here's your place. Now where am I?"

"Ha! Where am I? Who am I? What is reality? Over here, McKnight, between Grace and me."

78. *VICHYSSOISE*

McKnight slipped into his chair very rudely before all the ladies had been seated. He grabbed the already full glass of white wine that was to go with the first course of vichyssoise and slugged half of it down. Pinckney had found out about Kimberley! Pinckney! Kimberley! Oh God!

Frowning with sympathetic worry, Grace asked quietly, "McKnight, are you sure you're all right?"

"Oh, yes, yes, actually must, must be a flashback to when I was uhh grappling with the killer." McKnight polished off the rest of his wine.

"I can certainly imagine that it must have been a terrible shock to be confronted like that by someone you trusted."

"That's not the only shock." McKnight shoveled several spoonfuls of vichyssoise down the ol' gullet.

"What do you mean?"

"Have I ever told you the whole story, Grace, about That Fateful Day?" By then everyone in town had suffered through McKnight's account of That Fateful Day, which grew with every telling, but Grace settled in to hear it again with the latest embellishments.

"There she was, see, brandishing the gun right in my eye. It was an antique Smith and Wesson revolver with rosewood grips."

"So Herbert, what's going on in the world of Monopoly?"

"Tournaments galore, Ivy, thank you for asking. Hoping to convince Gardy to come with me to the next big one in Hawaii. Big one on the big one – island that is – heh heh. The old gal needs a vacation. All this stuff with Eunice has taken its toll let me tell you."

"When is the tournament in Hawaii?"

"Two weeks from tomorrow so that'll give me enough time to finish building the kink free hose barricade in our garage. It'll keep Gardy from running into walls and flowerpots."

"Ha! She missed her calling as a demolition derby champion. Maybe you should put a barricade in front of the tearoom."

Madeleine's eyes swept around the table, making sure that everything was going along well. She was quite irritated that one of the waiters had poured the white wine before people had sat down. Although she had to admit that cooking with caterers beat can openers and casseroles hands down. From now on she would stick to caterers and her trusty hardboiled egg cooker. "So, Cuppy, how's the search for a house going?"

"Nothing so far. At first I had a small place in mind but the more I think about it, I might like something bigger. As long as it doesn't have a yard. I don't even want a window box. Maybe one of those grand old apartments in the city. Tall ceilings, huge windows, nice architectural features – a bunch of them have recently been redone, so I wouldn't have to do anything. Just move in."

Pinckney was keeping her eye on McKnight. Something was up with him and he was drinking even more than usual. His voice was getting louder and she could hear him telling Grace about That Fateful Day. So she was distracted and Merit was not sure how to start a conversation with a woman whom he regarded as terminally stupid, but he tried.

"Good soup."

"Yes."

"Nice wine."

"Yes."

Pinckney knew she wasn't helping things along but she could never think of what to say to Merit Wilcoxen. He was so literary. Taking an encouraging gulp of the white Burgundy, she turned toward him and smiled. "I really like champagne the best. Do you have a favorite wine?"

Across the table, Ivy could hear Merit launch into his two favorite topics: wine and himself. Maybe Pinckney wasn't so dim after all. Neither was Gardenia, Ivy admitted ruefully. She was still quite miffed that Gardenia had solved the case. If only Merit hadn't been so unreasonable. He was probably relieved that Ivy had not figured it out – thinking it would only encourage her. Ha! As if she needed encouragement! Although, she had to say, he had been genuinely concerned for her safety. Perhaps they needed some joint project to bring them together, to smooth over the bit of distance caused by her investigation. The dump! That's what they could start doing together: going to the dump! They could clean out all that old junk by the side entrance and get rid of the kink free hoses at the same time. Oh there was so much to look forward to!

"Oh Dash dear, it is so wonderful to have you back in the land of the living so to speak my vichyssoise is better than this but that's all right and now I can order the Chinese Chippendale bridge for the park and give it in memory of my mother and get rid of all the kink free hoses I never want to see another one again."

"Gardenia, you never cease to amaze me."

As Gardenia babbled on, Dash slowly took in the dear old dining room. All Madeleine's accretions, as he called them, had been taken down. The heavy, voluptuous curtains (she'd called them drapes!), not at all suitable for a dining room, the murky mirrors that he'd smashed, the jaundiced wall paper, which she had called Renaissance, and the too thick rug. Fortunately, she had not gotten rid of the old threadbare oriental rugs. That would have been the last straw. There might have been another murder in Deer Creek. The rugs had actually been sent to the cleaners with a view to future sale but Dash had rescued them just in time. At least he had not had to buy back his own rugs. Although the cleaning and repair bill was a humdinger. Dogs are our best friends the man had told him.

79.   SALADE AVEC HOMARD

The soup bowls were cleared away and a lovely spring salad with slices of lobster, artfully carved to resemble little claws, appeared. Dash turned thankfully to Grace, who was on his left. She was finding it a bit difficult to extract herself from McKnight however.

"The dame was tough but I forced a confession out of her, see, then jumped over my desk and grabbed the gun. It was an antique Smith and Wesson revolver with rosewood grips and an ivory dragon carved on it."

"McKnight how thrilling. I'm sure Ivy would love to hear all about it too." Grace gratefully turned to Dash, who lifted his wine glass and his eyebrows toward her.

"How long are you going to be in Europe?"

"At least a month. I don't have a specific return date. It kind of depends on my mother and just what I feel like at the time. Father Wedgewood is going to join us at some point too." Grace was not entirely sure that she was looking forward to a Europe that contained her mother and Father Wedgewood, as much as she loved all three of them. Dash interrupted her fleeting vision of Olivier in Florence.

"Did you really tell Mad that you are going to teach her how to needlepoint when you get back?"

"Yes, she asked me to, although I am not sure that she will have time with all the other things she is undertaking."

"What do you mean? What other things?"

"Well, the real estate class and the interior design course; and then just tonight, Ivy suggested inviting her to join the garden club."

"I thought Ivy was kidding."

Dash launched his eyes to the far end of the table where Mad was laughing at something Herbert had said. Did she think that Dash wanted her to be one of those Deer Creek women – selling each other houses and then slathering them with fabric? His ballerina was dancing away. Did she really think Herbert was funny?

Ding ding ding. Pinckney was standing up and gently striking her wine glass with a teaspoon. Ding ding ding.

"Everybody, everybody – hi – I have something to announce."

The chatter died away and they all turned to regard Pinckney with curious surprise.

"I have something very important to tell you all. I know that you have been wondering what has been going on over at the village hall."

If McKnight hadn't been so close to an alcoholic coma, he might have had a seizure. Pinckney, his beloved, was going to reveal his unforgiveable transgression. How could she be so vindictive in front of all their friends? She had been so kind right before they came over here for dinner. McKnight swayed toward Ivy who pushed him back upright. Pinckney pretended not to notice and continued.

"I want to put an end to all these rumors that are flying around." Pinckney paused momentously to build the suspense. McKnight was afraid that he might cry but then an amazing religious peace settled upon him. It would all be over soon. He just had to keep his head above plate level.

"Gardenia and I are the ones who redecorated the Garden Club of St. James's closet!"

Impressed silence greeted this revelation.

Grace started clapping so everyone joined in. Merit threw in a few gallant "Huzzahs," as he was sitting between the two clandestine decorators. He then stood and led everyone in "Here's to Pinckney! Here's to Gardenia!

Here's to the Garden Club of St. James!" Merit sat down but then surged up again, "Oh, and here's to the Deer Creek Garden Club!"

McKnight was coughing and clawing (carefully) at his Hermès tie, the one with the bunnies and shotgun shells on it. Ivy pounded him on the back while Grace patted his shoulder and handed him a water goblet.

"You must be so proud McKnight. And you didn't know at all? Isn't it astonishing what secrets people can keep? Even from our nearest and dearest."

McKnight could see a Kelly bag in Pinckney's future.

80.   CARRÉ D'AGNEAU

The conversation picked up momentum again as the main course of rack of lamb with roast potatoes, baby carrots, haricots verts, wild rice and thick, rich gravy was served. The delicious scents of rosemary, mint sauce and red currant jelly wafted and mingled around the dining table then gently faded into the collective memory of many such happy occasions in the beautiful old room.

Gardenia had been smiling regally and nodding her head in acknowledgement of the toasts and cheers. What dear friends she had! Not to mention her dear Herbert! He had been so sweet to throw out her clothes and towels that night and clean up the bathroom. Even though it had been that lovely new suit, pale as creamy moonshine with infinitesimal glints of silver. And he had never said anything about it. That's what a long marriage could produce: unspoken trust, understanding and loyalty. Although maybe she needed a little less Monopoly and a lot fewer kink free hoses – no kink free hoses as a matter of fact. Oh well, you couldn't get rid of everything.

Gardenia summoned the memory of that critical night at the mulch site. That maniacal drive home had happened after Eunice had called her a traitor and Gardenia had run to her car and turned right as usual out of the mulch site to get home, but then halfway there it struck her that she had forgotten the shovel, so she kept going around to the right back to the mulch site.

By now it was dusk but when she pulled in she could still see the shovel leaning against the wall of the shed where Dash had left it. Everybody else had left but then someone appeared out of the dark. It was Eunice, who started calling and marching toward her.

"Gardenia – I've got to talk to you!" It was Eunice, who was going to malign and harangue and attack Gardenia again and again with unending malice. With renewed violence, all the poisoned arrows that Eunice had shot into her plans and her soul over the years once more found their marks. In a dark silence of bitter rage, Gardenia raised the shovel and strode into battle to meet her enemy. It was true what they said about seeing red.

❦

81.   *MOUSSE AU CHOCOLAT*

In dawning horror, Dash turned to Gardenia.

"When did you become an interior decorator?"

"Oh Dash dear, Pinckney and I aren't real decorators, but we knew that we had to do something to keep feelings from being hurt because there are so many garden club members who are professional decorators – truly marvelous too so contemporary and historic – how could we possibly choose with the closet getting so damp and shabby?"

Holding his head still and his eyes open, Dash regarded her with newly discovered appreciation. "Indeed."

The beautiful old white linen tablecloth and the napkins embroidered with his mother's monogram, the delicate crystal, the burnished silver and the Royal Doulton china with naval battle scenes on it brought Dash a great sense of comfort. His ribs still hurt a bit from where Gardenia had clobbered him with the shovel, but it was as nothing compared to freedom and the realization that Mad need not become a professional interior decorator. He would tell her that he needed her more than ever at the company now that the development project at the mulch site was as dead as Eunice. He had driven by the other day to see what was going on. All the mulch was gone. There had only been that one pile anyway, Eunice's shroud. Perhaps it would have extra fertilizing power.

Cole had been lying under the dining room table, minding his own business and sniffing the soothing aroma of leather and feet all around him. He was thinking about the UPS truck. It was so much better than the golf cart.

It had lots more room, you could walk around in it, and so far at least, it had not driven into a pond. Cole drifted into a dream. The UPS truck appeared in the distance. He kept running and running but he couldn't catch up! He was almost there! Cole jumped as high as he could – bang! – went his head against the bottom of the table.

Dash smiled at his dear cousin Gardenia. He had to hand it to her. She was the one who had solved the case and saved him from life in prison. Pointing out to the police that since she had cleaned the shovel right before taking it over to the presentation, then the only way that That Miss Sigman Person's (which is what they all called her now) fingerprints could be on it, was if she killed Eunice. Of course that had precipitated That Miss Sigman Person's unfortunate demise and the destruction of McKnight's car, but it had saved his bacon. The fact that McKnight's account of the confession corroborated this theory, was legal icing on the cake of justice. Oh there was so much to look forward to!

Good ol' Gardy. There was more to her than met the eye. A mysterious muffled thump from under the table brought everyone to attention. Dash took advantage of the perfect timing to stand up and lift a very full glass of champagne. "To Gardenia, who swings a mean shovel!"

THE END

CPSIA information can be obtained
at www.ICGtesting.com
Printed in the USA
BVHW032145090621
609254BV00006B/47